TRAITORS
IN HIGH PLACES

Professor Andy Crane should have knocked when he walked into the office of Bliss Mansfield, president of the university. But he didn't and that omission changed the course of his life and, in other ways, the political history of the United States. Dr. Mansfield was speaking fluent Mandarin Chinese when Crane walked in unannounced. All Crane was able to catch were the words "sleeping giant," they chilled him to the bone. Twenty-five years before, in a pitch dark Korean village, he had heard the same words spoken by the same voice. And thus began the unraveling of the greatest conspiracy of modern times.

THE KOREAN CONSPIRACY

Melford S. Weiss

MANOR
BOOKS
INC.

A MANOR BOOK

Manor Books, Inc.
432 Park Avenue South
New York, New York 10016

ISBN CODE 0-532-19198-6

PART I

ONE

He hadn't planned on seeing the president, so he hesitated in front of the open door before making up his mind. The secretary's desk was empty, unusual but not particularly alarming, yet there was a letter still in the typewriter only partially answered, and that was strange. It was as if she had suddenly been interrupted in the middle of a pertinent statement.

Andy Crane stepped softly onto the thick pile carpeting of the outer office. This is ridiculous, he thought, I should leave and come back another time. But he didn't. Instead, he let his eyes wander across the cream-colored walls to the easy chairs where waiting visitors could pass the time reading copies of the *Alumni Newsletter.*

The doors to the president's chambers were slightly ajar, yet he sensed that the president had intended for them to be closed. Quietly, with unaccustomed caution and without really knowing why, he moved closer. Now he could hear the university's chief administrator talking into the receiver, his voice almost but not quite a whisper.

"Shr...shrde. Wo jr dau. Parsons jyang bu hwei bei... Ti ming de...Wo bu syang jr dau. Blaine yau wo chyu jying hsuan.. Bu...Ming tyan jyou keyi wo jr dau...Shr de. Dzai jyan. Chun swei dzu jyu ren."

Andy was stunned. My God! The president was speaking Mandarin. He couldn't believe it. He was so startled by his discovery that he failed to hear the door open.

"How long have you been standing there?" It was an abrupt accusation.

7

Andy began to panic. "I...I just came in."

The man's anger was subsiding, the tone more cautious yet still demanding. "What did you hear?"

Get hold of yourself Andrew. He hesitated for a fraction of a second before answering. "...Nothing."

He's afraid and he's lying, Bliss thought. Better take it easy, don't let him see you're upset, that's it, smile. "I'm sorry, it's just that you surprised me." Then in a voice made more sinister by its unexpected softness, "what did you want?"

"I was going to see you about the speaker for the Cultural Affairs Program. I can come back later." Andy realized an apology was in order. "The door was open."

The president ignored him. "Perhaps we could discuss the matter tomorrow, say ten o'clock. You're Crane... anthropology, isn't it?"

"Yes, that would be fine."

"Next time please knock, won't you?" The attempt at humor was a feeble one.

Professor Crane hurried across the campus. The sun was unusually warm, a signal that the hot summer would arrive early this year. Despite the heat, Andy shivered and pulled his jacket close to his body. He could feel an icy fear creep under his flesh as if the old nightmares were coming back to haunt him. He was a very frightened man.

It wasn't so much that the president had caught him eavesdropping, or even that he was speaking Mandarin, although that in itself was surprising—his tones were really quite good, almost like those of a native speaker. What really bothered him was the conversation—the final expression. It was such an odd phrase with which to end a dialogue. Chun swei dzu jyu ren, "sleeping giant". He had heard those words before. It was a very long time ago, in a half-forgotten country far across the ocean.

Late for his luncheon date with Leslie, he rushed along the tree-lined path to his office. He didn't like to keep her waiting. She was always prompt.

By the time he reached the department, his hands were shaking so badly that he barely managed to unlock the door. The perspiration that had covered his forehead was already beginning to drip down his neck; his throat was parched. Somehow Andy was able to light a cigarette. Inhaling deeply, he forced himself to calm down while he searched his memory. Maybe it was Taiwan? No, it couldn't be. That was only two years ago. It must have been long before that.

He sat in the dark deliberately making himself concentrate. For a moment he thought about Su-lin. That wasn't it either. Then he remembered. It was cold...and dark, dark because there weren't any lights on in the village. Korea! That was it, it was in Korea.

He hastily scribbled the phrase on a sheet of paper, stared at it, wrote it down again, and then a third time. He put the paper aside with his lecture notes.

But the Korean War had happened over twenty-five years ago.

TWO

President Mansfield slowly walked back into his office, poured a third cup from the coffee brewer and sank deep into the cushions of his executive chair. He turned it so that it faced the picture window behind his desk. The sun was bright, and for a second the glare hurt his eyes. Beneath him, the people appeared as dolls wandering aimlessly in a toy village. They seemed to have no direction, no purpose, puppets without strings dancing away their precious lives.

May third marked Bliss Mansfield's fifty-first birthday, and he was enjoying the best days of his life. The image of an eminent university president, he had been mentioned, although not yet seriously, as a contender for the United States Senate. A man full of promise; the day belonged to him alone. He basked in the warmth of that thought. Had he not been referred to, well suggested was more like it, as a candidate? And why not? A doctorate from Chicago, author of the best-selling *Justice in America,* a consultant to the House Committee on racism, and now the president of a prosperous and promising university.

His reputed sense of fairness and cautious advocacy of affirmative action had made him popular with both faculty and students. Perhaps his insistence on an expansive budget wasn't appreciated by all the legislators, but neither did they consider him irresponsible, a charge commonly hurled at presidents these days. The bill for the new medical school had just been passed making him the odds-on favorite of the community.

Bliss was seen as a reasonable man, reasonable in that

10

he understood the realities of compromise but never bent under them to the extent of forgetting his principles. His bursts of enthusiasm and excitement were genuine. His appearance as a man of decision was heightened by his rangy good looks, the shock of tousled hair reminiscent of the Kennedys, a touch of silver in the sideburns, and pleasant yet provocative blue-gray eyes. He always looked right at you.

President Mansfield liked to think he stood for progress, a better world for people of every class and all colors. Deep within him burned a dream. He was not merely idealistic, he was committed.

Closing his eyes, he continued to think. Why? Why now? The phone call had been unexpected. They had been instructed not to call his office and never in Chinese. What was so important that it couldn't wait? He smiled. Somehow they had done it. Arranging for Parsons to withdraw would make him a viable candidate indeed. The party's nomination meant the primary, and in this state winning the primary was as good as winning the election itself. Senator Mansfield, Senator Bliss Mansfield. The honorable Senator from the State of...

He had sent his secretary on an errand and was certain he had closed the doors, well evidently not. There wasn't anything to suggest that Crane, had understood the conversation. He had been frightened because he had been caught eavesdropping, that's all it was.

Mansfield grinned, the master once again. Swinging his chair around, he reached for the noon mail. A meeting at two with the Dean of Engineering, old Barrington is going to badger me for more research funds and his graduate program in Bio-Mechanics...Three-thirty is that Woman's Studies coordinator. He recalled her memorandum; the campus is just not safe, particularly the wooded path in back of the library. Why were there no lights? I'll have to check with Facilities and Planning and have them get on it...The dinner at the Lions is for

11

six. They're going to honor me as "citizen of the month"...
He stopped. Dammit! Even if he understands Mandarin
he couldn't possibly know...and then he thought he
remembered. It was in the Faculty Bulletin, only a few
lines but it had caught his attention. Crane, hadn't he just
written a book? What was the title?

Shi-nan: a Taiwanese village in transition, that was it.

As he realized the implications he experienced some
difficulty in breathing, his breath coming in short bursts
like a jogger at the end of a two-mile run. So Crane spoke
Chinese, that's why he was so nervous. He pressed the
secretary's intercom, and asked for the personnel file on
Andrew Crane in Anthropology. When it arrived he
spread the folder on his desk and began reading.

Andrew Marcus Crane, born Brooklyn, New York,
1932. Graduated from Boy's High School in 1949. A B.A.
in History summa cum laude from New York University
in '58. M.A. awarded from Cornell in 1961, Ph.D. in
1966. From '66-'68, Assistant Professor, SUNY
Binghampton, '68-'70, Assistant Professor at Columbia."
Looks like he's on his way up, Mansfield thought.
"Came here as Associate Professor in'72. The next year
he received an NSF grant for fieldwork in Taiwan. Then,
Research Fellow at the East-West Cultural Learning
Institute in Hawaii...returned in '75." Enjoys moving
around, doesn't he?

Area of specialization: Chinese culture and society,
overseas Chinese social organization, peasant societies,
social anthropology. Fellow: American Anthropological
Association, Society for Asian Studies...Hmmm,
impressive publication record. He read on.

Glancing at the transcript from New York University,
he noted that Andy had first enrolled in 1954. He found
the records from Cornell. This was what he wanted.
Crane passed his Chinese foreign language exam in 1959
but he enrolled at Cornell that very same year. So he must
have learned his Mandarin elsewhere and it wasn't in

New York.

Bliss was becoming agitated. He didn't like the conclusion he was considering, not one bit. Quickly he leafed through the remainder of the folder. Offer of employment...letters of recommendation...social security identification. Where the hell was it.

He discovered that Crane had been married in 1954 but a change in his health care benefits indicated that in 1972 he was claiming no dependents.

There was a gap in the records. 1950 through 1954 were unaccounted for. The time when a young high school graduate could easily be drafted and sent to Korea. But university personnel files tended to be academic, they didn't often contain information about military service. Bliss smoked two cigarettes. He had to know. Those were four very important years.

Had he not been so preoccupied with Andy Crane's military career he might have also noted the void for 1971.

THREE

Leslie Pace was ten minutes late for her luncheon date with Andrew Crane. She couldn't help thinking it was more like ten years.

At six-o-five on the morning of July 29, 1942, Simon Purcell Pace and the former Beatrice Eddington of Lake Forrest, Illinois became the proud parents of a six pound five ounce screaming baby girl. They named her Leslie after a distant relative who had been a suffragette. She was also a Leo but the stubborn and aggressive qualities associated with that sign would not emerge for another twenty years.

As an infant she was coddled, spoiled and protected by her doting parents, four grand-parents, her older sister, Belinda, one maid, one gardener, one chauffeur, a maiden Aunt and a succession of governesses. She walked at fifteen months but could recite the alphabet at two and was learning how to read by four, the same year Andy Crane made the Boy's High frosh football squad.

She adored playing with dolls, teacups, ribbons and nannies, became overly excited when she rode her pony or sailed on Lake Michigan, despised visiting relatives, and attended church each Easter Sunday because that was what her parents expected. For the next eight years she was enrolled in Town and Country Day School and did more of the same except that she no longer went to church. In her last year she menstruated two days before the family moved to New York's Westchester County.

At thirteen she learned her first lesson about becoming a woman.

"Bee, what are you doing?"

14

Captured by her reflection in the lighted mirror, Belinda Pace was rapidly falling in love with herself. "I'm putting on make-up squirt."

"Why?" She had always been fascinated by all the creams, lipsticks, eyeshadow, powder, perfume and deodorants that crowded her sister's dressing table.

"So that I'll be beautiful when Michael calls for me."

"Don't you want to be beautiful just for yourself?"

"No silly, girls always make themselves pretty for boys." Belinda was sure that once Leslie grew up she wouldn't be asking these inane questions.

"Bee, why do boys like pretty girls?"

"Oh, I don't know, probably because they're boys. Listen Les, I'll let you in on a secret. Most boys are really dumb but they like to think they know everything. We girls just play along with them or else they won't take us out. It's like a game."

Leslie thought she knew all about games but this must be a new one. "Do you really have to pretend you're dumb?"

"Uh-huh, if they ever found out how smart we are the game would be over."

Leslie didn't think she liked this game. "Well, it sounds pretty stupid to me."

Belinda smiled at her naivette. "You know, sometimes I think you're right, but you'll learn."

"Learn what?"

But Belinda never answered her question. Michael was at the door and unlike the other boys she knew, he didn't like to be kept waiting.

Her second lesson was more poignant.

Sweet sixteen is a very special time in a girl's life, particularly so if she comes from a very upper-middle class family. It's not that she becomes a woman, that rite is formally recognized and socially sanctioned when she makes her debut. Nor is she really more aware of hormonal changes in her body than she would be at fifteen or even fourteen. If anything it is an awakening of the spirit when romantic fantasies assume larger-than-life proportions and where spur-of-the-moment giggles or outrageous tears are as natural as breathing.

For Leslie it was an age of discovery. There were new dance steps to learn, old gothic thrillers she would force herself to stay up all night to finish and tennis lessons that emphasized a correctness which seemed to have little to do with the game itself. She was continually going to slumber parties where friendships vowed never to betray each other's secrets, even upon pain of death.

Her gawky limbs and baby fat permanently gave way to full hips, budding breasts and a flat tummy. Silky hair now cascaded across her shoulders drawing your attention to the promising curves below. While tiny freckles surrounded a pert nose, her mouth surprisingly revealed a woman's sensuality.

Leslie was well aware of the facts of life yet the sperm and eggs she studied in biology appeared unrelated to the forbidden desires of her own flesh. So at times she found herself confused, anxious and just a little bit afraid, all perfectly normal emotions. Most of the anxiety had to do with boys. Sometimes she swore they must have originated on another planet, they were so different.

The Junior Prom at Mrs. Dobbs School for Young Ladies was a significant social event. Not to have a date (the headmistress called them "escorts") was disastrous and an overt admission of failure. Leslie didn't worry about such things because her good looks and vivacious personality guaranteed success, whatever that meant. The school grounds and manicured lawns were brightly lit by paper lanterns suspended from wires so they would sway with the evening breeze. The girls graciously advertised their fashionable evening gowns while young men, uncomfortable in their formal wear, paraded about desperately trying not to stare at Dianne Van Giff's backless, strapless Dior creation.

Leslie's escort was overwhelmed. "God, Les, but you're beautiful."

"Why thank you Ned and you look so handsome." She knew she should say that, all the boys at Choate liked to be told they were handsome.

The evening got started with the dance itself, the orchestra making it a point to alternate between fox trots and fast music. Leslie liked the electrifying beat of rock and roll. It was good to lose yourself in the demanding rythm allowing your body and particularly your hips their free expression. But the slow ones were so much more romantic. As she danced with her partners, occasionally touching and then ever so slightly pulling away she could feel her breath quicken and hear her heart beat faster. Ned's courage that night was fortified with his roommate's smuggled bottle of vodka. The fiery liquor made him relax so that he was only a little embarrassed by the rising stiffness in his trousers.

Promptly on the hour, Mrs. Colson announced that the ball was over and cautioned princesses about turning into pumpkins lest they stay out too late. But for Ned and Leslie the night had just begun. She responded, perhaps a bit too eagerly, when Ned suggested they drive out in back of the tennis courts.

It was warm as they lay on his blanket. Leslie's eyes were half-closed as she waited for her boyfriend's kiss.

"Gee Les, there's a full moon out tonight and if you look closely you can count the stars in the Big Dipper."

She answered "uh-huh." Kiss me you fool, who cares about the damn dipper.

"Did you have a good time at the prom?"

"How are your grades, I'm not doing so well in math."

I feel like screaming. "Ned Sheridan, I didn't come all the way out here with you to talk about math."

He put his arm around her.

"That's better."

Silence.

"Well?"

"Well, what?"

"Aren't you going to kiss me." She realized she was being aggressive but the music and the dancing had made her impatient. Besides, necking was so much fun. And soul-kissing, when it was done really well, almost took your breath away. She found it terribly exciting when a boy touched your breasts and once she had even let Harold Carpenter put his hand underneath her panties.

Needing little encouragement, Ned reached for her and as their lips joined he let his finger stroke the back of her neck. Now their kisses lasted longer, they explored each other's mouths with daring thrusts of their tongues, he was sweet although his breath was heavy. Ned's hands cupped her small breasts while she matched his growing excitement. He became bolder and after unhooking her brassiere ran his fingers across her body. Slowly he started kissing her neck, then her shoulders. He placed his mouth over her erect nipples teasing them with his teeth and then his tongue.

"Ohhh, oh Ned, it feels so good." His hand slipped under her gown and carressed the creamy whiteness of her inner thighs. She knew she ought to stop him but she didn't. His fingers found her opening and she sighed with an almost uncontrollable passion. Moving closer and without quite realizing it, she put her hand on his zipper.

Ned groaned. "Don't stop, touch me, please don't stop."

It wasn't difficult to remove her dress and her pants slipped easily down to her ankles. His penis was swollen with its tip beginning to feel sticky. Not knowing what else to do Leslie began to rub it up and down hoping it would make him feel better. She hadn't wanted to go all the way but he was becoming more and more amorous. Ned's lips brushed her belly and started to move onto her pubic hair.

"No! I don't want to. Please don't do that."

18

They continued to kiss and touch and finally, when Ned could no longer stand the tension, he spread her legs apart and moved on top of her.

"Ned, don't...Ned...not there...here...no, lower...lower...ouch."

"I'm trying...wait a minute...Oh no, I can't." His semen spilled all over her thighs.

He apologized. "I'm sorry...I couldn't stop."

They dressed in silence there being little they could say. When they reached her home she ran to the door. Leslie undressed and lay on her bed, awake, alert, curious and disappointed. She was no longer excited.

Is this what it's supposed to be like, all that sweating and groping? And for what? Do Belinda and Michael do this every night? Good Lord, he couldn't even wait. What was I supposed to do? Now he'll probably want to marry me he'll feel so guilty.

Leslie was wrong about marriage. Ned never called her again. But two years later in November, she married Dexter Parkins III. He was fresh out of Harvard Law, a friend of the family, a fair to good tennis partner, and he needed a wife. Her mother was delighted.

"Dex, why did Thomas really give the Malone boy a suspended sentence?"

"It's politics, honey, Patrick's father is a councilman. He's got clout, and besides that they belong to the same club."

"Be serious now."

"Okay, it's not that critical an issue. It was just a first offense. Kids go joy-riding all the time, and no one was really hurt."

"But he didn't care, he hit the old woman and wasn't even sorry. Will she sue?"

"I doubt it, Malone's lawyers offerred her more money than she had ever seen before. No, she'll settle out of court."

"Why don't you do something about it. I mean it's not fair, is it?"

"No way, I'm just a very junior assistant D.A.. Besides, the law's the law."

"You're evading the question counselor, the law's the law doesn't answer anything." She was baiting him now.

"Leslie, you ask so many questions you ought to be a lawyer yourself."

She was becoming annoyed. He only pretended to talk to her, treating her as if she was some kind of simpleton, as if he couldn't take her seriously. "Well I might at that."

"Don't worry your pretty little head, just be a good wife and enjoy life. Better finish dressing. The Fairchilds will be here soon." He bent down to kiss her before stepping into the shower.

Leslie Pace Parkins was rapidly becoming disillusioned. She had assumed that marriage would bring people closer, so that they could really share their thoughts. She wondered just what she had ever shared with Dexter. Certainly not serious conversation. As far as he's concerned I might as well live on Mars. Why does he need a wife anyway? She suspected she knew the answer to that one. At least he screwed her regularly although she had to admit without much fuss or bother. Slam, bam, thanks for the use of the hall ma'am. What he really needed was a hostess.

She wanted so desperately to confess her concerns to the other women but they were more like Belinda and her mother. They smiled a lot, occasionally giggled, shopped in the city, put on too much make-up, played tennis, played bridge, and rarely said anything worth remembering. Yet they were accomplished performers at charity balls, country club dances and dinner parties. It was as if a woman was judged by how well she arranged the centerpiece and if her gatherings had just the right number of bankers, lawyers, councilmen and bachelors. Somehow there must be more to life.

It was actually more fun talking to the men, that is if they would listen. Most of the time they complimented her figure and hinted at adultery especially when they were drinking brandy.

Leslie had an inquisitive mind, she read voraciously and had been a fine student. Recognizing her academic talent, Mr. Jenkins encouraged her to go to Vassar but at the time she hadn't realized that she had the right to make her own choice.

Good God! It was all such a bore.

"Les, what are you doing?" It was the summer of '63 and the rain was gently falling on the garden of their North Shore home. Leslie didn't hear him. Her pen clenched between her teeth, she was to busy practicing for the S.A.T.'s.

"I said, what's that your reading?" Dexter walked over to the desk.

"Don't bother me now hon, I'm studying. I've got to score at least in the six-hundreds if I'm going to go to college."

"What's this about college?"

She looked up at him. "I'm going to college in the fall."

"But we'll be moving to Washington"

"It's okay, there are colleges in Washington, there's Georgetown and American University and..."

"Hey, you're serious aren't you?" he exclaimed. "Look, I don't need a co-ed for a wife. I've got an important job with the commission. There'll be social responsibilities. When will you have the time?" Her anger surged. "Then we'll just have to skip the dinner parties."

"You can't mean that."

Now she was furious. "You damn well better believe it." She marched into her bedroom and slammed the door.

It wasn't their first fight but it would be their last. Leslie filed for divorce and in the fall of '64 enrolled at Radcliffe.

She graduated with honors in '68 and went on to study criminology under Olmstead. In 1974 she reclaimed her maiden name and received her Ph.D. Leslie taught at Oakland University in Rochester, Michigan before accepting an Assistant Professor's appointment at the university. Her first day on the campus she met Andy Crane.

She graduated a bit sooner than he had spent in the building...

FOUR

They drove across the city to a favorite restaurant. It wasn't that they didn't want to be seen by their colleagues, it was more because they preferred being by themselves.

Leslie was in a talkative mood and one of her favorite subjects was the circumstances of their first meeting.

"And, do you remember...I was so excited. Imagine, me, Dr. Leslie Pace, a professor at a real university. Classes hadn't started yet and I spent the entire afternoon walking around and staring at all the buildings. I felt like a small-town girl who had just discovered the big city. And then I saw you strolling across the quad in a T-shirt and cut-offs. Well, there wasn't anyone else around so I had to ask you where I could find the Administration Building. You pretended to be serious and then looked straight at me and answered with that shit-eating grin all over your face,'do you need help registering for classes'? I was so embarrassed. I thought you were terrible. Andy. You're not listening."

"What's that? I'm sorry Les. Oh I noticed you all right and even started to say something really clever and sophisticated, but I couldn't think of the right words. I thought you were ravishing and wanted to fuck you right there, on the lawn."

She laughed suggesting both intimacy and understanding. They had come a long way since then. "I wish you would have. Do you realize we wasted a good four months?"

The clouds began to shut out the sun and threaten them with a spring shower. Le Buffet was almost empty, most of the regular customers having returned to their offices. A lone candle burned casting deep shadows.

"When you asked me out for dinner I wasn't sure. You reminded me of an aging jock out to make the new girl in town. Andy. You haven't heard a word I've said. You just sit there and stare at the door. Are you expecting someone?"

Yes, it's almost as if she was right, he thought. Mansfield will walk into the restaurant, he'll order a martini, casually reach inside his jacket and take out a gun. Then he'll say, "Crane, I'm going to have to kill you. Chun swei dzu jyu ren." He'll laugh and squeeze the trigger.

Andy's accidental meeting with Mansfield had left him badly shaken. He was sure Mansfield didn't believe him when he tried to pretend he had just walked in. What was there about the conversation on the phone that had made the President angry and then defensive? What was he so afraid of? Why?

"Les, something happened this morning..." He told her about his unexpected encounter with Mansfield.

"Okay, so our beloved leader speaks Mandarin. Strange, but why worry about it?"

"No, it's more than just that." He explained about the final phrase. "Look, it doesn't fit. I mean you don't end a normal conversation with words like that. It's almost as if they had some kind of a special meaning."

He seemed so concerned, no not concerned, almost terrified. It was so unlike. Andy, always vibrant, outgoing, even sarcastic. Something must really be bothering him. "Andy, what do those words mean?"

"Literally translated... 'the sleeping giant.' "

He had captured her attention. "Sounds like a secret

24

password. The kind we'd make up when I was a kid and wanted to get into my sister's tree-house."

"Doesn't it? Like a signal of some sort or maybe, maybe it's a nickname, but whose?"

Her curiosity was becoming more intense. "Let's go back to the conversation itself. What was he saying?"

Andy paused and tried to remember each word. "I didn't hear all of it. When I walked in, I think he was being told about a nomination. Then he said, 'I don't want to know.' Wait a minute, he was being told that Parsons would not get the nomination and...and that Blaine would ask him to run. Then he referred to tomorrow being soon enough for something and after saying 'dzai jyan'—good-bye, he ended with...your password."

"Parsons must be Congressman Duane Parsons. He's on the House Ethics Committee that's investigating those alleged Korean bribes to legislators. He's very popular. I'd think he was a shoo-in for the nomination."

Andy continued. "Blaine is the state party chairman. He's an old political pro, like Daley used to be in Chicago."

Leslie wasn't satisfied. Something was still missing. Andy wouldn't be upset over a political conversation, even in Mandarin. "Andy Crane, I know you. You're not telling me everything. It's about that cryptic declaration of yours, 'sleeping giant.' "

But Crane wasn't realy listening. Korea, that's where he'd heard it and Pasons was investigating Korean bribes. It still didn't make any sense. He'd been in the village and it was dark...nighttime. The woman was sleeping and he remembered waking up. There were voices coming from the adjoining hooch. I opened the door...

"Leslie, you're going to think I'm crazy. I know I heard those very same words and it was back in Korea. When Mansfield repeated them over the phone I broke into a cold sweat."

25

Their conversation was interrupted by the waiter who presented them with a '69 Robert Mondavi Cabernet. They ate their meal in silence.

He was not really eating his food and he hadn't even touched the wine. Whatever happened this morning must have really disturbed him. Leslie knew that Andy had served during the Korean War, but he had never talked about it. In fact it was like his wife, a topic he deliberately avoided. She knew that they had been married almost sixteen years before she was killed in a tragic accident. But that was all she knew. There was so much more she had to learn about this strangely sensitive man with whom she was beginning to fall in love.

The threat of rain had ended, the sun was shining again. They returned to her apartment and Andy spent a lazy afternoon trying to finish a new political thriller, "The Chancellor Manuscript," while Leslie wrote the first draft of a research paper.

In the evening they made love. It was well past midnight but neither of them was really sleeping. Leslie rubbed her eyes and turned to face him.

"Andy, about this morning, it's probably just a strange coincidence, the whole thing. Just wait, Parsons will be nominated for the Senate, and Mansfield, well, he was probably speaking to his wife. I'll bet she's Chinese. Your secret code is really lover's talk for 'I want to get laid.' You know what I think, it's that book you've been reading that's giving you these spooky ideas."

Andy stared at the moon through the open window thinking about what she had said. How he wished it were as simple as all that, but the President's wife was as blond as he was. Crane lay awake for a long time before he finally drifted into a restless sleep, then he began to dream.

...It had been cold, so cold that he hugged the body of the girl sleeping beside him more out of a need for warmth than anything else. He had insisted on escorting

her home and checked out of the compound at 2010 hours. They were both young and very lonely. Bound together by the evening's unpleasant incident they undressed silently, and after a quiet and gentle coupling, fell asleep in each other's arms.

FIVE

While Professors Crane and Pace were having lunch, Bliss Mansfield was on his way over to the Anthropology Department. He had told his secretary to cancel the appointment he had with Dean Barrington. *I must know more about Crane; I must know if he was sent to Korea. If anyone can tell me it will be Luke.*

Lucas T. Gargurovich was a living legend. Beyond being merely an elder, he was at the very least, a celebrated ancestor. At six foot four he topped the scales at a hefty 310 lbs. His double chin could have competed with his immense gut if it had not been hidden by a heavy white beard complemented by a magnificent handle-bar mustache. Lucas had survived three administrations. He ran his department like a fleet admiral, but he ran it well. His students often jokingly referred to him as Dr. G. because there was some difficulty pronouncing his name correctly.

Luke swiveled about in his built-to-specifications chair when he saw Mansfield approaching. "What does that son-of-a-bitch want?" he muttered, loud enough to be heard in the outer office.

"Relax, Luke. I'm only here for a friendly chat and some coffee."

Like hell thought Luke, but he replied, "Well then, welcome to these digs. Get that, anthropology—these digs, hah."

"You're always saying you'd give me a tour if I came down, well I'm here and I've got about an hour."

Lucas beamed. "Come on, *el presidente*, we'll show you how we earn our keep."

Bliss found it hard to concentrate. As they walked through the labs watching students cataloging samples and painstakingly separating artifacts from rubble, he asked some questions, nodded in agreement most of the time and pretended to listen to Lucas. When the tour was over, both men retreated to his office to enjoy a special blend of Ecuadorian coffee while rekindling their friendship.

"How's the old commander doing these days?" Bliss began the gambit.

"Gettin' tired Bliss, it's been a real long time since my Navy days." Lucas had been a lt. commander in the Pacific theater during the "big war", and had never quite gotten over the experience.

"Do you still tell the story about when you were off New Guinea and the Japanese destroyer came up behind you?"

"It was the first time I had been in combat. I was trying to act like an old salt but when I turned around..." Lucas rambled on.

Waiting patiently for the right opportunity, Bliss asked "I wonder what our younger colleagues think about your war stories, old man."

Lucas laughed. "Half the time they think I'm making them up, but then they don't know what those days were really like."

The president pretended to agree with him.

"Anyway the military isn't popular today. They're always accusing anthropologists of working for the CIA. Most of them never been in the service. Walter's been to Korea, that's Walter Maris, but he was a cook. Matt and Warren are the only old war-dogs."

Bliss had to take a chance. "How's Andy Crane doing?"

"Oh, Andy's just fine. He wrote a book about that Chinese village he studied, *Shi-nan,* damn good research. What you interested in him for?"

Startled by the directness of Lucas's question, he

quickly lit up a cigarette and coughed. "Crane's been recommended for full professor, hasn't he?"

ªYou bet," Lucas continued, "he's one of our best. If we don't promote him he'll probably go to Harvard, 'ceptin' he and that classy gal over in Criminal Justice got a thing goin'."

Bliss was relieved, he tried again. "He was over in Korea too, wasn't he?"

"Uh-huh, they taught him Chinese at that school in California. Saw some action, was even wounded. Say, he was there 'bout the same time that you were, did you know him?"

Mansfield could feel his heart beating faster. "What outfit was he with?"

"Don't rightly know, he never says anything about it, think he used to have a girlfriend over there, believe he still gets letters from someone."

They chatted a while longer. The chairman made it a point to mention the budget request for a new four-wheel drive vehicle for the summer field school in Arizona. The president promised to seriously consider it.

Bliss was still uneasy. The visit to Lucas provided him with some of the answers but it also raised more questions. Where did Crane serve in Korea? When was he wounded?

His promise of a career as a U.S. senator hung in the balance. It would be inexcusable to let one man ruin him, and after all these years. Although he was reluctant to become further involved, he had to know, and that would mean a call to Washington.

Bliss walked quickly to a vacant pay phone near the library. He dialed a District of Columbia area code and then a number. A woman's voice answered.

"Barclay's Service; do you wish to leave a message?"

"Yes."

"Please identify yourself."

He whispered, "sleeping giant."

"What is your message?"

"I want the service jacket on an Andrew Marcus Crane, born in Brooklyn, New York, 1932. He served in the Army somewhere between 1950 and 1953. I think he was wounded in Korea. He may have studied Mandarin at the Army Language School in Monterey. I must know the units he served with. I want it personally verified."

"How soon do you need the request?"

Bliss raised his voice. "Immediately."

"Thank you." There was a click.

The answering service relayed Mansfield's message to the appropriate party. Within minutes a civilian clerk working for the Army received instructions. He searched the computer tapes and paper files in St. Louis and retrieved Crane's DD two-fourteen, Report of Separation.

A call went out to a light colonel at the Pentagon who spent two hours in the basement of the cavernous building looking for additional information.

Brice Stephens, an ex-sergeant living in New Jersey verified that Crane had been at Fort Dix in 1950 and a former Chinese instructor at the ALS remembered the young soldier who had graduated first in his class.

In Montana, Colonel Crowley (USA, retired) told the two men claiming they were from NASA, that Corporal Crane had served honorably under his command in Korea.

A Japanese nurse checked Crane's admission to the Army Hospital in Tokyo while Korean CIC. records placed him near Taegu in October of 1952.

This information would be forwarded to the caller within twenty-four hours.

SIX

The event was scheduled for Friday. It would take place at the west end of the Spradley quadrangle.

Ron Mabra removed his cap noticing the sweat staining the leather headband and wiped his brow with a damp handkerchief. He would have liked to have hung the weatherman who predicted overcast skies and a cooling trend. The heat was okay, but the accompanying humidity always made him feel uncomfortable beause his uniform would soon become soggy and stick to his skin.

Ron Mabra, the Director of Campus Security was tired. Twenty years with the Los Angeles Police Department, four teen-age kids and a bitchy wife made him that way. Shading his eyes from the sun, he surveyed the area. He usually did so before a Cultural Affairs presentation.

The quad first gave you the impression of being larger than it really was. Practically enclosed on all four sides, the buildings on three of them were from an earlier era, constructed of fading and overgrown ivy vines, a style in vogue when the university was still a college. The exception was the five-story administration headquarters that faced the speaker's area.

It was basically a grassy arena surrounded by oaks and maples, with a partially wooded enclosure towards the east. The trees protected the students from the sun, though most of them preferred to tan in the open. The woods had always been a favorite for romantic interludes.

A platform complete with podium and a loudspeaker had been moved in anticipating the event. Later, folding chairs would be added and, if necessary, a canopy to shelter the guests. The audience would gather on the grass but a few adventuresome individuals would sit in the lower branches of the trees.

Mabra nodded to Sergeant Anderson. "Do you have the schedule, Don?"

The Sergeant consulted his clipboard. "Right here, Chief. Shultz and Gibson will cover the parking lot and later move to the quad, Rizzo will be inside the building during the reception, and McAllister's on stand-by."

Ron didn't particularly like the beefy ex-Marine. There was something about the way he stared at you as if he secretly hated your guts. And he was always chewing that damned cigar. He never lit it, just sucked on the tip, rolling it between his lips until it disintigrated in his mouth. Someday Anderson, you're going to blow it. "Who's manning the switchboard?"

"It's Jennie's turn. She'll be in contact with the State Police and the hospital. The city cops'll be near the west gate but they won't come on campus unless requested."

There had always been a problem about jurisdiction. The university was nominally within the city limits which meant that the local force could legally interfere. Six months ago Mabra thought he had reached an agreement with Commissioner Blake, and his men agreed to stay off campus. But all day long they rode in their "green and white" up and down River Avenue, just waiting... "I don't expect we'll need them. It's just before finals so the campus ought to be quiet."

"Hey, Chief, don't tell me you really think there'll be any trouble."

"No, but it pays to cover your ass. You can never tell about these controversial speakers. Sometimes the kids'll cheer 'em when you figure they ought to be shoutin' 'em down and I've seen 'em listen to raving maniacs and applaud politely. It's like there's a special kind of chemistry between the speechmaker and the crowd.

Anything can happen. Remember when they almost got Maddox. One minute they were smiling and all of a sudden... If that coke bottle had been a little more on target they'd have busted his skull."

The Sergeant nervously stroked his leather holster. "Who's this Spaacklund, the one scheduled for Friday?"

"Some bigshot with the Economics Ministry in South Africa, supposed to talk about tariffs and trade." Mabra was concerned about him. Ever since the students at Stanford protested their university's involvement, anything connected with South Africa was potentially explosive. Besides, the topic didn't mean much, once you started talking you could say anything you damn well felt like. He kept his feelings to himself, no sense worrying everyone.

"Doesn't sound like much to get excited about."

"You're probably right."

"See you here Friday, Chief?"

"Yeah, Spaacklund will come on campus at ten-thirty. He'll be speaking at eleven. We'll go over the grounds again."

Jefferson White was only five feet, three inches tall, five-five, if you considered his oversized afro. What he lacked in stature he made up for in eloquence. A speech and drama major, he could mesmerize most audiences with his biting scarcasm and razor sharp wit. He was dressed in his self-styled uniform, a black turtleneck, black levis, and black boots with two-inch heels.

Jeff, he preferred the nickname, sat on a wooden stool in a deteriorating house with faded yellow walls, eleven miles from the campus. Ever since he could remember he had always wanted to be an actor. But the university theater had few challenging roles for blacks and he'd be damned if he would stoop to playing "Stepin Fetchit." Las year he had organized a rally for a visiting black legislator and was genuinely surprised when he found people eagerly responding to his passionage monologue. Now as the Black Student Union Leader, he found an outlet for both his frustrations and ambitions.

He patiently waited for his sometimes friend, sometimes enemy, Whitney Rawlins. The setting he had chosen seemed particularly appropriate for a meeting to discuss the South African speaker. The house looked like a picture he had once seen of a native drinking place there.

Whitney was uptight. That lousy cop had stopped him for speeding and he had only been going ten miles over the limit. He was sure it was his long hair and because he wasn't wearing a shirt. Pig! They were all pigs, fucking pig cops, nothing but assholes, dupes for their imperialist masters. He'd show 'em.

His feelings about Jeff weren't much different. Goddamned peacock, do anything just for an audience. His commitment to fighting social injustice is zilch. But needed the black activist. Phonwy or not he sure knew how to heckle a speaker. Whitney parked his '67 Ford two blocks from the house and walked back. He knocked three times.

"Come on in red-neck, grab yo lily white ass a beer."

"Shit, nigga, why do we have to meet in a dump like this?"

"It reminds me of my ancestral roots," answered Jeff.

Whitney laughed. "That's a crock, your grand-daddy wouldn't even piss in a place like this." He was referring to Jeff's very middle-class origins.

Whitney prided himself on his own folk heritage. A slim Georgia cracker with pale blue eyes, he was born in the hills where his uncle distilled moonshine and sold the white lightning to an Atlanta distributor. Having returned from Vietnam a bitter young man, he carefully learned to hate the system that spawned the "American War." He became an avowed Marxist, a radical who seriously studied political rhetoric and even believed it.

35

This wasn't the first time that White and Rawlins had cooperated in staging a rally or disrupting a speaker.

"Okay, whiteman, let us get down to logistics. My people'll be there early, we'll move front and center. I'll give the South African a few minutes and then challenge him with police brutality and genocide in the townships. That'll be your signal."

"Right on! We'll start in from the administration building chanting about the university's funds being used to support apartheid and join forces."

"Fantastic," exclaimed Jeff. "We can hold hands and form a line, you know, black and white together."

"Yeah, sure. You got another beer?"

Neither organizer expected it to be a particularly rousing demonstration. Yet it would be one of the few times black and white anti-establishment groups could ideologically cooperate. Both Whitney and Jeff understood that. The illusion of solidarity would be exploited by the two leaders.

"Hey, Rawlins, let's keep it cool, like no violence."

He suspected that Jeff was just chickenshit but he agreed. "Okay, only posters and obscenities, we'll keep it clean."

In a house similar to and not far from where White and Rawlins were planning their strategy, Arlen Robinson was waking up from the after-effects of a bad drunk. He hadn't made the track team and on top of that the university was threatening to expel him because of failing grades. Also, his girlfriend was pregnant.

Arlen had been recruited as part of a special program for ghetto youth and although he tried real hard to understand the teachers, very little of what they said made any sense. At first he faithfully attended the tutoring sessions but soon lost interest. If it hadn't been for Elvira he would have been long gone.

She stirred beside him. "Arlen, honey, what you

36

grinnin' bout?"

"Luck's about to change, girl. Las night this dumb honkie give me one-hundred bills. All ah gots to do is throw some kina bottle at the platform. I ain't even sposed to hit the speaker."

SEVEN

At exactly nine a.m. that Wednesday morning, while Leslie was teaching an introductory class, Andrew Crane was presiding over the meeting of the university-wide Cultural Affairs Committee. As a rule, Andy disliked committees of any kind. He felt they were often staffed by his less talented colleagues; those pompous windbags who were over-impressed by their own importance, and by junior professors, overly anxious to become the new leaders. Nothing of any lasting importance was ever accomplished by a committee. Parliamentary procedure would be used as a delaying tactic, democracy meant that each and every ridiculous perspective had to be considered.

Department meetings were the worst. After praising a colleague's meritorious research and teaching abilities, they would pass a blank sheet of paper around the table and each member would secretly vote his or her pleasure. The results were often astonishing. Nobody had anything bad to say about Joe yet they unanimously rejected his bid for tenure. Andy often thought you should have two faculties, and A and a B team. One group would attend to meetings so that the other could concentrate on scholarship.

Ordinarily he would sit and fantasize about Leslie's body. Last spring he arrived at a mandatory staff meeting in his tennis shorts and when asked about his dress, explained that he had just come from a really important engagement.

Cultural Affairs however was a different matter. He recalled its beginnings. Edna Bannister-Burke, upon her death, had willed the university a yearly stipend to be used to attract unusual and sometimes controversial performing artists to the campus. Originally they invited poets, musicians and dancers, but as times changed began to include more political figures; General Curtis LeMay, Marxist Angela Davis, and even two chiefs of state, King Hussein and Jomo Kenyatta.

Andy truly enjoyed meeting these, fascinating people. He had lunched with Dylan, shared the dinner table with Senator McGovern and Congresswoman Jordan. Once he had spent two hours sitting by the lake with Jane Fonda. He was convinced that these people by their reputations alone would have a more dramatic impact upon the students than the untold hours of boring and repetitive lectures they would be forced to endure.

"Irv," he was speaking to Irving Weiss from Economics, "You've met Spaacklund before, what kind of a speaker is he?"

"Well Andy, he's usually reserved but I've seen him make some pretty inflammatory statements."

"Such as?" asked Lorraine Malcom.

"He accuses the United States of hypocrisy, you know, openly condemming South Africa while covertly buying her exports."

"Sounds like he's just what our students want to hear." added Lorraine.

He paused to light his pipe. "Yeees, but wait till he gets to the where he talks about his 'natives' and our 'Negroes.' He'll claim that they have to prove themselves capable before they can have the same rights as others. He compares his country in that sense to the U.S. before the Civil War."

"Reactionary bastard, isn't he? Perhaps he should head our affirmative action program," Prescott Smythe, the only black on the committee sarcastically volunteered.

They discussed the flight and hotel arrangements, luggage transfer, security, and the afternoon gathering planned for Spaacklund with the Econ Department, adjourning at nine forty-five. Andy had fifteen minutes before his meeting with the President.

The sun was just beginning to make its presence felt when Bliss Mansfield reached the dirt path at the entrance to Emerson Park. Moving with the practised patience of a habitual runner, he continued past the golf course and did not stop until he arrived at the water fountain signaling the end of the two-mile track. Momentarily resting to catch his breath, he found he was thinking less about his upcoming meeting with Crane than his plans after Spaacklund's speech.

At first he had been reluctant. What if the disturbance got out of hand? If the police couldn't control the mob, someone could get hurt. He was not indifferent to human suffering and refused to recognize himself as a deliberate perpetrator of violence. The organizers would be protesting the university's financial involvement with the Union of South Africa. It was a cause he too had championed. No good could ever come from supporting the racist policies of apartheid. What right did he have using their beliefs for his own purpose? The debate with his conscience wasn't strong enough to override his growing desire for power, and when he thought about it later, the ends seemed to justify the means.

It was a positively brilliant idea, just the right kind of publicity with which to launch a campaign. A similar incident had all but guaranteed the Junior Senator from California his election. His thoughts became a curious mixture of fantasy and wish fulfillment.

I can see Walter on the evening news. "There is at least one university president who won't tolerate terrorism on his campus. He just might be the kind of a man we need in Washington these days." The front page headlines would shout: "President cracks down on demonstrators, restores law and order to the university."

40

Later luxurating in the warmth of a stinging shower, Bliss adjusted the jet spray to a lesser intensity. Lathering up for a second time, he turned off the hot water and defiantly refused to shiver. Then he remembered his meeting with Crane.

"Come on down Dad," Bryan shouted upstairs, "Mom's already got breakfast on the table."

"Yes, yes, Dr. Crane, the President is expecting you at ten, he'll be with you in," Macmillan, the secretary, consulted her watch "...in six minutes."

To pass the time Crane imagined her sitting at her desk without any clothes, scratching her crotch, and quickly suppressed an emerging chuckle.

The secretary removed her glasses and pointed to a chair by the wall. "Won't you sit there, please."

He wondered how she would react if he were to pick his nose...my, but we're in good humor this morning. He had been apprehensive about seeing the president so soon after yesterday's confrontation, but a new day had made the incident appear less threatening. There had to be a logical explanation for his speaking Chinese. He blocked the cryptic phrase from his thoughts.

"Come right in Andrew, let's sit here." He motioned him to a matched pair of leather chairs next to a glass table.

"Do you take coffee?"

"Thank you." Is he ever in a friendly mood.

"Macmillan, please bring us," he emphasized the *us* "some coffee." He closed the door.

The man's private chambers...leather chairs and wood grained paneling, a little heavy but not depressing; there's a lot of light from the picture window. Rosewood desk which must have cost a small fortune; the books on the shelves looked really used, not just decorattion. The expected administrator's journals were neatly arranged but there was also quite an impressive library on politics and philosophy. How about that, fresh cut flowers. His Klee and Miro prints even looked like originals. So this was the way presidents lived, Crane thought, unwilling to compare this understated elegance to the over-sized broom closet he euphemistically referred to as an office...

Mansfield was speaking. "Stopped by the bookstore this morning." He was holding a copy of Andy's book. "I'd be honored if you would autograph it for me."

Andy was pleased. "Be delighted," and he signed his name and the date on the inside cover. Macmillan knocked and entered with the coffee.

The president continued to study him. A good-looking man with a strong yet sensitive face. Mansfield suspected women must find him attractive. His easy manner was a little too pronounced but he was very adept at pretending it was just a friendly chat.

Bliss lit a cigarette, handed Andy the pack and watched him light one of his own. His hands were steady.

"I've always been interested in anthropology but can you tell me what it's really like doing fieldwork in an Asian village?"

Andy smiled. This man knows how to pick his topic. "It's a terribly exciting experience; challenging yet dangerous. You're all alone in a very small community in another culture, so markedly different from your own. In just twelve months you have to make friends, turn them into informants, and learn from their perspective a thousand and one new ways of..."

Mansfield listened attentively, his eyes never wavered. "No doubt Chinese is a difficult language to master?" he queried.

He's trying to make it sound like a casual remark. Okay, I'll play his game. Andy eagerly responded. "Yes and no; actually some of the rules are rather simple, there are no tenses and no different verb endings, but in speaking it, the tonal quality is everything. The accent or inflection on a word gives it a meaning. Like 'mai," he pronounced it with a falling and then rising rythem, "means 'buy', but 'mai'", spoken this time with a falling tone, "means 'sell'. It's difficult going to market if you can't hear the distinction." They both laughed.

"Yes, I know," the president added, "when I was growing up we had a Chinese housekeeper. She found it too frustrating to learn English so in order to speak to her we had to learn Chinese."

Ah, that explains it, thought Andy. He was going to ask which Chinese language she spoke when Mansfield abruptly changed the topic.

"Are the arrangements for Dr. Spaacklund satisfactory?"

They discussed the speaker and when they were finished Andy added. "Dr. Barth and I will be acting as sort of marshalls for the presentation. If anyone has any special questions or requests it might be best to ask us first. We'll be wearing bright blur armbands." Andy left the office feeling relieved. He couldn't help being impressed by the president. He knows how to manipulate a conversation, Andy thought, and he's well informed. The anthropoligist returned to his department to pick up some graduate papers he had planned to grade at home. He kept thinking about the comment the president had made about his family's housekeeper. Domestics would find it difficult to come to America given the exclusion laws at the time. Even so the chances are that she would come from Hong Kong or Southeastern Kwangtung province, say Toi-Shan district. She would speak either the Sze-Yap or Sam-Yap varient o Cantonese, not Mandarin, the language he was speaking yesterday.

But the thought passed quickly from his mind as he slid into his new Fiat and drove the twenty-odd miles to his country home.

The president also left his office. Whatever else Crane was, the man was no fool. He too was impressed by both

43

the confidence and caution Andy had displayed. He had not mentioned the telephone conversation even once, nor had he even hinted at it.

Later that day walking rapidly along a new bike trail, the President stopped near a pay phone and after he was certain no one was following him, stepped inside and dialed the Washington number again.

"Barclay's Service, do you wish to leave a message?" It was another woman's voice.

"Yes," Bliss answered.

"Please identify yourself?"

Instead of giving the correct code he said, "I'm the person who called yesterday about the Crane file."

There was a noticeable pause. "I'm sorry sir, I wasn't here yesterday...can you identifiy yourself?"

Perhaps it was an unnecessary charade, but any caller who phoned two days in a row had to use it..

His stomach was churning now. The antacid hadn't helped. So Corporal Andrew M. Crane, AUS 56322487 had been stationed in Korea with Military Intelligence. He was a clerk in G-2, a translator, and was privy to top secret documents...

The "village" couldn't have been more than a few minutes walk from his compound. I'll never forget the smell from the honey-buckets when the wind shifted; Mansfield thought. Crane was wounded in action on October 13,1952, later flown to Tokyo. But where was he on the night of the twelfth, and I don't recall that village being off-limits.

He was shaken, but he remained calm. This was not the time to panic. He recalled his conversation with Lucas. "Probably had a girlfriend; he still gets letters from Korea."

The evidence was perhaps only hearsay, but he could not afford to take the chance. He had to be certain.

EIGHT

The university seemed almost as crowded in the evening as it had been during the day. Students mobbed the parking lots, filled classrooms, smoked pot on the lawns, read in the library and drank dark coffee at the "Pub" till it closed at eleven. It hadn't always been that way. Faced with decreasing enrollments, and that meant a smaller budget, the President initiated the campaign to, as he put it, "open the doors to the people."

The strategy was a successful one. The experimental college and extension classes started at dusk, primarily attracting older adults and those seeking a different kind of challenge. Later, academic departments found it to their advantage to offer a full major to working students. There was even some humorous talk of a vice-president for evening instruction.

Bliss explained to his wife that he had to go to the campus to work on the budget. Alexa would miss him, but she had learned that a president's time is never really his own.

Driving the station-wagon he parked in the visitor's pay lot in back of the library rather than the administrator's reserved area. He knew that most classes had started at seven and usually run till ten. He arrived at eight-seventeen.

The evening was cool and he was comfortable, wearing his rust turtleneck and corduroy jacket, similar to the outfit Andy had had on that morning. They appeared to be about the same height.

"Good evening, Dr. Mansfield."

He was startled. "Evening Dr. Wheeling." He had met

her the other day and remembered she had her office in the library.

"What brings you to our busy campus at night?"

He thought quickly. "I have to do some homework," then smiling, "glad we keep our library open."

She nodded politely and walked on. Bliss was annoyed. He had not planned on meeting anyone tonight. Then he recalled the wooded trail, the one with no lights. He walked back and started up the path.

The evening was alive with the strange sounds of small night creatures. Twice he imagined he heard approaching footsteps but no one appeared. A full moon cast eerie shadows, its reflected light turned the trees into sinister guardians. The Anthropology buildings were dark save for a single light in the Archeology lab. He made his way swiftly through the breezeway and paused outside Crane's office. Slowly he inserted the master key in the lock. It opened easily and he stepped inside. For a moment he just stood there allowing his eyes to adjust to the shadows. Then he closed the window blinds and withdrew the pencil flashlight from his pocket.

It was really not a very large office. He was reminded of those bathrooms on airplanes, small but fully operational. There was a university desk and swivel chair against the window. The desk held a tensor lamp and was cluttered with papers and books; some were open and there were passages underlined in ink. Industrious, wasn't he?

Bookshelves dominated each wall, filled with hardbound texts, paperbacks and journals. The earlier works were stacked neatly with an attempt to arrange them in size place, but the later volumes were in dissarray. Social and cultural anthropology he mused...some sociology texts here and there...the last two shelves were dovoted to China, most of the titles in English but some with distinctive bright red characters. There was a smaller table and a chair...judging from the introductory chapters it was probably used by his graduate assistant. The file, an older wooden model without a lock was set against the wall.

Bliss had called Andy's residence earlier at eight-ten and when the professor answered he had immediately hung up. He knew Crane lived at least twenty miles from the campus and on those roads it would take him at least forty-five minutes to drive to it and park the car, that is if he left right away. It was now eight-thirty, he had twenty-five minutes of safe time.

Relax, there's no reason for him to come here. You've probably got all night. Letters. Where would he keep them? He began a methodical search. For twenty minutes Bliss hurriedly, yet systematically, examined every desk and chairs and even peered inside a large wooden Chinese statue with a hollow base. Damm! The letters, if there were any, must be at home.

"Briiing." He froze.

"Briiing...Briiing." Short of breath, Bliss waited in the dark silence.

"Briiing." Who could be calling? Why now of all times? The phone stopped ringing.

The president was about to leave when he noticed the memo sticking out from between Crane's lecture notes. He carefully removed it and stared at the words. They were hastily written not once or twice but three times. The third time they were underlined. At the bottom of the page was a single word, followed by a question mark, *"KOREA?"* It had to be deliberate. They were the very words he had used on the phone that day, the identical phrase whispered in a Korean village over a quarter of a century ago. The anthropologist knew.

He opened the blinds, re-locked the door and made his way cautiously back to the wooded path. Crane knows, but why hasn't he done something about it? Maybe he only suspects? He's really not sure? Maybe he doesn't remember? Could he be thinking of blackmailing me?

47

He's just waiting for his chance? Stop it! You're becoming paranoid. A lesser man would have panicked, and although Bliss was getting very close to that point, he was able to regain control. All these years of careful planning... he had to take one more chance. Crane had to be stopped. But how?

A lone light burned as he sat in his study drinking freshed brewed coffee and chain smoking. He continued to stare at the spotlight and the shadow it cast upon the garden for a very long time. Although he knew what he had to do, it wasn't easy reaching a final decision. Then, he picked up the phone and dialed a local number. Slowly he reached for his pen and began to write.

NINE

The house was a natural stone and wood fortress when seen from the road, but a virtual wall of glass facing the lakeside; all of it surrounded by redwood decking. Navaho ceremonial blankets and rough-weave Columbian rugs hung from ceiling height, vibrant colors lighting the dark walls. Eerie metal sculptures designed by a Calder devotee stood next to traditional hand-carved Chinese statues, an uneasy alliance of East and West to complement the shelves of endless books.

Your attention was immediately drawn to the stone fireplace where massive granite boulders spanned an entire wall giving the conversation pit a rustic charm. It was truly magnificent, a lasting monument to the architect's love-affair with gargantuan proportions. On cold winter nights burning logs crackled and blue-tipped flames almost touched the rafters. The house reflected the eclectic nature of its owner as chrome and glass tables, Mexican folk art and velvet couches blended together in the massive living room. A late afternoon sun highlighted spreading plants. It was home to a man whose yearning for the country was a direct result of growing up in city streets.

Andy Crane had spent the first seventeen years of his life surviving in Brooklyn, New York. He distinctly remembered the endless rows of seedy brownstones; a world of crowded apartments, discordant noises and overpowering smells. So he had spent the next twenty years escaping from the frustrating memories of depression-era blue-collar parents and the rest of his childhood past. The time had come to stop running.

Watching the ducks warily circle an approaching sailboat, he waved at Ian McGregor, the ship's master. "Beware the Loch Ness monster," he shouted.

"Yer daft," replied Ian as he passed out of sight.

For the next hour, Andy diligently applied himself to the war against ignorance, but the disappointing quality of his students' papers suggested he was losing the battle. He gave up. Leslie had called earlier. She was having dinner at the Pattersons and would be over about ten. There was something she had to tell him and she sounded excited.

His relationship with her had started out as just another experiment between two consenting adults, but both of them quickly tired of the charade. In the past year their feelings had grown substantially so that there was an implicit understanding, a feeling of trust and security in which both love and lust could flourish. The future was uncertain. Andy was not entirely free from the memories of Elaine's tragic death, and Leslie still sought proof of her independence.

Crane started to read again, but it was no use. He yawned several times and drifted into a deep sleep, waking about eight to answer the phone but hearing only a dialtone. Returning to his novel, he read till nine-thirty when there was a knock on the door.

"Hi, lover, did you miss me?"

"No, not really, I was too busy thinking about how I was going to make it with Farrah." Of course he had missed her.

"Liar!" she screamed and without so much as a warning playfully wrestled him to the floor and started to kiss his neck. "I'm better than her anyway."

"Perhaps," teased Andy, "but does it matter where I get my appetite as long as I eat at home?"

"Yes!" she shouted, "yes, yes, yes."

When they had untangled themselves and after opening a new bottle of wine, a Chablis this time, Andy inquired, "want to tell me about your evening?"

"Oh, do I ever. You remember Dave Snyder? Well, he coincidentally on purpose dropped over while we were having dessert and I don't think it was the cake he wanted. He just sat there giving me puppy-dog looks with those sad eyes, waiting for me to forgive him for being married."

"And with four children." Andy quipped.

"He apologized profusely, complimented me on my hair, and told me how well my paper was received by *his* friends at the sociology meetings. Then he hinted that your aggressive tennis betrays your true feelings, so you couldn't possibly love me, and that he and his wife had almost reached a new understanding."

Andy stopped her. "What, no proposition?"

"Wait, that comes later. He told me that this time he was going to ask for a divorce so I wished him the best. Then he waited until I was at the door, I suspect so the Pattersons wouldn't overhear us. He leaned over and whispered in my ear: 'Are you free tomorrow between two and four...my wife's going shopping.' "

"...and you told him?"

"Don't interrupt. I informed him that I was not interested, but he just shrugged his shoulders and asked, 'how about ten-thirty then, but it'll have to be in my office.' "

Andy laughed so hard he spilled the wine. Leslie was hysterical. Dave Snyder's attempts to acquire a "girlfriend" had been going on for five years before Leslie joined the faculty, and were, by this time, legendary.

Leslie recovered first. "All this talk is just making me horny." She gave him a suggestive leer.

She always amazed him. This young professional, so cautious, even why when it came to other matters, was a hellion when it came to sex. No, that wasn't quite right, she was a woman who enjoyed the act and wasn't embarrassed about admitting it.

He reached for her hips and backed her against the wall keeping her body pressed against his own. Their kisses were gentle at first but her rising desire had little need for foreplay. Lifting her arms and then her black sweater above her shoulders, he lowered his head and hungrily tasted her brown nipples. She was breathing deeply as her nails dug into his flesh, moaning as his tongue stimulated her breasts. Still holding her against the wall, he let her pants fall to the floor as he placed on hand under her backside, the other hand cupped her mound of dark pubic hair while his fingers stroked her dampness. Leslie's body was on fire. She reached for him but too excited to coordinate her movements and gasping as she reached her climax.

Later she lay beside him on the rug and when she was ready, opened his shorts and licked her lover's swollen penis. Straddling her chest, he rubbed himself in the valley created by her small breasts until he could no longer stand the pressure. He spread her thighs and penetrated her moist lips. Lying over her, he moved his hands down between her legs as he continued to thrust deep inside. Their orgasms were almost simultaneous, Leslie coming seconds before him.

Andy was returning from the bathroom when she started to get dressed.

"Thought you might be planning to spend the night?"

"Nope, I've got an early class and lots of preparation."

She was half out the door when she suddenly stopped. "I'd almost forgotten what I came over for."

"Really?"

She was blushing at his smile. "Be serious...Have you seen this evening's *Chronicle?*"

He shook his head.

"It's about Congressman Parsons. The president

52

must have gotten an inside scoop." She showed him the newsclipping.

"*PARSONS DECLINES NOMINATION*. Pleading ill health and over-extended commitments, Congressman Duane Parsons surprisingly declined the party's nomination and the opportunity to fill the Senate seat held by retiring Senator Wallace Riggs.

Parsons, the powerful chairman of the House Sub-committee on..."

TEN

When it was real quiet, and nowadays that was practically all the time, you could hear the cricket's chatter disturb the night's silence. They knew better than to sing during the day when they would have to compete with the jays and the robins or with the farmer's machines making their fields ready for a late Spring planting. The crickets brown-green colors allowed them to blend into the country grass saving them from nature's predators. It was as though they weren't even there.

It was the same for the leathery old man rocking back and forth, watching the weeds grow taller. His skin was the color of red earth and when he stopped moving it would be as if he too had disappeared.

Wes Baylor's service station, a weathered shack with forty years of constant exposure to the sun turning it white, and the single red gas pump, fronted on the old highway, two miles east of the railroad crossing. During the day business was erratic. You could count on Charley's dump truck at noon, Nora Preston and her five kids an hour later, but that was it. Customers were almost non-existent in the evening, the station having been that way ever since they completed the new freeway.

At first Wes complained bitterly but as the years passed he became resigned to sitting in the wicker rocker spending his days alone as old men had always learned to do. He was about to rekindle his pipe when he heard the car pull off the road and stop by the one remaining pump.

"Whut kin I do fer ya stranger?" He volunteered as he walked towards the vehicle. It was a new Buick station wagon with local plates. The driver's face was hidden in shadow but you could tell he was wearing a jacket. He was alone.

"Fill her up."

Wes walked slowly to the pump, pulled on the hose and proceeded with his job. He tried to make conversation. "You from the college, Mister?" He was noticing the decal on the window. There was no reply.

Wes mumbled and grunted. "That'll be ten even."

The stranger took out his wallet and gave him a ten dollar bill.

"Check the oil, Mister?" he inquired.

"No thanks."

The old man was about to return to his solitude when he heard a second car pull up. It was an older-model pickup.

Well ain't this sumptin, he thought. Next thing ya know we'll be havin' a party.

The driver opened his cab and walked up to him. "I've been having some trouble with the battery, could you check the water?"

This one had the look of a hunter about him. Hair cropped real short, almost a crew cut. Wearing levis and dusty cowboy boots. His outfit sure fit the old truck, but there was somethin about the way his eyes searched the area which reminded West of his Sergeant during the big war.

"Is it all right if I use your restroom?"

"Yep, through the door in the back."

Wes bent over the hood, raised it and opened the caps. Sure enough, there was hardly any water. How'd he drive out here anyway? He was busy filling the battery so he couldn't see the Buick's owner pass the other man a thick envelope.

The plain manila folder contained a description, six foot-one, one hundred and eighty-five pounds, blond hair, hazel eyes, and a photograph taken from last year's Faculty Profiles of Professor Andrew M. Crane. There was a map of the campus, a hurriedly-sketched diagram of the Spradley quad, but one that showed all entrance and exit points, and the information that Crane would be the only adult male wearing a bright blue armband.

At 11:30, the man with the look of a hunter picked up the telephone and dialed an unlisted number in New York City.

Dominic Vereste was ten years old when Andy Crane broke his leg as a senior running back during the city's All-Star High School Football classic.

On that day he was busy shaking down a skinny third-grader for lunch money. The kid only had thirteen cents so he held his head in the toilet bowl while he flushed. At fourteen he shoved his switchblade into the gut of a rival gang leader from the Red Hook section of Brooklyn. Taken to Juvenille Hall but later released due to lack of evidence, he went home to his Sicilian mother whose broken English was almost unintelligible and who worked part-time as a domestic. Dominic's father had been killed in a construction accident when Dominic was only seven.

In 1960 St. Mary's reluctantly granted him a general diploma, and he enlisted in the Army completeing basic and advanced infantry training at Fort Benning where he qualified as an expert with the M-1. He went on to Jump Training and Ranger School at Fort Campbell. Ordered to Vietnam, he was promoted to Corporal six months later. Unfortunately his military career came to an abrupt end when he stomped all over his fire-team leader during a routine patrol. This time there were witnesses.

Reduced two grades but honorably discharged, the Vietnam veteran enrolled in the Police Academy, spent two years on foot patrol, and at the age of twenty-six volunteered for a S.W.A.T. team. During a demonstration, he shot a sixteen-year-old civilian. Termed a "bad shooting" by a Review Board, he was allowed to resign from New York's finest.

By the time he turned thirty, he could list under occupation, enforcer, syndicate muscle and hit-man. He had a promising future.

Rain had been expected but the sky was only overcast before night fell on what had been a muggy unpleasant day in "Fun City." Dominic had just finished his daily workout at Paddy's Athletic Club, the name given to a third-rate Manhattan gym. His muscles stretched as he toweled off after his shower. Deliberately tightening his stomach, he paused to examine the pleasing result in a full-length mirror. He then spent fifteen minutes styling his thick shoulder-length black hair. Dressed in a T-shirt and chinos, he swaggered across Forty-Second Street, ignoring the midnight cowboys and porno flick hustlers who vied for his attention, walking towards Angelo's Bar and Grill over on Eighth Ave.

"Hey, gimme a beer Angie," he ordered the bartender.

"Sure Dom, anything you say." Angelo despised the egotistical hood but knew better than to argue with anyone working for the "Romano Family."

The cool liquid couldn't begin to quench his thirst. "You seem Bitsy tonight?"

"She don't start datin' till nine. Wait a couple of minutes, she'll probably be in for a drink."

Demanding another beer, Dominic thought about Bitsy Ricco. He was bored and when he was bored he became frustrated, and when that happened, he looked for Bitsy. Never much good with women, he easily tired of bullshitting a broad just to crawl in her pants. What's the difference, a fuck's a fuck.

At ten minutes after nine an ominous sky turned black, and accomanied by thunder and lightning, released its fury on the dry New York streets. Bitsy had just started to work her "stroll," the northeast corner of Eighth Ave. and Fortieth Street when the torrent started, immediately causing her translucent blouse to cling to her body reavealing large, over-ripe breasts. Her twenty-five dollar hot pants were waterlogged and her spikes ruined by the time she found shelter at Angie's.

"Jesus Christ, are you soaked. Hey, Bits, over here, you wanna drink?"

"Thanks," she purred. "I'm glad there are still some gentlemen left."

Bitsy, real name, Rosalina, was an oddity among working women, a street hooker who really liked to ball.

"Here, take my handkerchief and dry your hair. Angie! get this lady a drink and then go get her a towel." As he watched her move, he was becoming increasingly aware of her body and of the rising bulge in his pants.

"How's tricks?"

What a weird sense of humor. "Are you kiddin, the only John's left on a night like this are the freaks."

"You need some bread?"

"Naw, my old man can carry me." Bitsy noticed Dominic staring. She was proud of her breasts, full yet firm, not like Dee-Anne's watermelons which almost reached her gut.

He was still reluctant to come right out and say it. "You wanna come home with me, huh?"

Why not, if the rain don't stop it's better'n nothin. "Why Dom, I'm so gald you asked." But they sat there a while longer making small talk, that is Bitsy did most of the talking. Dominic was hardly a conversationalist and never spoke about his work.

The storm turned to a shower and they took a cab to his apartment. He turned on the lights.

Bitsy was shocked by its spartan appearance. "Hey,

58

Dom, you ain't got no furniture here."

He gave her a nasty look. "I don't need much."

She would be careful next time. "Okay honey, what'll it be?"

Dominic blushed. "Half n'half."

Bitsy did a slow striptease. Removing her blouse she cupped her breasts and let her fingernails stimulate her nipples. She didn't quite know why, but it always turned men on. Her lace panties were next. Some guys got all hot when she played with her pussy, and even wanted to eat it. Dominic wouldn't go for that. His understanding of women was limited to the thrust of his cock yet his prick continued to grow as he watched Bitsy slide her fingers inside.

Dom stood by the bed and let the young hooker open his zipper. She inspected his penis and when she was satisfied that it was clean, held it between her thumb and index fingers. Slowly and with practised expertise she started to rub until his swollen shaft turned red. Softly kissing him, she licked up and down each side. Then placing his tip between her warm lips she began to suck. Take it easy girl, too much pressure and he'll get it on in your mouth. Actually Bitsy didn't mind sucking him off, it would be a lot easier and she wouldn't have to douche. But the deal was for half and half and she intended to keep her part of the bargain.

Spreading herself on the mattress, she opened her legs letting him mount her while guiding his cock with her hands.

"Come'n baby, move it. That's my man." Her hips matched his excitement.

When she left, Dom opened a bottle and poured himself another drink. He felt good, a little tired but relieved, his demands being easily satisfied. Falling into a relaxing sleep, he was dreaming about Bitsy's talented tongue when the ringing of the phone disturbed his fantasy. He listened intently to the caller.

Dominic Vereste was a bully and a braggard, but he had certain redeeming qualities. He was reasonably intelligent and in excellent physical condition. When he was working, he listened carefully and did exactly as he was told. An expert marksman who had never missed a moving target, he was also expendable.

ELEVEN

The day before Spaacklund was scheduled to speak, Bliss Mansfield neither ran in Emerson Park nor did he go to his office at the university. His behavior was unusual, the president being a man who prided himself on daily physical conditioning and duty.

Bliss hadn't slept well at all, tossing about most of the night and waking at four only to discover he was covered with sweat and felt feverish. He breakfasted alone on warm tea and unbuttered toast before retiring to his study where he sought sanctuary from his family's well-meaning, but nevertheless annoying concern.

It just wasn't fair, his career and ambitions ruined by a single conversation. The decision he had reached yesterday was a logical one; engaged in a war you had to expect casualties. This wasn't a theoretical exercise any longer. Bliss hadn't thought about Korea in years; there was really no need to do so, but he should have known it would come to this sooner or later.

The phone rang once. "...Yes?"

"President Mansfield?"

"Speaking."

"This is Mr. Haber representing Dandridge Realty. If you recall, sir, we met briefly the other day and spoke about listing your property. Do you still want us to go ahead with those plans?"

He hesitated. What would he gain by changing his mind. "Yes... go ahead."

"Very good sir, we should have it on the market by twelve noon tomorrow at the latest. Would there be anything else we could do for you?"

It was his last chance. "No, nothing." The phone call concluded the matter. By noon, Friday, Crane would no longer pose a threat.

Leslie was up earlier than usual rubbing the sleep from her eyes and splashing cold water on her face. While the coffee was brewing, she returned to the bathroom and vigorously brushed her teeth.

Sitting at the oversized butcher-block table she often used as a desk, she could imagine the sun starting to rise, it seemed, over the sky blue waters of the olympic pool. Leslie had leased a two-bedroom apartment in a fashionable complex near the campus that catered, although not exclusively, to those men and women who enjoyed an active, hedonistic lifestyle. Before she became so involved with Andy, she was a frequent habituee of the Friday, four-to-six happy hour at the clubhouse and often found that the time passed so quickly it was much later before the party was over. Other evenings were spent sipping wine in the Jacuzzi pool while aimlessly making small talk with the residents. Wednesday nights she taught a class from seven to ten. Most of the time she had worked hard and had been lonely.

Older than the flight attendants, secretaries, models, call girls and other unattached young beauties, she was not so old as to be mistaken for their maiden aunt. At thirty-five, Leslie Pace was curvaceous with a shapely figure that was enhanced by dark curls which easily fell past her shoulders. Still very much an "outdoors gal," her skin was bronzed in the bright days of Spring and Summer.

Aware of her body, and ever since she had first made love with Andy, of its many sensuous and erogenous zones, she was not a woman to be taken lightly. She demanded sensitivity and honesty in her relationships with all people, but particularly those with men.

As a professional woman, she tried to appear

confident, poised and rather aggressive. To trifle with her mind was as serious an offense as tampering with her body. Graduate school had been a challenge, one she had successfully met, so she was incensed when a colleague referred to her as the department's "token woman." If it took determination, grit or sheer staying-power to be accepted as an equal, then she would meet that challenge too. She was also adept at hiding her insecurity.

While Leslie regarded her marriage as a bad scene, actually a silver-spoon trap, it had not discouraged a loving, sharing commitment with one man. Her fantasies about her relationship with Andy frequently included marriage.

Starting on her second cup of coffee, she re-read her notes, checked a reference in a book borrowed from the library, and looked forward to the interdisciplinary Arts and Sciences seminar sarcastically called by the students, "revolution and rubbish."

The special class in Room 361 of the Arts library was unique. Not only was it limited to a maximum of twelve graduate students in the social sciences, it was also staffed and regularly attended by three professors. It was further restricted to those students who were in their final year of doctoral candidacy, most of them already writing their dissertations. The seminar was as close as any student had come to being treated as an equal by his or hers mentors. The topic for this last meeting focused upon the character of the revolutionary traitor.

Professor Robert Dorn was speaking. "...Nonsense, how can you expect a man," he glanced at Leslie, "or a woman, to suppress their most demanding desires for a decade or more, and to pretend to go along with the system they have betrayed, without experiencing some serious psychological confusion?"

"Begging to differ with you," replied Tony Mott, one of the Psychology Department's better young minds, "but confusion is to a large measure a result of incompatibilities. A covert revolutionary then, would have to hold conflicting ideas about, let's say justice and morality, but what if he can compartmentalize his conflicts and separate them?"

Janis Wainright, Andy's most attractive student, joined the attack. "Take for example the Buganda Chiefs of Africa in the 30's. They had to participate in both a British and native world, each with different expectations about loyalties. Most of them managed to be quite successful in both systems."

At that point Lincoln Ong entered the arena with a personal anecdote. "I'm an American but my parents are China born. They expected me to kow-tow to my elders and I still do. Yet when I'm with my American friends we behave as equals and no one bows down to anyone else. You would think there would be a conflict but there isn't. I can and do switch identities depending upon my audience. Do I seem particularly confused?"

Everyone grinned and there were a few laughs until Leslie interupted. "I think we may be missing the point, Janis, you should also recall that many of the Buganda chiefs couldn't handle dual expectations and committed suicide as a result, and Lincoln, your example is not unique. All of us are to a large degree situation oriented, but most of us are ordinary people without the burning commitment of revolutionary zeal."

"Just what kind of revolutionary are you talking about?" asked Angus Howe, the third faculty member, who thought the conversation was going nowhere. "Do you think he's dark and sinister, with a black beard, ready to hurl a home-made cannonball at his enemies, or is he like the late Mao Tze-tùng, leading his followers on the long march, or even Jesus, wandering in the desert and experiencing visions?" He paused to pour some water and continued.

"No, they were open about their motives and their dreams of a new social order. They didn't have to hide and pretend."

"Would you call them confused then" asked Jehan ElGuindi, the Egyptian polysci major.

"Oh, no" replied Howe," at least not in the classical sense of psychological disorientation. I doubt if they were really so different from many of their contemporaries...perhaps a bit more outspoken."

Len Springer, the only admitted Socialist in the class rose from his seat and shouted. "That's not the kind of a person we've been discussing. This is a man who is willingly planning to betray his people. Unlike, let's say 'the man without a country,' he shows no remorse. He knows he's right, he's always known. I can't help conclude that his normal everyday life is nothing more than a charade, he's just waiting for the right moment to make his move."

"And how might I ask is he going to make that move?" quizzed Alexander Owusu, an Ashanti with tribal scars on his cheeks.

Len continued. "By using the system he hates so. He'll rise within it, gain access to political or economic power, and destroy it from within."

"I would think," it was now Alexander's turn, "that anyone who could rise to such an important position would, how do you say it, lose some of his revolutionary zeal in the process. You know the best way to tame a radical is to make him part of the system."

"But that's not what happens" exclaimed Len loudly. "His success only intensifies his dissatisfaction and makes all the social injustices even more evident. Each time he wins he becomes even more committed."

Professor Pace defused what seemed to be turning into a personal debate. "Since you both seem to already know how a covert revolutionary thinks, I would like to know how he became one, that is," she added a bit sarcastically, "assuming they are not born that way."

Not to be overshadowed, Dr. Dorm replied "I wouldn't

be so sure about that Leslie, perhaps it could go back to genetics. Individuals open to change have selective advantages for surviving."

He changed his grin to a more proper expression. "Seriously, the answer seems to lay in an individual's life-history, that is how our fictitious fanatic views it. Oh I grant you it may be related to a particularly stressful period of history where chaos reigns, but it ultimately depends upon very personal experiences. Let us say a man grows up in an ordinary environment but is exposed at an early age to a grave social injustice like racism or bigotry, either involving himself or his family. If our fanatic was religious he might blame God or Satan, but if he is perceptive and can see beyond the immediate, he'll blame the society itself, and there's a damn good chance that's where the blame really lies."

"Oh, then our revolutionary friend is a realist," Lincoln interjected.

"Absolutely" replied Dorn, "chances are he is also rather clever and, I would suspect, better off than most of the population."

Alexander interrupted him. "That's logical, he might even be a member of the elite. You must have time to reflect upon poverty, starvation or inhumanity. Most people are too busy surviving to afford that luxury."

"Agreed," Dorn continued with enthusiasm, "but the inhumanity you mention doesn't have to be so pronounced, it's all in the mind. The point is this, if what our friend sees is reprehensible to him, than it's real enough."

It was Howe's turn. "As a historian I'm more concerned with the sequencing. First he must be aware of injustice; perhaps he meditates upon it, maybe for many years and it grows like a cancer. Now he holds the society responsible. But here's where the argument is weak. Almost all of us go through such stages, but when we try to do something about it, it's usually not outside, but within the rules. Let's say as a young man I was appalled by the ignorance I found about me, so I became a teacher, that would hardly make me a revolutionary."

"But you are" piped Janice, "after all, you challenge the establishment every day in your classes."

"True, but I hardly need to be covert about it. A university is an accepted arena in which to raise those challenges."

Leslie again. "Maybe what you needed was a revelation an experience that transcends the ordinary, almost a religious conversion."

Edward Wright, an American Studies scholar who had been silent up to now spoke out. "Yes, that would explain it. Remember that Korean Minister's sect, the moonies? They claim to have been disenchanted with life as they saw it. The answer he supplied seemed simple enough, so they saw the light, and boy, are they ever committed."

"Weren't they brainwashed?"

"Yes and no," Edward responded. "They were subjected to intensive re-socialization programming, but those that converted were well on their way, that is they were psychologically ready to accept new answers. I just read a recent study where it says that the Chinese Communists were most successful with those POW's who were ready alienated from America before they were captured. I guess just being in combat could do it all by itself. It wouldn't take much convincing to drive them over the edge."

"Yes, but look what happened when they returned home," Dorn added. "They were once again re-programmed and seemed to make the adjustment. You could call them temporary converts at best."

"How do we know they all readjusted?" asked Jehan, "perhaps they were sent back, told to fake it, and wait."

"Wait for what?" asked Len, "a secret signal, a rising of the moon so to speak?"

The clock announced that the seminar had officially

ended and another class was scheduled for the room. Dorn and three others left for the coffee house to continue the conversation.

After the seminar, Leslie walked a way with Angus Howe, another faculty member, who asked her to join him for lunch, but she declined the offer and returned to her office. She had received the proofs for her article, "The Police Investigator as Sociologist," and was anxious to mail the proofs back to the editor, it being the first professional article she had written as a new Assistant Professor. It was important because the publish or perish philosophy was very real.

Yet as she stared at the papers, her thoughts drifted back to the seminar. Why not? The Irish, before the Easter rising, had secretly trained men for just that moment. During the day they might behave like ordinary farmers, biding their time and waiting...The Germans had sent what they referred to as 'sleepers' back to their Scottish and British homes long before an actual declaration of war. They, too, were told to establish themselves in the community and await further orders...and Rudolph Abel, who had been a Russian spy for twenty years before he was discovered. What was his mission?

She didn't know why, but she was more than disturbed by those thoughts.

At that moment, Andy wasn't concerned with revolutionaries or speculative philosophy or even Parson's refusal to run for the Senate, although he had to admit that last night he had been surprisingly unsettled. He was concentrating very hard on the tennis game and his only concern was with winning. Billy Ridges, the club pro, had taken two sets; the first a rather shameful 6-1, the second he had barely lost in a 7-6 tiebreaker. But Ridges was slowing down. It was now 5-4 and Andy was serving...

He raised his racquet back, leaned forward and smashed the ball into the net. The second serve was a hair short of being wide, yet Billy returned it with such force that Andy barely reached it. Billy met the ball and it dropped over the net. "Love-fifteen." Andy needed the next point. His service was deep, returned down the center, he hit it and the ball went to the baseline. Don't let up now, keep putting pressure on him. Two more return rallys. Billy was out of position and had to lob the ball high into the sun. Andy easily put it away. The game continued to see-saw back and forth...thirty-all... forty-thirty...deuce...add-in...deuce...add-out...deuce.   Andy was really sweating. His wristbands felt waterlogged. Wiping the perspiration from his eyes on his clean shirt, his legs started to buckle. Good God! That son-of-a-bitch is a human backboard. He never misses.

Then he noticed that Billy had moved and was standing rather close to the center of the court. Too close, Andy concluded. His first serve was an ace, barely catching the outside corner. Billy didn't even have enough time to bring his racquet into play. Now you've got him, just one more point and it's all over. Andy brought his arm up and bore down hard. He could almost feel the ball flying across the net.

"Sorry, long," shouted Billy.

Andy walked back to the service line. On his second serve he kept the ball deep and to his opponent's forehand. Billy returned the shot almost at his feet and Andy had to scoop it up. The pro's next return came about shoulder height and Andy handled it beautifully with a backhand slice. Now it was Billy's turn to be surprised. He hesitated too long and managed only a weak return but the professor was at the net and sent it racing down the sideline well out of reach. The game was over and they shook hands like the good friends they were.

"Andy, when are you going to stop killing yourself?

You're getting too old for kid stuff. Go play doubles with your girl friend."

He laughed. "If I'm getting so old why are you out of breath?"

Crane's love-affair with tennis began when he was a kid and accompanied his parents on a rare visit to friends on Long Island, and actually saw the game being played for the first time. Westhampton was a summer home for the more affluent and it was not unusual for a family to have their private court. He was impressed with the grace and agility of the players. Their movements seemed fluid yet precise. The men had a poise and confidence that hid their human frailties, so evident off the court.

It was only after he had become an anthropologist, that he perceived the "tennis match" as a ritual where mortals used psychological and social skills to enhance their prestige and where spectators could also play games of their own choosing. The court was more than merely a playing field, it was a stage where people acted out dramas as large as life itself.

Back in Brooklyn, the realities of street life demanded expertise in stickball and football, so Andy didn't start playing until his graduate days at Cornell. With his natural athletic abilities and his eagerness to learn, he became a relatively good player in a remarkably short time. Tennis also held for Andy another kind of reward which had little to do with the game itself. In the academic world, rhetoric and pretense often substituted for knowledge, but on a tennis court you had only to prove yourself; your skill would be as evident as your pretense. Nobody would be fooled for long. At the university, one's own future also depended upon the goodwill and cooperation of colleagues, administrators, secretaries and government agencies. Your research grant might be delayed because the Dean's assistant forgot an important form. Similarly, plans for team-teaching depended upon the willingness of your partner.

On the court, you and you alone were responsible. Victories were not shared, nor could you blame others for your defeat.

Andy showered quickly, grabbed a sandwich and beer at the club bar and rushed home. It was his job to see that Dr. Spaacklund was met at the airport, and Andy was both excited and a little apprehensive about meeting the South African official. Tomorrow was going to be an eventful day.

Dominic Vereste arrived at the airport in the early hours of the morning carrying only an overnight suitcase. Although his body was tired from lack of sleep, his eyes remained alert. He was met by a man with short hair who hustled him into a waiting car, drove him to an apartment just outside of town, and who later explained his assignment. Dom listened carefully and remembered everything. He gave the man a list of materials he would require.

The afternoon was unseasonably warm, causing the muscular student to take time out from jogging and rest in the shade of the maple trees surrounding the quad. Because he was wearing a T-shirt emblazoned with the university's initials, gray sweatpants and white sneakers, no one payed him particular attention as he wandered about Spradley Hall. Smiling at a secretary on the fifth floor, he inspected the janitor's station, a small cubicle facing the speaker's stand. He made a mental note of the stairwells and the elevator location before he left the building.

As he continued to walk around the campus, an overweight coed wistfuly admired his broad shoulders and long black hair.

TWELVE

At dawn, on a Friday in late May, the sun was just beginning to make its presence felt. The wind was quiet and there was yet a hint of moisture on the grass. Robins called to each other as they eagerly explored the wet ground searching for their breakfast, while garden spiders were busy weaving their treacherous webs. The campus glistened in the early morning light, a silent sea of green; the man-made buildings and concrete footpaths seemed oddly out of place.

The silence was largely illusory. Already the parking lots were beginning to fill with early-risers. Smells of brewing coffee and freshly baked bread mixed with bacon sizzling on the grill. Cooks, clad in white were busy preparing breakfast while students, paid the minimum wage as busboys, stacked dishes and filled sugar bowls. The cash register was ringing up the first sale of the day.

By six-thirty, the Residence Halls were starting to become alive. Lights switched on in dormitories and sounds from electric razors competed with showers and toilets as the student body hurriedly prepared for a new morning. Outside the library doors, a throng of red-eyed and anxious scholars gathered awaiting the seven o'clock opening. Inside, the library personnel braced themselves for the morning onslaught.

Early-bird joggers waved to arriving bike riders and to the fishermen who were moving out in small boats on the river. Married students in Collegetown were busily dressing hungry children while readying their infant's bottle for the first feeding.

The night-shift security and maintenance people

anticipated the arrival of their replacements while a few secretaries, graduate assistants, administrators and even professors began their work, on what promised to be a warm and humid, yet clear and sunny day.

His name plate identified him as Anthony Pereira. Dressed in an immaculate and newly-pressed green uniform, with the University's gold crest centered over his shirt pocket, he remained indistinguishable from the other members of the maintenance crew. A blue baseball cap completely covering his close-cropped black hair was pulled low over his forehead so that his face remained partially in shadow. Several keys hung from a brass ring attached to his belt. Like many other blue-collar employees, he carried a faded canvas bag which should have contained a change of clothes, lunch sack and a thermos filled with black coffee.

The uniform did little to disguise his bulging muscles. A careful observer would have noticed this, and the fact that he shied away from the other men. But no one was watching.

He was replacing Alden Findley, who at this moment was rapidly pacing the hospital's waiting room. Findley had received a call informing him that his wife had suffered a heart attack and was on the critical list. She was calling for him and he was advised to hurry.

Director of Security Ron Mabra nervously smoked while staring out the kitchen window. His four children were arguing about school and their continuous shouting made it difficult to think. Last night he had received word from a reliable source that a demonstration was planned for the South African's speech. When he asked for details, his informant abruptly hung up. He didn't like it. Not one damn bit.

"Betty," he growled at his wife, "I have to get over to the campus." He put on his belt, removed the pistol from the locked drawer and slammed the screen door on the

73

way out.

When Bliss Mansfield arrived at his office at seven-thirty, Macmillan had just finished making coffee.

"Good morning Sir, hope you slept well. The doughnuts on your desk are fresh. You look like you're losing too much weight. They'll be good for you."

"Good morning Macmillan. Thank you for taking such an interest in my weight, but I've already had breakfast. What's my schedule?"

She gave him a scowl but was secretly pleased. "Two long-distance phone calls but nothing urgent. An appointment with Vice-President Hadley at nine. Dr. Spaacklund from South Africa will be in the V.I.P. lounge at ten-thirty, he'll be speaking on the quad at eleven. Luncheon at twelve forty-five with the Alumni Boosters. I've kept you free to work on the budget after three."

"Is that all?" asked the president.

"Oh, yes, your wife called to tell you to remember to pick up your new suits at the Custom Shoppe. I personally prefer the herringbone." She smiled triumphantly and marched out of the office.

If Bliss was agitated or even overly concerned he didn't show it and his hands were steady as he poured coffee. Despite his speech to Macmillan he devoured the doughnuts and began reading the agenda on his desk...

Classes began on the hour forcing students to scurry about the campus, and causing some anxiety for Chief Mabra. He would have preferred to make his final check of the area in peace and quiet and without distraction.

The groundkeepers had been riding their mowers and the fresh smell of newly-cut grass was pleasant. Despite the continuous foot traffic, the quad was still empty save for two young lovers sitting on a blanket near the trees and oblivious to the rest of the world. The Chief envied them.

He was watching the maintenance workers setting up the chairs and checking the loudspeakers system. "Clarke, look in those woods again."

"Jeez, Chief, I just came from there, what the fuck am I supposed to be looking for anyway?"

"How the hell should I know, anything that's out of place or unusual, something that doesn't belong—like a stick of dynamite."

Officer Clarke didn't appreciate his joke. He shook his head and walked back towards the trees.

"Don, I want two more men in uniform right here on the quad. I also want Baker and Donaldson in plainclothes, one near the platform, the other in the back," bellowed Mabra at the Sergeant.

"Ok, but I'll have to pull them from the parking lot and the dorms."

"I don't care where you get them from. Just make sure they're here."

"Yessir."

The chief was understandably concerned. He had been hired to maintain order at the university and to see to it that any demonstration was peaceful and that nothing more than obscenities were hurled at overly unpopular speakers. Last year, when he had received permission to arm his security police, and to upgrade their status and salary, he noted that student opposition had been minimal. Perhaps they too, were tired of the lawlessness that characterized the sixties. He strapped his four channel "Handi-Talkie" to his belt. The units cost $1,400.00 each and had a range of thirty-five miles.

"Chief one to Sam two-two, how do you read me?"

"Loud and clear Sir," answered Billy.

"What do you see from your position?"

Billy was stationed on the roof of Spradley Hall and enjoyed an unobstructed view of the quad as well as much of the campus.

"Everything's A-Ok Chief, the traffic's a bit heavy on

75

West Ave. Otherwise things are pretty normal."

"Good, but keep your eyes open."

"Sure thing...ten-four."

Mabra relaxed for a moment. Billy would remain on the roof during the entire speech, and Justin would patrol the corridors of the admin building, particularly the fourth and fifth floors.

When the light came on, Peter Spaacklund released his safety belt, lit up an American cigarette and leaned forward in his first-class seat to watch the countryside below. There are no mountains and oceans here he thought, just the endless fields of farmers laid out so precisely, like the squares in a quilted blanket. No wonder these people have no sense of urgency.

Peter Spaacklund was not a native of the "white tribe," the name that Afrikaaners sometimes called themselves. His ancestors did not come to the Cape over 300 years ago, nor did they help to organize the "great trek" into the interior in 1835. Coming from England to Rhodesia in 1963, they arrived in Johannesburg two years later, the day that Rhodesia broke away from Britain and when Peter's younger brother Robbie, was murdered by rebels near the Zambian border.

Nevertheless, Peter had the true spirit of the "Voortrekkers" and shared the belief of their Calvinist forefathers that the destiny of his adopted country rested upon white domination and management of black labor. He did not care to dissect the race-relations policies of his own country with the same critical scrutiny he applied to what he termed the American hypocrites. He wasn't the least bit hesitant about presenting these views to a university audience either.

While Professor Andrew Crane was welcoming the speaker on behalf of the Cultural Affairs Committee, and Professor Leslie Pace was carefully putting the finishing touches to the natural curls of her long dark hair, Dominic Tereste alias Anthony Pereira, was diligently applying the muscles of his broad shoulders to a long-handled broom.

He appeared to be engrossed in sweeping the fifth floor corridors, all the while watching the movement of people, particularly the times between rounds for the young security officer. He took his frequent cigarette breaks in the janitor's cubicle, standing by a window where he could view the quad below. Paying attention to the University Police, he noted the walkie-talkies strapped to their chests. It was almost 10:30 a.m.

University students are notorious for their unpredictability. It would be reasonable to assume that just before the start of finals week they would be huddled over scribbled semester notes, overcrowding the reserve book room desperately reading the assignments they had ignored since the first week of classes. But the day was warm, the sun was shining, and perhaps spring fever was too overpowering.

Chief Mabra almost had his first coronary as he watched them fill up the quad in front of Spradley Hall. Some were barefoot though most of them, he noticed, at least wore sandals. Levi's and "short-shorts" hugged their slim figures and often left little to the imagination. Deeply tanned hairy-chested men, pimply boys with scruffy beards, braless coeds wearing T-shirts, who bounced and jiggled as they swung their hips, returning vets garbed in faded fatigues, beaded necklaces, silver chokers, buttons for all causes, and gaudy medallions. Tall, thin, fat, slender, sexy, grotesque...he was overwhelmed. Quickly he looked for trouble spots. There, in the center, Jeff White's Black Student Union, the mean faces of dark young men and women, many with cake-cutter handles protruding from their pockets, conspicuously crowding towards the front of the mob near the speaker's platform. He noticed that they were not carrying placards or bottles. Thank God for small favors, the thought.

"Sam two-two to Chief one," his portable squawked.

"Go ahead Billy," he replied.

"There's a group of about forty civilians. They've got some picket signs. Now they're lining up in formation. I think they're planning to march to the quad."

"Any sign of weapons?"

"No Sir," snapped Billy.

"Keep an eye on them and let me know if the situation changes, ten-four."

The chief checked his men's positions, mopped his brow with a handkerchief and re-checked the safety on a four-inch, thirty-eight caliber Smith and Wesson.

The VIP lounge had velvet curtains, deep pile carpets, and comfortably-cushioned leather chairs arranged in informal conversation areas. A table set against the wall held silver coffee urns, and attractively-prepared trays of snacks, cheeses, cakes, and cookies.

Near the stone-fronted gas-jet fireplace were gathered about thirty men and women making small talk in muted tones. Most of the men wore light-weight jackets and ties or cord suits while the women were clothed in a colorful variety of pant-suits, skirts and dresses. A uniformed security guard was positioned by the open door.

While Dr. Spaacklund was quietly discussing international policy with Margret Green, the Chairperson from the Economics Department.

"So you can see Dr. Green, the stability of the Krugerrand, now makes it the inevitable standard of, and I don't mean to be facetious, 'dollar diplomacy.' "

About five persons were listening attentively.

"Don't tell me the striking Dr. Pace had to actually bother with make-up," Andy teased. Leslie was wearing a revealing and uncomfortably low-cut white blouse with a

78

black and white stripped blazer, matched by grey bell-bottoms. If she leans forward any more thought Andy...

She smiled, accepted the unspoken compliment and returned her own.

"And what nice tight pants we're wearing today Dr. Crane..." They had not seen each other for about forty-eight hours and were almost like teenagers in their anticipation.

"How are you and our mysterious president getting along?" She inclined her head towards Mansfield.

"He's all smiles today, grinning just like a Cheshire cat."

Prescott Smythe, the Black historian was speaking to Bliss.

"I hear our enlightened speaker is quite an advocate of race-relations," he sarcastically challenged.

Bliss refused to be baited. "Come on Prescott, what's a university for if we can't tolerate a bigot or two? Besides I heard that when he spoke at Swarthmore he was so ridiculous the students didn't even bother to boo him."

"Now that's what worries me. I think..."

Bliss interrupted him to accept a note from the security guard, glanced at it and put it in his pocket.

"What was that all about?" inquired Prescott.

"Nothing to get excited about," said the president. Then he smiled. "Seems the Black Student Union's out in force today."

Prescott, who had been informed about the demonstration, just shrugged his shoulders.

"Ladies and gentlemen, it's about that time. I suggest we move towards the speaker's platform," announced Andy.

Twenty minutes before Spaacklund was scheduled to speak, officer Justin Bailey was making his rounds of the building's fifth floor. Justin was exceptionally intelligent, a quick study, who had spent the previous four years as a

79

Military Policeman, two of them in Vietnam. He was also enrolled at the university and in less than a year would receive his bachelor's degree in Criminal Justice. A pleasant, easy-going young man of twenty-four, he took the responsibilities of his new occupation seriously.

His hand rested lightly on the handle of his revolver and as he walked down the empty halls he kept thinking. There was something odd about that janitor. It's in the way he moves...too sure...too light on his feet...like a street fighter, almost...and he's got a fighter's body too...lean and muscular. He's trying to act nonchalant, but his eyes are watching everything.

Dom saw the officer walk past him, then deliberately turn and start back. He tensed.

"Excuse me sir, but I don't recognize you, may I please see your identification card?"

"Sure."

Stepping back a foot, Justin studied the card. It was all in order...but something was wrong. That's it, he thought, he didn't just show me the card, he removed it from his wallet. Justin was cautious. It's probably only my nerves, he decided, but I'm going to call control to verify. His left hand moved towards his portable.

Dom slammed his fist into the officer's midsection causing him to buckle. Justin grabbed for his stomach, Dom caught him with both hands and smashed his knee into the officer's chin. He carried the unconscious body into the men's room, removed his weapon and communicator, and set him down on a toilet seat. Taking a thin metal wire from his pocket he bound the officer's hands behind his back and tied them to the flush valve. Quickly he taped his mouth, pulled down his trousers, then locked the door and slid underneath the stall. If anyone were to come into the men's room, it would appear that Officer Bailey was answering nature's call.

Five minutes before Spaacklund would start to speak, Dominic locked the door to the janitor's cubicle.

80

Opening the canvas bag he removed a ten by eighteen inch case. The Charterarms AR-7 weighed four pounds and came in three pieces. He assembled it in less than fourteen seconds, mounted a Weaver K-2 scope and attached an illegal custom-made silencer. Inserting a seven-shot clip of 22 caliber long rifle CCI Mini-Mags, he opened the small window facing the quad, taking up his position. If you were standing less than five feet from the rifleman all you would hear would be the sound of the bolt action. If you glanced at the window when the weapon was fired you would notice a faint spark similar to the flint striking in a cheap cigarette lighter.

Spaacklund placed his glasses in the pocket of his jacket, grasped the podium with both hands and startled the audience.

"If America is the land of freedom and equality, then it is also the home of racism and bigotry. It is a nation that for over 200 years has lied to its people and deceived its citizenry. Your leaders have publicly stated at the United Nations that they are appalled by aparthied, yet they continue to support the system they condemn in the international marketplace. In fact, each year the United States keeps increasing its illegal trade with my South African Republic."

"Right on," cried a voice in the audience. "Way to go," shouted another. The crowd was relaxed, the mob smiling. It appeared that the speaker was saying just what most of the students wanted to believe.

"... I have more respect for our Black African neighbors who refuse our products. At least they are honest, if unfortunately misguided."

There was something about that last sentence. It wasn't so much what he said, it was more the way he said it. You could feel the crowd strain. They were growing more alert as their eyes focused upon the speaker. Jeff White cupped his hands over his mouth and shouted.

"Excuse me Sir, but would you please repeat that last

sentence. I didn't catch all the words."

Spaacklund challenged him. "Which words were you referring to?"

Jeff moved a few feet closer. "The part about your Black African brothers," he shouted.

"I have no black brothers," was Spaacklund's angry reply.

Jeff now knew how to bait him. "I heard you talk about your black brothers. Are you calling me a liar?" Without waiting for a reply he turned to his followers and cried out.

"Didn't you hear him call me his black brother?"

"Yeah...Sure did...that's right, man."

"How about your black sisters," he continued to taunt him.

"What are you talking about?" replied Spaacklund in a high shrill voice.

Jeff shouted back, "your mother, your big black beautiful mother." He turned again to his people. "Do you know this man's mother, his beautiful black mother?" He was leading them on.

"No, I don't, but my daddy sure does...Hey, ah knows his mother, she got a white ass...fuck his mother...yeah, fuck his sister too."

Spaacklund clenched the mike tightly in his fists. "You scum, you filthy lying scum," he screamed.

Now, thought Whitney. "Let's move out." He ordered his people to march. They came around the building and charged down both sides of the quad waving picket signs and chanting, "racist pig, go back home, racist pig, go back home."

Their appearance caused a natural diversion and Mabra's men turned towards them. It took less than a few seconds but Spaacklund, now incensed and irrational leaped off the platform and pushed a very surprised Jefferson White to the ground. Bo Williams, a senior halfback, reacted first and grabbing Spaacklund's shoulder wrestled him down. The security guards immediately started moving through the crowd. Sergeant Anderson thinking he saw the flash of a knife, drew his revolver. Holding his pistol high above his head, he charged into the crowd, lost his balance, and as he fell, accidentally discharged his weapon. Whitney Rawlins couldn't resist the temptation, he screamed into his megaphone.

"They killed him, the pigs shot him!"

The crowd started to panic. It was Chief Mabra who reached Spaacklund first, grabbing his collar he dragged him to his feet and was literally carrying him away from the center when he heard the shot. Turning just in time, he saw Arlen Robinson remove a bottle from his paper sack, pull his arm back and let the glass container sail towards the wooden platform.

The roar from the explosion was deafening. The platform erupted in a blaze of fire. Dean Elwood was screaming as his clothes started to burn. The crowd became a mob, they ran in all directions, trampling those who couldn't get out of the way. A student blindly lunged for Anderson's pistol which now lay on the grass but Andy who had been sitting closest to the platform reached him first, and pinning the student's arms to the ground with his shoes retrieved the weapon. Andy stood up and desperately looked for Leslie. The fire had now engulfed the platform and was a vivid orange spreading rapidly towards the nearby brush. Billy McDivitt saw the holocaust from the roof and called in the city police. Seconds later, lights flashing and sirens screaming, they raced onto the campus.

Dominic waited until the man with the blue armband was centered in the cross-hairs. He held his breath and slowly released it as he squeezed the trigger. No one was paying any attention when Andy Crane lost his balance as the first shot grazed his forehead. When he fell a second bullet pierced his thigh.

The medical report indicated an abrasion on the lateral aspect of the right supra-orbital ridge. He suffered no other head injuries and his pupils were equal. The second bullet entered the upper thigh and traveled obliquely and downward exiting in the lower third of the thigh, medially, near the patella. It passed in front of the femur, so there was no possibility of damage to the sciatic nerve, and went through the belly of the quadriceps muscle. The wounds were debrided and dressed.

Antibiotics were prescribed and the patient was advised to rest and use crutches for the next few days. There would be some pain and soreness for a month or so but he would suffer no permanent damage.

Leslie visited him at Township Medical Center that evening.

"Well, well, how's the campus hero?"

Andy groaned. "My head's splitting and I feel like throwing up, but I'll be OK if you'll crawl in the bed with me."

"Only if you promise not to throw up." She was relieved to find him in such good spirits.

"What happened after the medics carried me off?"

"Just about everything. The city police invaded our campus and locked up half the student body, Dean Elwood, the man who caught on fire, was pretty badly burned but they say he'll recover. Let's see now, the fire engines came and sprayed water all over. The only thing that really burned was the platform. After they took you to the hospital, everyone just went home."

"Who tried to kill me. I felt this sting in my head and then I fell and was shot again in the leg."

"Oh, it wasn't you they were after, it was Spaacklund. Somebody dressed like a janitor tied up poor Justin Bailey in the john and then he must have fired at Spaacklund from the fifth floor."

"Did they catch him?"

84

"I think he got away in all the confusion. Mansfield was very upset, he's calling a press conference in the morning. Oh Andy, I'm so glad you're all right!"

He grinned, "I'll survive, but I'll have to use these crutches for the next few days. They'll be letting me out of here tomorrow morning. Will you come and get me?"

The visitor's bell rang and a nurse politely informed Leslie that she would have to leave.

"I'll pick you up bright and early, get a good night's sleep." She bent over and kissed him softly on the lips.

But Andy would not sleep and tossed restlessly throughout the night. He woke up and glanced at the clock, it was just after two. Laying back he tried to dismiss his thoughts but it didn't work. The bullet and the pain brought back vivid memories of a time some twenty-five years ago in a forgotten Korean village. He could remember it all so clearly, as if it had only happened yesterday.

Graduation from high school meant that you would be drafted. But to a young man, with an adventuresome spirit, the Army was a welcome relief from the city streets. Not that Andy believed in the military mystique, nor did he understand what the killing would be all about. None of that really mattered, not at barely eighteen.

He was an ordinary recruit save for a special talent, an ability for foreign languages; so they sent him to the Army Language School in Monterey. After he had mastered Mandarin, they ordered him to Korea.

At least he hadn't been sent up to the front with the twenty-fourth Infantry Division. He was instead, stationed with a special intelligence unit located three kilometers south of Taegu. He would spend his days reading classified documents in Chinese while sitting across from his Korean counterpart, Mr. Han, who would read those same documents in English. The Army works in mysterious ways.

Andy's sexual experience was limited to traumatic

scuffles in the reclining seat of an old car or an occasional tryst with the neighborhood slut. He was totally unprepared for Lilly. Her real name was Kim Suk-ja and she worked in the Major's office. Slim, petite and with silky long black hair that fell to her knees when she untied her braids, the young soldier found her irresistible. Unlike the other girls, prostitutes who grabbed you on your way to the E.M. club, Lilly remained aloof. In fact she hardly went to the club at all. Andy kept his passion a secret, dreaming about her at night and when he masturbated.

Sergeant Conrad had been in the service ten years, six of them in Asia. When it came to Oriental women, he just assumed they were all whores who sucked cock for a thousand hwan, about two dollars in military scrip. On the night of October 12, 1952, he accosted Lilly on her way home.

"Hey you girl, suckahotchie an do, two dollar?"

Lilly tried to ignore him.

"You goddamned yellow bitch, you hear me." He shoved her once and when she refused to stop, a second time. Andy had been watching them. He became so incredibly angry that he lunged at Conrad and sent him sprawling in the mud. He would have kicked him senseless if Lilly had not begged him, "Stop, Andrew, I want no trouble, please."

She had called him by his first name, she knew him, and he was in heaven. Insisting upon escorting her home, he checked out at the gate at 2010 hours.

Perhaps they were both lonely, or maybe just bound together by the evening's unpleasant incident. They made love, a quiet and gentle coupling of two souls rather than two bodies. The Korean night was very cold.

Andy tossed restlessly in his sleep. He thought he had heard voices in the adjoining hooch. He listened.

"We must hurry Lieutenant. Sung will be questioned in the morning. They do not know he is Chinese and they

86

must not find out."

"What should I do?"

"When the MP's come to take him to the interrogation center you will accompany them. They will have to drive through the village. There will be a diversion..."

The two men must have moved because he couldn't hear them anymore. Lilly stirred besides him.

"What's the matter Andrew, why do you wake up?"

"Shhh, I heard two men talking next door. One of them is an American. I think they're planning an escape."

The voices returned.

"...I'll do my part, see to it that you do yours, Chun swei dzu jyu ren."

Andy rose quickly and slid the screen door open. He thought he heard footsteps, but the dark was silent now.

Corporal Crane returned to the compound just before midnight. The Duty Officer was asleep and he didn't want to wake him. It could wait until morning.

But at 0330, on October 13, 1952, Andy and all the men in his barracks heard the first sounds of the shelling. Ten minutes later the compound was burning. The young soldier grabbed his M-l and ran outside. Through the haze of an orange sky he could see smoke and fire everywhere. He thought he heard the loud report from a rifle and felt a sharp pain in his chest...then nothing.

When he regained consciousness he was in a Mobile Army Surgical Hospital. Delirious for three days, he tried to tell the medic what he had heard that night but no one would listen to him. One week later he was evacuated to Kimpo and then flown to Tokyo where he received the Purple Heart.

Finally discharged in Oakland, he promptly spent his accumulated pay in the bars he frequented all night. He had nightmares for three months where he would wake up screaming about two men in a Korean village who were shooting at him. He remembered their words: "I'll do my part, see to it that you do yours. Chun swei dzu jyu ren."

In the Spring he enrolled at New York University, married Elaine Bravermann, and his nightmares ceased.

There was no mistaking that last phrase, it was identical to the words the president had spoken a few days ago. Andy couldn't help but have the strangest feeling that those shots had been meant for him and not for the South African.

THIRTEEN

While Andy complained about being forced to ride in his wheelchair to the hospital exit where Leslie was eagerly waiting, President Bliss Mansfield was about to hold a press conference in the V.I.P. lounge.

Two of the three local affiliates had set up bulky TV cameras. The third used a mini-cam. Coffee and doughnuts, Macmillan had called them "breakfast staples," had been prepared for the reporters, and the tan leather chairs by the fireplace. Additional folding chairs had been brought in earlier and the curtains opened to catch the sun's morning rays.

The reporters greeted each other loudly and almost immediately began to scribble pre-conference notes. They drained their paper coffee cups and then used them as ashtrays. The scene might have resembled the war room at the Pentagon during the 1940's. Duane Onstott, the University public relations man was busy handing out prepared statements, typed just minutes before, when the president walked in.

Flanked by two campus security guards, he could have passed for a visiting head of state. His striped maroon and white tie handsomely accented his tailored dark blue suit. Silver streaks in his sideburns added a dignified touch to his otherwise sandy hair. He marched with the purposeful stride of a man with a mission. The reporters and cameramen were duly impressed. He spoke directly into the microphones.

"Ladies and gentlemen, this is a serious matter, so let's dispense with the frivolities and get down to business. Mr. Onstott has passed out my formal statement, I'll start with the questions."

Kyle Emory from local *Chronicle* was the first to be recognized.

"Mr. President, what actions are you planning to take against the rioters?"

"That remains to be seen, Kyle, pending the recovery of Dean Elwood, the man who was seriously burned in the fire. I have already suspended the leaders of the demonstration and the student who threw the bomb. I will insist that they be expelled from the University. Our lawyers are drawing up the proper papers to institute criminal proceedings. I will strongly support their recommendations."

"What about the sixty students who were arrested by the police?"

"That is a police matter and I am sure they will be dealt with accordingly."

Emory continued. "Were the students responsible for the shooting?"

Bliss appeared pensive. "That again is a police concern. All I can say at this time is that their behavior during the speech certainly appeared to encourage the shooting. Their guilt or innocence is a matter of law and will have to be decided in the courts. Yes, the gentlemen in the front row wearing the denim suit."

"I'm Sean Mallory from UPI, President Mansfield. Who is this Dr. Spaacklund and what was he doing on the campus?"

"Mr. Mallory, Dr. Spaacklund is a government economist from the Union of South Africa. He is an expert on international trade and was invited by our Cultural Affairs Committee as a guest speaker."

"Do you usually let racist on campus?"

The audience was momentarily stunned by the question. If Bliss was surprised he wasn't going to show it.

"Mr. Mallory," he replied in an even tone, "I was present during his speech and there was nothing inflammatory or racist about Dr. Spaacklund's few remarks. Perhaps if he had been allowed to speak longer...This, sir, is a university, an appropriate setting for dialogue between people of all persuasions, many of them controversial." He hesitated and let his eyes wander over the audience. He focused on Mallory and continued.

"But while we encourage debate and discussion, we do not condone violence, we never have, and as long as I am president, we never will. Mrs. Lacy?"

She was a stunning woman in her early fifties. "Sandra Lacy from the *Evening Star,* Dr. Mansfield. I understand that the man who was shot was a member of the committee which invited Spaacklund to speak. Do you think, perhaps, that the bullet might have been meant for him?"

"I never try to guess the intentions of a bullet, Mrs. Lacy."

The reporters laughed.

"But I can see absolutely no reason why anyone would want to shoot Dr. Crane." The cameraman's lights were bright. He started to perspire and pulled at his tie. Quickly, he recognized the next questioner.

"Jim Carson from the *Campus Informer.* Sir, do you feel that because the police were armed, it might have added to creating a tense situation, one in which a riot may have been encouraged?" Perhaps the question was not appropriate, but Jim Carson, as a Student Senator, had been violently opposed to arming the security police.

"Mr. Carson, the campus police did not start the incident, nor did they at any point fire at the demonstrators, they were not responsible for viciously insulting the speaker, they didn't throw a firebomb, neither did they shoot at Dr. Spaacklund. As I recall, they responded properly and immediately to stop the riot, without the use of firearms. Does that answer your question?" He didn't wait for a reply.

"Martin Thomas from the *Daily Telegram,* Mr.

President. Do the police have any suspects in custody?"

"I'm afraid you'll have to ask Chief Mabra or Commissioner Blake from the city police." He nodded to a young lady in the back row.

"Lisa Manners from the *Courier*. Do you plan to run for Senator?"

The audience was quiet. Ever since Parsons had declined the nomination, Bliss' name appeared more and more as a preferred candidate.

"Ms. Manners," he replied. "Under our present two-party system, it is proper to be nominated before running for public office, however," he softened his tone and almost smiled, "when and if I am nominated, I would be more than delighted to comment upon that question." The crowd was with him. He made his first speech.

"I will not tolerate violence of any kind upon my campus at any time. Both this nation and this campus were founded upon freedom from tyranny and terror. I intend to see that we keep it that way."

"Thank you Mr. Candidate," replied Lisa Manners. The crowd applauded. Bliss fielded more questions and responded favorably.

"One last question please." He recognized Tom Kite from the *Union Reader*.

"Wouldn't you say Mr. President, that this unfortunate incident was tailor-made for your Senatorial ambitions and will surely give you state and national publicity?"

Bliss laughed, clever son-of-a-bitch, he thought, he's absolutely right.

"I would have preferred to stick my finger in the dike," he replied. The audience clapped.

"I'm afraid that will have to be all today. I have a very hectic schedule. Mr. Onstott will remain to answer questions."

"See you in Washington" a voice shouted from the back of the room. Bliss walked out of the lounge and returned to his office, the security guards matching his stride.

Leslie drove through the lush green countryside to Andy's home overlooking the lake. She made a fresh pot of coffee while he changed into a pair of shorts. They sat on the deck soaking up the warm sun. Andy stared at the lake. It was a silent, almost bright blue mirror. The ducks were once again swimming by the shore and in the distance he could barely make out Ian's boat drifting. A bull frog could be heard calling to his mate while black and yellow butterflies danced about orange flowers. The intricate web of a garden spider was illuminated by the sun. He closed his eyes and drifted into a deep sleep.

Something's bothering Andy, Leslie was thinking. He was silent during the drive and had remained so. Her attempts at conversation were ignored with a nod or an occasional "yes" or "okay." She was glad he had accepted her but her concern for him was growing. He just wasn't himself. He was keeping something inside him and he was refusing to share it with her. That disturbed Leslie the most. Sharing was an important part of her life and her relationship with Andy. He had held her when she cried and had been sympathetically understanding, soothing her anxieties during the first weeks of the semester, when she felt uneasy about her acceptance at the University. She had trusted him with the painful memories of her marriage and divorce and he had helped her face them for what they were. The sad lessons of the past, he had called them. Their lovemaking had been gentle yet exciting. She admired this considerate lover who had taught her to enthusiastically respond to the pleasures of the flesh without, for the first time, feeling guilty. He was her man and she desperately wanted to share his anguish and help to make it better. Oh, Andy, she thought to herself, what's really bothering you?

She fed him ice cream with chocolate syrup for lunch and tried to make conversation.

"I called Janie, your TA, and she'll take care of the Social Anthropology exams. She'll leave them in your office when she's finished the grading."

"Thanks," he replied.

"Do you feel up to going out for dinner?"

"Not really, why don't we eat here."

"I looked in the fridge and I'll have to go out and buy some food. There's a shop down the road about three miles."

"Okay." He returned to his ice cream. Dammit, Leslie thought, can't he say anything.

"I promised one of my students I'd meet with her this afternoon, about two. Will you be all right?"

"Sure, I'll just rest and maybe catch up on some reading. Going to take my car?"

"Uh huh," she replied, still annoyed with him.

She started to leave and hesitated. "Andrew Crane, I love you very much!" When he didn't respond, she slammed the door and left. Andy poured himself a beer and returned to the deck. He sat there looking into the sun and remembered.

The M.P.'s would take the prisoners to the interrogation center early in the morning, the earlier the better. Sgt. Conrad had once told him they were likely to be nervous and frightened and it would make the interrogation easier. There would be a diversion, that's what the man had said. He recalled the shelling of the village and the compound about 0300. Yes, that would surely create one.

They would have to leave the jeep and take cover by the side of the road. In the confusion, a prisoner might be able to escape, and if he was helped. He returned to the conversation he had overheard. A Lieutenant, that's what the man had called the American. Andy had known the officer's at Division headquaters, there were Lieutenants Cook and Rafferty, but weren't they already in the compound when the attack began. Lt. Marcus was the

94

Duty Officer, and he was asleep. He couldn't remember anyone else.

"Sleeping Giant," what did it really mean? Was it some kind of code? His thoughts flashed back to the president's office. He had been upset, not angry, when he had caught Andy listening. He knew he had overheard the conversation, yet he didn't mention it when we met to discuss Spaacklund the next day.

Just before he fell asleep, he was thinking, I wonder if Mansfield served in Korea?

FOURTEEN

That afternoon Leslie parked Andy's red sportscar in the faculty lot and walked rapidly towards her office.

Lucas waved to her. "Well if it isn't the prettiest filly in the faculty stable. How're you and how's my Andy getting along?" He joined her and they strolled together.

"Oh, he's okay Lucas, at least physically, but he's been so darn moody today, just sits there on his deck and stares at the sun." Lucas was a father-figure to her and she wanted to talk to someone.

"That's not so good." He became serious. "I've known people in the Navy like that, after getting shot. They're depressed for weeks, even months. What's he worried about?"

"I don't know," confided Leslie. "He won't tell me, but I don't think it's only the shooting. It's something else, much deeper. Like he's just beginning to remember something that happened a long time ago and it's bothering him." She thought of Andy's experience during the war.

"Lucas, wasn't Andy wounded in Korea?" she asked.

"Yes, I believe he told me that there was an attack on his unit down in Taegu, he was hit in the chest, received a Purple Heart. You know, speaking about Korea, the president stopped by the other day, was asking all kinds of questions about Andy."

Leslie brightened. "He's up for promotion to full Professor, isn't he?"

"Yep, but those weren't the questions he asked. He was wanting to know about his military service. He even wanted to know what outfit Andy was with."

"Did you tell him?"

"Don't know myself. Bliss was rather nervous, none of his usual confidence."

That seems odd Leslie was thinking. "Lucas...was the president in the Army?"

"Uh huh, he was a forward observer with the Field Artillery."

"Was he ever in Korea?"

"About the same time Andy was."

Leslie continued to quiz him. "Does the president speak Chinese?"

"Don't think so, at least he's never spoken any when I'm around. Why are you asking these questions anyway?"

They had reached Leslie's office, "Look, do me a favor, don't tell Andy what we were talking about. He'll probably be upset if he thinks I've been prying and we want him back to his old sarcastic, free-wheeling self, don't we?" She smiled at him.

"Okay, but if something's bothering him and I can help let me know. Give my best to the wounded hero."

"Sure will," replied Leslie as she left him and entered her faculty office.

Maryanne Wallis sat down and quickly lit up a cigarette. She was an attractive redhead with a mass of freckles over her body. When she leaned over to pick up a book her overdeveloped breasts moved with her. It was rumored that she didn't wear a bra because they couldn't make one large enough. She was Dr. Pace's first graduate student and, like Leslie, new to the campus. Her independent study focused upon police procedural techniques and how they were selectively utilized in the investigation of a criminal act. It was her hypothesis that the nature of the crime, the type of suspect and the social climate in which the act took place were significant in determining the manner in which the investigation was

97

conducted and the extent to which the police would pursue it. She strongly suspected that race, social class, and public opinion could be as influential as actual evidence. Both the nature of her study and the fullness of her figure had insured the enthusiastic cooperation of campus and city police.

"Okay, Dr. Pace," she said, "take a young black male, a known radical who has been leading demonstrations for years...he's at a rally and all of a sudden there's a shot...the speaker has been killed, but the police can't find the weapon...who's the logical suspect?" She continued without waiting for an answer.

"Would the police carefully scrutinize all the possibilities? ...like other people who could have pulled the trigger? Would they really consider that the victim could have been killed for reasons having nothing to do with the rally? Or take a gangland murder, let's say in New York, maybe the gangster was executed by a jealous husband and not a rival mob, but would the detectives think about that possibility?"

"I see what you're getting at," replied Leslie, "but the police operate on the premise of motive and opportunity and they're usually right. The most obvious suspect is often the killer. That's not really the issue though, how are you going to demonstrate that they failed to pursue legitimate possibilities?"

Maryanne thought for a moment. "Take yesterday's attempted assassination of the South African. The prime suspects are two student dissidents who organized the demonstration. They're the logical candidates, and the police will make every effort to tie them to the shooting. My boy friend's on the campus paper, and he went to the president's press conference. All the reporters, with one exception, seemed to think it was the work of radicals.

"Who was the exception?" Leslie inquired.

"Some lady from out-of-state. She even suggested that Professor Crane and not the speaker might have been the intended victim."

"But that doesn't make sense."

"Of course not, there's no reason for killing Professor Crane, but it's still possible." Maryanne was excited now.

"Let me suggest another answer, maybe the president himself arranged for the incident in order to get publicity when he runs for Senator, then it wouldn't really matter who was shot. Let's try this one. Perhaps the South African government ordered his murder and staged it at a rally, to throw suspicion on someone else?"

Leslie laughed. "Maybe it's also part of a world-wide conspiracy and Spaacklund's the weak link in the chain?"

"Yes. I mean no, Dr. Pace, I don't see how it can be any more than what it is—yet the other suggestions are probable. I'll bet the police don't even seriously consider them. Now if it was the President of the United States who was shot at..."

They finished their discussion considering the differences between probable, pausible, possible, and impossible. Leslie was secretly delighted with her student's creative imagination. On her way back to Andy's, she stopped at the market to pick up a two-inch filet, lettuce, cucumbers, tomatoes, green onions and mushrooms for a salad, and some coffee. She had noticed that Andy was almost out of beans.

Her conversation with Maryanne was not only interesting, it was intriguing. Just suppose Andy had been the sniper's intended victim all along, and just suppose the fire bombing of the stage and even the demonstration was to create a diversion. She knew the logical conclusion was that the sniper had missed Spaacklund and had accidentally hit Andy. Yet, perhaps Maryanne was right. Even if other possibilities were suggested, hadn't that woman reporter suggested one, they would be dismissed. Why would the sniper wait until Spaacklund was in that mob scene? It would have been much easier to shoot him at the podium.

99

Leslie was still confused. All the pieces didn't fit. What's all this got to do with the president asking Lucas about Andy's military service in Korea? That was over twenty-five years ago. Or about the president speaking Chinese? What had Andy heard that he couldn't remember? It all comes back to those words, what were they? What was going to happen now?

Part of the answer to her questions would come when Andy returned to the campus tomorrow.

It was well after midnight but Chief Mabra sat in his office, his elbows resting on the desk. The quiet was a welcome contrast to the noisy confusion of the day. A single lamp burned softly as he studied the papers layed out before him.

He was openly disappointed in Don Anderson. The Sergeant had not used good judgement when he drew his thirty-eight. It was departmental policy that police officers should only draw their weapon to defend themselves, or in the defense of others. When you take your gun out you should be prepared to use it, and there was no way he was going to do that in the crowd without the danger of hitting an innocent civilian. Tomorrow he would convene a "shoting board" consisting of himself, the Lieutenant and two other Sergeants. He was sure Anderson's action would be determined unjustified, not consistent with department regs. He would suspend Don for thirty days, and have to think about letting him go.

He dismissed the Sergeant from his mind and picked up the police report. Something was wrong. No, by Jesus, everything was wrong, nothing made sense.

"Can I come in?" Betty Mabra knocked loudly on the door. "I knew I'd find you here. I couldn't sleep and thought you'd like some company. Want me to make some fresh coffee?"

"No thanks, hon. I'm really finished now but I can't figure out any of this."

100

"Want to tell me about it?" She really wasn't interested, but after being married to the law officer for almost twenty years, she knew what he needed. "It's about the shooting, isn't it?"

"Yeah. I interrogated those two kids, White and Rawlins, separately. They admitted they planned the demonstration but both of them insisted it was supposed to be peaceful. They denied knowing anything about a bomb or a sniper. I know both those young men. Rawlins is a pathological liar and you can't trust him, but White seemed to be telling the truth. I believed him. He's a radical who's long on rhetoric but short on action, not the kind to get involved in a shooting."

He paused to light another cigarette. "And why Spaacklund of all people? Here's a man with a very limited reputation as a rabble-rouser. I checked him out at the last place he spoke. Hell, most of the time he couldn't even attract a crowd. He's just not a candidate for an assassin's bullet. Okay, even if he was the target, then the sniper couldn't have picked a worse time to fire. Spaacklund was a good three feet from Crane when I started to drag him away from the crowd. It was impossible to get a clean shot. If I wanted to kill him, or wound him, I would have fired when he was alone at the podium."

Betty interrupted him. "Maybe the sniper's not very smart?"

"Uh-uh, I'll get to that later. The fire bombing makes no sense either. A student bomber would have used gas and soap, but the police lab said it was napalm—you only get that stuff from the military. And that kid, Robinson who hurled the bottle claimed he had been paid one hundred dollars just for throwing it at the platform. I believe him too. He still had eighty dollars in his wallet when we apprehended him, and his girl friend swears he was telling the truth. Why would anyone want to set fire to the platform, except to create a diversion?"

101

"He's smart all right. Justin's no fool. Anyone who could knock him unconscious, disarm him and then tie him up had to be experienced. The phone call to Findley, the uniform, ID card, the tape and the wire, it had the earmarks of a professional operation. There wasn't any noise from the rifle, so he had to be using a silencer. It was the kind of thing you would expect from the syndicate or the CIA. There were no fingerprints either.

"So it looks like you've got a mystery now."

"I guess so. Aw, let's forget it and go home."

But the chief could not forget. He had been in police work for close to thirty years. The entire incident only made sense if Crane and not Spaacklund was the target. But why should anyone want to kill Crane he wondered, where's the motive? I'll have to find out more about Crane.

The city below was alive. Thousands of lights gave it a brilliance and vitality that had been immortalized by Tony Bennett's sentimental yearning when he sang about his "city by the bay." Prevailing winds had kept the fog offshore so that the reflections from both the Golden Gate and Bay bridges illuminated the dark waters.

The view was breathtaking, an unforgettable panoramic vista from the glass enclosed Carnelian Room, fifty-two stories above the ground, high atop the Bank of America building. They would have enjoyed the scene too had their thoughts not been occupied with other, more pressing, matters.

Seated apart from the dinner crowd, they were finishing their brandies. The man with the deep tan and the pleasant smile contemplated the golden hues of his grand marnier as he felt its warmth spread throughout his body.

"We must reach a decision," he said to his companion.

Across the table, Chao Ping-ti nodded affirmatively. He was well in his sixties yet the clear lines of his smooth face suggested a much younger man. When he spoke his voice was strong with the responsibility that comes from command and decision.

"The anthropologist is alive and well. Let him be."

"But what if he knows?"

"He does not know, he may only suspect."

"Yet he will seek answers. We remember the trouble he caused the Company in '71. He's not a fool. What if he makes the connection?"

"He cannot. He will look for the 'sleeping giant' and his answers will end there. We will watch him."

"And the sniper...He has already seen and heard too much?"

The older man narrowed his eyes and looked down on the shining city.

"See to it that he forgets."

The man with the deep tan and the pleasant smile was the first to leave. He started to climb the steep hill but apparently changed his mind and hailed a taxi.

The Chinese gentleman made a phone call and fifteen minutes later was met outside the building by a green Mercedes. The German sedan joined the traffic and headed in the direction of the airport.

FIFTEEN

It was the dawn of a new day. An unusual spring morning; frost clinging to the windows and a wind that more properly belonged with the icy gusts of past winters.

Leslie was opening her eyes as she cuddled beneath the heavy blankets.

"Andy, I'm freezing, come back to the bed and keep me warm."

"Sorry, but I've got a lot of catching up to do today, get your body out of bed, there's a fire going and the coffee will be ready in a minute."

Leslie was relieved. Last night she recalled almost crying herself to sleep, and here he was, cheerful and full of life at, my God, it wasn't even seven. She searched in the dresser for one of his flannel shirts and wool socks. Then she hurried to the comforting warmth of the blazing fire.

"What do you have to do today that can't wait till a decent hour?"

"I've got a proposal to finish. How would you like to go to Hawaii this summer?"

"Oh boy, would I ever, when?"

"First week in July, I thought we'd go to Washington first, I want to visit an old Army buddy."

"Anyone I know?"

"I don't think so. His name's Bruce Jones. He's at the Pentagon."

Leslie was going to tell Andy about the conversation with Lucas and her growing curiosity about the shooting, but when she had returned for dinner, he had still been sleeping. Later she was so frightened by his strange sobriety and awful silences that she was literally afraid to bring the subject up. Now she was excited over Andy's rebirth into the human race. It would have to wait.

Leslie drove to campus and let him out by the bookstore. Andy struggled with the crutches, unsure of his balance and his ability to master his new wooden helpers.

His office was cluttered, the usual disarray of open books, papers, notes and journals save for the neat stack of corrected exams. Janice had been in earlier that morning. She had stayed up half the night grading them. Andy opened his briefcase, spread the proposal on a yet unused portion of the desk and started to write.

Michael Francis O'Hara had just been transferred to the day-shift janitorial crew. It was tantamount to a promotion although he would have to forego the privileges of "free night-time telephone service." He noticed Andy's open door.

"Hey Professor, how's the leg?"

Andy looked up. "Fine, Mike, a little gamey but I'm getting around."

"You usin' them?" He pointed to the crutches.

"I'm trying to," replied Andy.

"That little cock-teaser of yours came in earlier, she said she forgot her key. It's okay to let her in, huh?"

Andy grinned at Mike's description of Janis, cock-teaser was indeed a fitting adjective for the diminutive, blue-eyed graduate assistant who often licked her lower lips while she rubbed her hands slowly over her thighs. "It's okay, Mike."

"Say, what wuz you doin' in your office the other night?" Mike didn't want to go back to his broom and was enjoying the conversation.

Andy showed his surprise. "What other night?"

"Let's see, must have been last Wednesday, 'bout 8:30, I wuz clean'n' outside when this broad calls me on your phone." He smiled sheepishly. "I wuz going to go inside when I seen you there in the office, just standing in the dark. You didn't answer the phone."

"Are you sure it was me, Mike?"

"Sure, who else would be in your office. Anyway he was a big guy about your size."

"What did he look like?"

"Couldn't tell cause it wuz dark, but I seen him when he left though he didn't see me. He wuz wearin' a turtleneck and jacket like you always got."

Andy thought back to Wednesday. That was the day he had visited the president and he was wearing his rust turtleneck and corduroy jacket. He remembered the phone call, the one with no answer. If someone wanted to break into his office, he would call to make sure Andy was home. Glancing at the door he saw that the lock seemed in order. That meant the intruder had to have a key. He looked about the office. Nothing seemed to be missing. Then he noticed the memo with the words. He looked directly at Mike.

"It must have been a student searching for an exam, probably thought he was going to flunk the course."

"Gee, shouldn't we call the police?"

"No," said Andy. "I'll handle it myself."

The Firehouse had been a gentlemen's club for over twenty years until it was partially destroyed in the infamous fire of 1913. It was rebuilt in 1918, renovated twice during the 30's and restored to its original splendor in 1962. It sat atop a hill looking down at the river that flowed past the university.

The dining room was noted for elegant French and continental cuisine served by a staff of very experienced waiters, the youngest having just turned fifty-five. The high, beamed ceilings and dark mahogany interior gave it the flavor of another era, a time when everything seemed much simpler. It was also reputed to have the finest wine cellar in the state.

Andy was finishing the '64 George Delatour B.V. Private Reserve, an uncompromisingly mellow California cabernet. It was almost ten and the cavernous room was deserted. He stared at the flickering candles trying to make up his mind.

"Leslie, since you've known me, have I ever seemed irrational or paranoid?"

She thought that was a strange question. "No, I still can't tell whether you're serious or sarcastic, and lately you've been awfully moody, but certainly not paranoid. Why do..."

He interrupted her. "Suppose I told you that I think someone's trying to kill me."

She looked straight at him, he was very serious now.

"I think the sniper at the demonstration meant to kill me and not Spaacklund." He hesitated before continuing. "I think President Mansfield's behind it all somehow."

Leslie knew he wasn't joking.

He spoke about Korea, the conversation he had overheard in the village and the cryptic phrase Mansfield had whispered over the telephone. He ended with the break-in of his office.

She was becoming frightened. She told him about her meeting with Lucas and about the President's odd questions. They sat for a long time before Andy ended the silence.

"Just suppose that Mansfield was in Korea and it was him I overheard that night. Let's say that he was involved in the escape plot and that those cryptic words identified the operation. What if someone found out about the incident and is trying to blackmail him. An investigation at this time could ruin his chances for the Senate. So when he discovered that I speak Mandarin, he found out about the units I served with in Korea. He can't afford to take any chances because I might remember him. Maybe he even thinks I'm the blackmailer of his accomplice.

When we go to Washington. I'll check Mansfield out with my friend in the Pentagon."

"I don't think it's quite that simple Andy. Remember the phone conversation that Mansfield was having in Chinese, the one you told me about? Well that doesn't sound like a blackmail attempt. I think the caller was giving him information about Parsons as if he were pulling the strings. I'd say Mansfield's in this thing up to his neck."

"Christ, do you know what you're suggesting?"

She nodded affirmatively. "Look, I'm a criminologist. That sniper was no student, he was a professional killer and they're expensive. If the demonstration was planned just as a diversion to kill you , it all had to be organized. That takes people, money and know-how. And it's not what they teach you in Psych 1A."

"I don't think the riot was originally planned with me in mind, the event was scheduled before Mansfield caught me in his office. I think it was an afterthought."

She thought about it. "Yes, that would make sense, but Andy, I'm the one who's scared now. Why don't we go to the police?"

Andy shook his head. "With what? We have no hard evidence, only some extraordinary coincidences. If I go to the authorities now, they'll say that the bullet must have scrambled my brains. No, we need proof."

Leslie remembered her afternoon session with Maryanne. Andy was right, the police would think he was mad. A professor accusing the president of plotting his death, and all of it based upon a phone conversation and a mysterious phrase he once heard in Korea more than two decades ago.

"Andy, if he tried to kill you once, what's going to stop him from trying again?"

"I don't think he will, another attempt so close to the last one is bound to make someone suspicious. I don't think either Mansfield or his people can afford to take that chance, not when he's this close to the nomination. I'll be safe for a while."

"What are we going to do?"

If Andy was frightened neither his voice nor his manner suggested it. "We are going to do some fieldwork, my dear Dr. Pace. There's a lot more than meets the eye concerning our beloved President. Let's start with Bliss Mansfield himself."

Dominic Vereste paused to wait for the light on 45th Street. It had been a week since the shooting but he couldn't get it out of his mind. Goddamn fuckin' luck, he thought. I had him in the cross-hairs and was squeezing the trigger when he had to jerk his head. Shit, it the Family finds out I took that contract, they'll have my ass, and my hair. They'll make me cut off all my freakin' hair.

He was so engrossed in his reverie that he failed to notice the two men park their Buick across the street and move towards him.

"Dominic Vereste?" the taller of the two men was addressing him.

"Yeah."

"I'm Detective Maitland and this is Detective Collazarro," they flashed their gold shields. "We'd like to hve a word with you, can we go inside?"

Dominic figured they probably would have at least two more cars on the block if they were serious, besides he didn't like street scenes. "Yeah, sure," he replied.

They walked upstairs to his second-story apartment.

"Now what the hell do you want with me?"

"We're investigating the murder of Tony Loggia. We understand he was your friend."

Their eye's searched his apartment. Something's wrong with these guys, Dom thought. They forgot to make me spread, and no shakedown. Besides, Tony's been dead for three months.

"Lemme see them shields ag..." He felt only a little pain

as he fell to the floor.

The article was buried in the back pages.

"Dominic Vereste, an associate of Louis Romano and a reputed enforcer for the Romano Family was found dead in his apartment on 47th Street. He was shot once through the forehead in what police assumed was a gangland killing. He was wearing a long black hairpiece when he was discovered by his landlord, Mr..."

PART II

PART II

ONE

It was the start of a beautiful spring weekend. The road beckoned to the red Fiat as it raced down the highway. Mild temperatures and a warm sun heightened their sense of adventure while wind rippled through Leslie's hair, giving her a feeling of freedom and abandonment. They were both laughing because it was a good time to be alive.

Earlier during the week they had gone to the library and had read Mansfield's brief biography in the Association of University President's Directory.

Born in 1927, the only child of Alden and Agatha Mansfield...graduated from Elkton High School, 1945...from the State College in 1948 (with honors) in political science. From 1949-1953, service in the United States Army. Honorably discharged as a Captain in 1953...Ph.D. in political science from Chicago in 1957; Assistant Professor, Ohio State, 1959; Associate Professor, Purdue University, 1963.

He had come to the campus overlooking the lake in 1964 as Dean of the College of Arts and Sciences; Vice-President for Academic Affairs in 1969; Acting President, 1973...Appointed by the Board of Trustees to the Presidency in 1975. Married Alexa Parkhurst, 1953. Two children, a son Bryan born in 1959 and a daughter Erin, in '62.

They stopped for coffee at a roadside diner and by noon were once again on their way.

"Start at the beginning," Andy had insisted. "If you really want to know someone,you have to understand how he grew up, where he lived, his neighborhood, his family, friends..."

"But what are we looking for?" quizzed Leslie.

"Patterns," Andy replied. "Consistencies, behavioral regularities and social patterns, his most important experiences, how he handles stress situations. Is he a leader or a follower? What kinds of people does he respect? Whom does he listen to, what does he believe in?"

"But where do you start Andy, and how do you begin?"

"I honestly don't know. If I knew the answers then I wouldn't have to bother with the questions. We can't assume anything about him. What makes perfectly good sense to us, won't to him and vice versa. He'll see different meanings in almost anything but in his way they'll be very important. We have to learn to see the world from his viewpoint, his perspective. It's one of the very first things you learn in anthropology."

"Doesn't sound terribly scientific to me. No wonder most people think anthropologists are a little weird."

Andy smiled at her. "You'll see, before we're finished we'll know more about Bliss Mansfield than even his mother."

Leslie was skeptical but deferred to Andy's experience in the field, and remained silent.

Mansfield's father had died while Bliss was overseas, but his mother was still living in the same town where he had grown up. "Elkton, pop. 3,357," the sign read. They drove to a gas station and looked in the phone book. "Agatha Mansfield, 912 N. Sycamore." Alden and Agatha, Andy thought, what typically beautiful turn of the century names.

They drove to the four corners of the town. It was what you would expect to find in America's heartland; small shops catering to the decreasing needs of a dwindling number of regular customers; a local market where the proprietor still sold you groceries on credit, payable at the end of the month; a drugstore, a hardware shop, the

114

bank, an old fashioned candystore where the kids met after school; the furniture emporium and mortuary owned by the same family, "E. Gorseline & Sons." There was a hand-lettered poster on the window of the Grange Hall advertising a 4-H exhibit.

They asked directions and drove down a road badly in need of repair past the Farmer's Co-op and the John Deere Tractor sales. They turned right at St. Cyril's Roman Catholic Church and drove for two more blocks until they came to North Sycamore.

The house was set back from the street surrounded by a huge lawn, now overgrown and clearly in need of a gardener's care. The two large oaks were in full foliage and cast deep shadows over the front porch. The wooden house was of typical period design, painted white with green shutters, and faded lace curtains still hung in every window.

Andy tried to imagine what it was like when Bliss was growing up. The paint would be new, the curtains clean and smelling as fresh as the roses lining the walk. Alden would be sweating as he mowed the lawn in his undershirt and coveralls, while Agatha served lemonade to her son's thirsty friends. She would wave familiarly to her neighbors as they strolled by commenting upon how fine the house was looking. In the evening, when Bliss was asleep, they would sit on their rocking chairs and she would be knitting a new sweater. They would gaze at the bright stars above, silently thanking God for their good fortune.

The doorbell no longer worked, so they knocked on the peeling screen door.

"Wait a minute now you two, I saw you drive up to the house in that bitty red car. I'm 'bout to fix some tea."

She let them in. The living room had about it a musty smell of old books. Yellowed wallpaper featuring small floral patterns blended with the heavy furniture of

115

another era. She was wearing a shapeless dress that had seen better days. Her frail body, pinched with wrinkles and suffering from rheumatism, was a contrast to her eyes which were bright and alert. She spoke with a vitality that belied her 75 years.

"Young lady." she pointed the way to the kitchen. "Why don't you bring out the tea and cookies while I meet your young man. If you've come to chat you'll have to sit and stay awhile." She motioned Andy to make himself comfortable.

He liked her immediately. What a woman. She doesn't even know us, or what we're here for but she welcomes us into her home and serves us tea. I wish I had known my mother better, he thought.

Leslie and Andy had secured authentic but dated press cards, from one of Leslie's students. They were going to pose as reporters claiming an interest in Mansfield's childhood, a normal curiosity about a Senatorial candidate.

Agatha, "Aggie" to her friends, was eager for the company and the conversation. No sooner had they introduced themselves and turned on the tape recorder when she launched into a delightful and nostalgic account of those days when both she and Bliss were much younger.

"We was poor, but proper folks, and we wasn't living in this fine house—that was when Alden got his own bus'siness. We'd been t'town for about two years, Bliss was nine then. Alden was working at Dempsey's service garage, believed in workin' and payin' our own way. Well it's Bliss you're wantin' to know about. He was a fine boy, did his chores right proper and then some. Helped out extra, too. Workin' at Lyle Cassady's farm, he was always there for the hay'in'. On the weekends he cut grass for the folks that could afford it. Every Sunday he came to church, that is until Alden stopped goin' after the accident. You ain't Catholic, are yuh?"

"No Ma'am."

"Anyway, he was always bringin' home A's from the schoolhouse. Miz Mitchell can tell ya, she lives over on Dawson with her sister. We got him a puppy, collie I think it was. Loved that dog, trained him and cleaned out his pen every day. Cried' bout a week when he ran away..."

"Did he have many friends?" Andy inquired.

"My word, did he. He was school president in the high school and they made him captain. Used to catch the ball that Eddie Hall throwed to him. Eddie's the bank manager now, you know."

"Mrs. Mansfield."

"Call me Aggie, son,"

Andy liked that. "Aggie, you said there was an accident?"

Agatha Mansfield lowered her eyes and brought her voice down to a whisper. "It's sumthin' that never should have happened," she began.

On July 28, 1938, Bliss Prescott Mansfield was a very frightened eleven-year-old boy. He had seen the entire accident.

Karen Merino was a shy little girl. She wore a pink dress with a blue border. When she smiled her braces flashed in the sunlight. Her black hair done up in pigtails moved with the summer breeze. Karen was riding her new bike. She was so excited, it was going to be her birthday present but she got it two weeks early. She was riding without using her hands.

"Bliss, look at me, see what I can do."

And then it happened. The car, it was a sports car. Bliss remembered later that it was red and didn't have a top. It must have been speeding over a hundred miles an hour. It made a screeching noise as it careened off the curb and smashed into Karen's bike and then it kept on going. It never stopped.

She just lay there on the ground. She wasn't even crying but her stomach was all bloody and he could see "things" hanging out. He ran across the street shouting for his mother.

"Mommy, mommy, she's dead, she's dead, she's dead."

"Bliss, what hap...Oh my God! Holy Mother of Mary, Bliss get in the house."

The ambulance arrived at eight, twenty minutes later and rushed Karen to the hospital. The Sheriff came at 8:18 but Bliss didn't know that. He was lying on his bed hugging his teddy bear and crying hysterically. "Why didn't he stop, it's not fair God, he killed her." He hadn't held his teddy in over five years.

Bliss was wrong. Karen did not die. Long after the operation her stomach continued to ache, and she would walk with a slight but noticeable limp, but she would live.

Deputy Don Purdee came to the house later that evening. He had spent the last summer as a counselor and knew how to handle kids. Although he was a serious young man he often smiled. Bliss liked him.

"Young fealla," he addressed Bliss. "It seems you were the only one who saw the accident. Can you tell me about it?"

"Begging your pardon, sir, but it wasn't an accident. I mean the car didn't even stop and he was going so fast. I'll just bet he wanted to hit her."

The Deputy continued. "Did you see the driver?"

"Yessir, I sure did, he wasn't a boy, he was older than I am but not as old as my Dad. He wasn't wearing a shirt and he had a lot of hair on his chest."

"What did the car look like?"

"It was one of those sports cars, bright red." Bliss hesitated.

"Go on," said the Deputy.

He grinned. "I can even show you a picture. It's in that magazine." He looked up at his father. "Dad, you know, the one you were reading last night." His father nodded.

118

"I remember it because I wanted a car like that when I grow up, but I don't think I want one anymore." He was about to start crying when Deputy Purdee put his arm around him.

"Let's go find the picture Bliss." It was an egg-shell blue Dusenberg SSJ with a long sloping hood, raked windshield and tall wire wheels.

"There, I told you, it's exactly like the red car, only this one's blue."

The Deputy was silent. It had to be the one. The description of the driver fit and there was no other car like that in all of Brown County. It belonged to Barry McCann who was home for the summer. His father was Angus McCann who owned half the town, and of the half that was not yet his he had an option to buy. Deputy Purdee decided he'd better speak to the Sheriff right away.

Aggie Mansfield finished her story.

"They wouldn't believe him, he was only eleven. Sheriff Miller made like he was mistaken, but he wasn't and we all knew it. How do you explain that sort of thing to an innocent boy?"

A cloud cast its shadow across the sun. There was the slight hint of a chill and the tea was cold. The interview was over. Leslie tried to encourage Aggie to go on but she knew the woman would talk no more. Old people seldom like to recall unpleasant memories. They left the house in silence.

"What now?" Leslie asked.

"First thing tomorrow we're going to check the newspaper's back files, but let's get to a telephone, we're going to call a Miz Mitchell and a Mr. Eddie Hall. What was the name of that girl again? Karen, that's it, Karen Merino."

Ed Hall was anxious to talk to the two reporters and invited them to come by about seven. Miz Mitchell was resting but her sister said it would be okay to visit tomorrow morning. There was no "Merino" listed in the phone book.

"Okay, Sherlock Crane, I like your style, but I'm also hungry and where are we going to spend the night?"

"Got one more thing to do," replied Andy. "I want to stop by the Sheriff's office."

Deputy Davis told him. "No sir, never heard of a Dupree but Ralph Miller's still alive and living over at the old folk's home over in Clinton. Sunday's visiting day."

They had dinner at the Regency Cafe and checked into the Red Horse Motor Inn out on the highway. Leslie was delighted when Andy signed the register as "Mr. and Mrs."

Ed Hall greeted them boisterously as they came up the driveway. He was in his early fifties wearing a tightly-buttoned brown vest which did little to disguise his spreading paunch. Aggie had been mistaken about his title, he was the vice-president. He had married his high school sweetheart, the older daughter of the bank president, produced four sons, had been to Europe once, nine years ago, and emphasized the fact that Bliss had caught his passes, when he had been the Elkton Eagle's reigning quarterback.

They were seated in the living room, Mrs. Hall served Leslie iced tea and brought the men mugs of cold beer.

"Yessir, old Bliss is sure gonna be our home town hero. I always said he'd amount to something big, though if you had known him a way back in high school, who'd have ever expected it?"

"Why is that?" asked Andy.

"Well, he was always quiet. I mean he wasn't a leader then, more like a bookworm, always going to the library every chance he'd get. Even turned down a date with Norrie Dressler, she was, beggin' your pardon ma'am, she was, well that kind of a girl; and all because he was

120

writing a paper for Mrs. Goldsmith. She was one of the Commies, got fired two years later but she and Bliss were always having these long debates about the meaning of life and things like that."

"You mean Bliss was a Marxist?" Leslie interrupted.

"No, ma'am, he was a good American, blieved in God and democracy. He just liked to talk to her, that's all. But you know when the School Board fired her he was the only one in the entire school, who wrote a letter saying it was wrong.

"Now Bliss was a good football player too. He was no natural athlete, he had to work real hard at it. Once I threw the ball to the sidelines, I was the quarterback you know. Well, I did it to kill the clock, but Bliss must have jumped five feet just to catch it and then he ran all the way for a touchdown. We made the county finals that year."

"Wasn't he student body president?" asked Leslie.

"No, that's not right, he was only president of the junior class. That was when the Japs bombed Pearl Harbor and we had to put them in those California camps for their own protection. Bliss almost lost the election on account of that. He was always sticking up for the little guy."

They visited "Miz" Mitchell at her sister's early the next morning. She was a quiet woman who had been confined to a wheelchair for the past ten years. She talked on and on about Bliss, raving about his curiosity and how he was always asking questions. She knew he would make a fine Senator. She refused to talk about the accident except to mention that it was a "disgraceful shame."

Later that afternoon they went to the offices of the Elkton *Crier* and poured over the back issues. There was only one small article that referred to the accident.

"Karen Merino, the ten-year-old daughter of Martin and Paula Merino of 925 N. Syracuse Way was injured when struck by an unidentified driver. She was taken to the emergency room at the County Hospital and is expected to make a complete recovery."

It was continuing to be a hot day. They drove the thirty miles to Clinton. The old folks home run by the county was a little more than a few buildings and two "dormitories," set apart from the rest of the town by a once green, crumbling picket fence. The buildings, like most of the residents, seemed badly in need of repairs.

Nurse Dorothea Francis was distinguishable from the patients only by her white starched uniform.

"Can I help you?" she volunteered.

"We're looking for a Ralph Miller, used to be Sheriff over at Elkton."

"What do you want to see him for?" Her tone was caustic, not suspicious. She seemed anxious only that these strangers not be bothering old Ralph.

Leslie surprised herself by the ease with which she lied.

"We're writing up a local history of Elkton. We were told he was one of the town's first lawmen. Maybe he can tell us what it really was like back then."

Nurse Francis visible relaxed her features and lowered her voice. "Well, I don't know what the old man can remember, if he can remember anything at all. He's drunk half the time and probably out of his head the other half. Oh yes, it's against the law for the residents to drink, but it helps them pass the days. Just talk kinda slow and loud. If you have to, shout. He doesn't hear so good."

She led them past the men's dormitory and to a man sitting on the grass. Judging from the iron-gray stubble on his beard, Ralph Miller hadn't shaved in a week. His eyes were vacant and set in deep sockets. His parched skin was like drying leather, from which bones protruded. Saliva dribbled down his chin as he turned to look at the visitors.

Andy was patient. He sat next to the old man letting him feel his presence. Lighting a cigarette he placed it between Miller's lips. He looked into his eyes and after a while spoke in a soft yet fatherly tone.

"Tell us about it Ralph, tell us about the accident with the little Merino girl."

Nurse Francis must have been wrong. When it came to certain things Ralph Miller had a fine memory. They listened attentively while he told his story.

At exactly eleven that July evening Sheriff Ralph Miller drove the four and one-half miles to the hilltop estate and residence of Angus McCann. Ralph knew Angus well. The Sheriff had dated Angus's younger sister Lucy during high school and it was Angus who had later "suggested" that Ralph be made a Deputy and then appointed to fill Sheriff Kimberley's term. His suggestion was the same as a command and Sheriff Miller was not looking forward to the visit.

"I'll call the Mister, he's expecting you." He was ushered into the big house by the housekeeper.

"Well, well Sheriff, what can I do for you," his voice boomed. Angus was all smiles yet his eyes belied the greeting. They were like ice, cold and knowing.

"Its about your son, Barry, sir."

"Yes, speak up man, what is it?"

Son-of-a-bitch, he's daring me to come right out and say it. "Can we speak alone sir, that is, in private?" God, how do you tell this man that his son's been identified as a hit-and-run?

"If you insist." Angus led the way to his library and sat behind the desk.

Rosewood, the grain matched the floor to ceiling bookcases, the smell of leather bindings. Warmth, security, money, gold money and unlimited power. His hands played nervously with his notebook. "Uh, have you seen Barry, Mr. McCann?"

"No, should I, he's away visiting my brother over at the college."

123

"Are you sure?"

"Of course I'm sure, don't you think I know where my own son is? He just called a few moments ago. Do you want to ask the housekeeper? What's this all about?"

Maybe I should just come out and say it. No, better not. "Was he driving his car?"

"No, he borrowed mine. Totaled his last month. He's not in any trouble is he?"

Sheriff Ralph Miller might not have been a very perceptive man but he understood all right. Angus's brother would provide the necessary alibi. An investigation would reveal that Barry's fraternity brothers at the Deke house would "swear" he had wrecked his car. The car, of course, would never be found. No doubt the housekeeper would verify the phone call. This was not the first time Barry had been in trouble.

Ralph's term was up in the fall. He could also really use the "bonus" he was sure to receive for his "integrity," and after all, the doctor had said the little girl was doing just fine. Her hospital bill had already been pre-paid by a mysterious benefactor. Yes, he would have to conduct an investigation officially, but first...

"Bliss, it's very important that we go over everything again. We wouldn't want to make any mistakes, would we?"

"No sir, Sheriff Miller," replied Bliss. He was just a little nervous. He had never been inside the stationhouse before, although his father had pointed it out to him on several occassions.

"Son, what time was it when you saw the accident?"

"It wasn't no accident Sir, I told..."

The Sheriff interrupted him. "Let's forget that for the moment. Bliss, was it dark yet?"

Bliss had to think. He didn't know the Sheriff was going to ask these kinds of questions. "It was getting dark, but Mom always lets me play outside after supper. I could see just fine."

"What was the Merino girl wearing?"

"I'm not sure...maybe it was a dress. Yes, she had a dress on."

"No Bliss, she was wearing dungarees."

The boy was puzzled, he distinctly remembered she was wearing a dress, a pink dress with a blue border.

"What kind of a car do you think you saw?"

"It was like that car in the magazine, the blue one."

"But you said it was red?"

"Yes, it was a red car in the street."

"Did you ever see the car before?"

"No, sir."

"Then why are you so sure it was the one you said you saw? Maybe it was another one just like it?"

"Golly, I don't know. It was awfully like the one I saw. Are there other cars like that?"

"Oh, yes, lots of cars look the same. How fast was it going?"

Bliss smiled. "Very fast, I'll bet it was going over a hundred miles an hour."

"No, now, cars don't go that fast Bliss."

"They don't?" He was really confused now. He wished his father was here.

"No, and anyway if it was really going that fast how could you have seen the driver?"

He was beaten. "Not very well, I guess."

"Do you think you could identify the driver if you saw his picture?"

"I'll try, I think so."

"Look at these pictures Bliss, look at them real good. You wouldn't want to get an innocent boy in trouble. Now would you?"

"No Sir, I'll look."

Bliss stared for about fifteen minutes at seven high school graduation photographs. All the young men were wearing ties and jackets. The one he had seen didn't even have a shirt on, thought Bliss, so how could he really tell?

"I'm sorry Sheriff, I don't recognize him but..."

"Thank you son, you've been a big help to all of us. We're really proud of you and I wish all our citizens would...Never mind, go on home now."

Mr. and Mrs. Mansfield were told that Bliss could not identify the driver, that he was not so sure about the car, that it was dusk, and that he couldn't even swear to what the girl was wearing. The Sheriff thanked them for their cooperation and commended them for reporting the accident in time to save the girl's life.

Alden and Agatha were new to town, having lived there for less than two years. Mr. Mansfield worked at a local garage and was saving his money to put a down payment on his own shop. One week later the bank surprisingly approved his application for a loan. Mrs. Miller persuaded Mrs. Mansfield to run for the school board. She did and easily won. Karen Merino and her family left town. Some people said they had inherited money. Deputy Dupree was notified he had passed the examination for the State Police and Barry McCann transferred to a college in Pennsylvania. He drove there in his new Cord 810, its blunt coffin-like nose breaking the wind before him.

Leslie was furious. "Where was his lawyer? Not even his parents were there...how can they call that sham an investigation. Just try to imagine it, a terrified eleven-year-old boy all alone in there with a scheming Sheriff who makes you almost doubt your own name. I don't think I could have done much better. You'd think we were in Nazi Germany."

Andy didn't really hear her. He was thinking about a trusting boy who believed in himself and in others, in his parents, in God, in law and justice. He was curious, always asking questions. He must have asked a lot of them about the accident. I can imagine the answers he got.

"He didn't realize it right away, at least not everything. Remember, he was only eleven." Andy was saying. "It's my guess he suppressed most of what he learned, pushed it into a dark corner of his mind. He was an introspective boy, a thinker. Still, there must have been times when he remembered and felt the shame and guilt; the powerlessness of not being able to do anything."

Leslie continued. "By the time he was in high school, it was too late to actually do anything about it, so he starts to identify with other causes, other injustices—the concentration camps for the Japanese-Americans, the school board firing his teacher. There must have been others. He doesn't even want to take advantage of the school slut."

"So what does he do? He reads, he debates, he keeps on asking questions and develops into a serious student. He even tries harder, like jumping for an off side pass and scoring the touchdown. I have the feeling he was pretty much of a loner, even back then. Too much success leads to a lot of resentment. Ed Hall was the quarterback and Bliss the pass receiver. They should have been good friends, but judging from what we heard yesterday, its no secret than Ed doesn't really like him."

"I wonder if he became a Socialist like Mrs. Goldsmith?"

"I don't think so, this all took place during World War II and every small town boy I've ever known was a patriot. But his teachers must have introduced him to other philosophies, other alternatives. He would have learned a lot about money and power politics and the injustice that supports it."

It was getting dark now. Andy turned on the headlights as they headed back towards the university.

"From what we've learned so far, I like the young Bliss Mansfield. I mean I really like him. He had a lot of guts. Are you sure he's the same person you heard in Korea?"

Andy replied. "I never said he was the one, but the

phrase he used over the phone was the same one I heard in the village. They've got to be connected."

Leslie closed her eyes and rested against Andy's shoulder. The car stereo was softly playing the music from the "Tennessee Waltz" and the glare from the on-coming headlights made her drowsy. "Andy, could we be wrong about the president?"

"No, I don't think so." Andy switched stations and thought about a boy who had learned very early about the way rich and powerful people could corrupt the law and suppress the truth, and how they made innocent victims suffer. He wondered what it would take before such a boy would act.

TWO

The car was a Mercedes 600 limousine. It had been scrubbed and polished that afternoon so that the soft leather inside was free of dust and the chrome grill with the distinctive logo sparkled in the early evening light.

It had a half-landau top which could be removed while the front remained enclosed. There was a bar cooled by the air-conditioning system, curtains, reading lamps and a writing table. The rear seats could be partially reclined for utmost comfort. A sliding glass partition was operated from both the driver's and passenger's compartments, and hydraulic locks would automatically close the trunk and doors. All interior appointments were of a hand-rubbed burled walnut.

The car was limited in production to about fifty each year, and similar models were owned by the Pope, Hugh Heffner, Arab oil sheiks, European heads of state and the late Elvis Presley. It had a V-8, 6.3 liter displacement, almost 300 horsepower and had not been brought into the United States since 1972 because of American emission control standards. This particular model cost $57,000.00

It was Mitchell Potter III's personal car and it arrived at the Mansfield's circular drive at precisely seven. The uniformed chauffeur stood by the door, and with a style born of long experience assisted Bliss Mansfield and his wife to climb into the enormous luxury of the interior. They began the ninety-minute drive to Terrace Hills.

This was not the first time that Bliss had visited Mitchell's sprawling estate, although he had not been there so often as to be unaffected by its elegant charm. It's too bad the sun had set, he thought. He recalled the magnificent expanse of manicured lawns, background for the oak-lined drive winding its way to the mansion. The tennis courts were just of the west wing. They were designed as a smaller replica of Forest Hill's center court, complete with spectator stands. From the court you could gaze down at the rose garden, a dazzling array of color and symmetry. There was a private lake past the woods, stocked annually with trout and bass.

Yet the most impressive feature was the house itself. Its immense majesty was softened by the attention to fine detail. Modeled after an Elizabethan manor house, the ancient timbers and leaded-glass windows suggested a serenity far from the hustle of the 20th century world. It was a place where men of power and substance could meet privately and discuss the important affairs of the day without being disturbed by the ringing of telephones, the nagging of secretaries and the other necessary nuisances of the executive life-style.

A request to spend an evening at the Potters was tantabout to a command; that is if you wanted to be considered a part of the world of political and corporate decision-makers. It was even rumored that the President of the United States himself awaited an invitation. Bliss had few illusions concerning his own position. He had been asked, or rather summoned, so that the party bigwigs and their wealthy contributors could get a first-hand close-up look at this aspiring Senator. The fact that he had been invited tonight was an indication that his candidacy had been given very serious consideration.

Mitchell Potter III, resembled in every way the aristocratic gentry of the political elite. He was tall and slim waisted, his features finely etched into a face pleasantly tanned by endless hours on the courts. A graduate of Exeter and Harvard, a former member of the eastern establishment, he had served as an Interior Undersecretary and an an Ambassador to the Court of St. James's. Beneath his cool exterior, some called it his "British affectation", was an experienced political in-fighter, a man schooled in the ways of Washington, a generous friend and a deadly enemy. He had been divorced for the past five years, so it was his daughter and not his daughter and not his wife who acted as unofficial hostess.

"A real pleasure to see you this evening, Bliss. So glad you could make it." He smiled at Alexa, whose youthful figure was adequately evident yet tastefully hidden.

"I will always wonder why such a beautiful young woman stays with such an old man." He nodded to Bliss who silently accepted the compliment.

Patricia Potter Sims, his jet-set daughter, a product of Brearley, Gstaad and Acapulco kissed Bliss lightly on the cheek. Turning to Alex she crooned. Come with me darling, while the men work we'll play." She led her to the champagne bar.

Alexa Parkhurst Mansfield was no stranger to the rich and the powerful, although her tastes ran towards the intellectual. Her father had been a professor of philosophy at Chicago, her mother an editor for a top publishing house. She had lived most of her life in university towns among scholars, Nobel laureates, authors, poets and assorted artists. She had just turned fifty, yet her face and particularly her figure suggested a much less matronly woman.

"You know you husband is really quite a man. How, in heavens name did you manage to catch him?"

Alexa was becoming annoyed with her presumptuous hostess, but mindful of Bliss' aspirations pleasantly replied. "I met him when he was at Chicago. He was exciting even then. He'd just come back from the Korean War and wanted to learn about everything."

She remembered that they had argued all evening at a coffee shop about the philosophies of democratic and totalitarian systems. When the shop closed at two in the morning they walked back to his small apartment, continued the discussion, made love, argued again, and too exhausted for anything else, fell asleep in each others arms.....

"We were married right after he passed his doctoral

exams."

"Oh, it must have been so difficult for you, being so poor and all."

Alexa thought, this woman is downright insulting but she continued. "Yes, it was rough those first few years, he was an assistant professor and I became pregnant. But I learned how to be a faculty hostess and after he became an administrator life was much easier."

She was still not used to the loneliness that was an inevitable part of being a university president's wife. The long weekends he would spend at out-of-town meetings and conventions, but she recognized their necessity, now even more so, if he was going to be a U.S. Senator.

Patricia Potter Sims carefully re-evaluated the candidate's wife. She was tough and she would survive the rigors of a campaign. I've been insulting her all evening, she thought, and she's taken it like a lady.

"Alexa, let's get away from these people for a while. I've got something I really want to talk to you about."

Bliss noted that there were about seventy people at the gathering. Guests filled the living rooms and conversation areas, spilling out onto the patio while uniformed waiters insisted that drink and food, but especially drink, were easily available. Mitchell guided Bliss among the guests, pausing long enough to introduce him but not so long as to engage in meaningful conversation.

"Bliss, I'd like you to meet Al Aronsen, he singlehandedly runs Aronsen's Electronics."

"Read about the way you handled the demonstrations at your campus." He was an intense young man with large black-rimmed spectacles.

"Why thank you, Mr. Aronsen."

"Think those radicals will get a fair trial?"

"That's up to the courts now, I have the utmost confidence in Judge Higgins."

"Yes, I suppose so." Aronsen seemed a bit dismayed.

"Perhaps we can discuss the details later Al," Mitchell interrupted. "Bliss is going to be a busy man this evening." Without waiting for a reply he steered his away. "Al is in favor of the death penalty for shoplifting." Both men chuckled.

"Do I get to meet the candidate, Mitch?"

"Of course Senator; Senator Ellis, Bliss Mansfield."

"Heard quite a bit about you from Lawson, Mansfield." Ed Lawson was the Senior University Trustee. "You really asking for that much of a budget hike?"

Bliss responded. "If we really want that Medical Center and a quality staff, we'll have to pay for it, but it's money well spent."

Mitchell looked pleased. "Gentlemen, come now, this is a party, not a hearing, they'll be plenty of time for that later."

Bliss couldn't help thinking of a Spanish bullfight where in a tradition of anticipation the bull was first paraded around the arena, cheered, called by name, while all the time the matador was carefully watching for any signs of weakness. He pictured Mitchell carrying a concealed sword beneath a red cape.

By 10:30, some of the guests had departed, the women were still gaily commenting upon who-did-what-and-with-whom, and Bliss found himself being escorted into Mitchell's private office. Seated around a long low table were five men and a woman. Bliss recognized senior State Senator James Poswall, Assemblyman Eli Ricketts and former U.S. Senator Matthew Larkin. The woman was Marcia Hersey, the *Chronicle's* political writer. Of the two remaining men, the one with the pot-belly was introduced as Bob Lippincott, a manufacturing scion from the north-state area, the other gentleman, smaller and trimmer, was simply presented as Major-General

Jason Carterett.

"Now you know the truth, Bliss," Mitchell sighed. "Political decisions are really made in smoke-filled rooms by a select group of dirty old men and one charming woman."

When everyone finished laughing and, with the exception of the General, re-filled their glasses, they proceeded to flatter their guest.

"Bliss, you were just superb the way you handled the rioters...I've always admired you ever since I read your book...There's no question about it; a man of your character will cinch the election...It's so nice meeting you at last President Mansfield."

Bliss smiled, shook hands, poured himself another bourbon and settled down in a leather recliner. Mitchell must have given them a silent command because the conversations suddenly became serious. Poswall, Larkin, Hersey, Ricketts and Lippincott each gave him a critical commentary on their respective positions regarding labor, business, oil, energy, welfare, gun control, gambling, taxes and foreign policy. Bliss wasn't asked for an opinion, that would come later. These people were all power brokers and represented particular lobbies or concerns. They were only making sure that Bliss be made aware of their positions. It was understood that if he received the nomination he would have to come to terms with them.

Bliss turned to the General. "I missed hearing your comments, sir?"

"I'm a soldier, Mr. President. It's not my place to discuss such things." Then he smiled. "I've been a fan of yours for a long time and when Mitchell told me you would be his guest this evening, I just wanted to have the pleasure of meeting you."

The drive home through the silent night gave Bliss time to think. He hadn't really expected the meeting in

Mitchell's office. The fact that this group, he couldn't help thinking of them as sinister cabal, had not asked for his opinions was both comforting and disturbing. Satisfying in that perhaps they already knew how he felt and were accepting him as the party's choice. He didn't really think so, yet there wasn't any formidable competition. But they were the ones giving the advice, suggesting how issues ought to be resolved and even which issues were the important ones. He never considered himself a spokesman for these people, a mere conduit for their policies. Yes, if you become a senator you always have to take advice. But you had better make it clear that you're your own man in Washington.

His own man, now that was really ironic. He wondered how they would have reacted if they knew the extent of his other commitments, his "real" involvement with causes and issues.

His people had told him that Andrew Crane was no longer a problem. They would see to it that he didn't make any trouble and they would handle him in their own fashion. He was to direct his energies towards securing the nomination.

Alexa watched him sitting there next to her. He hadn't said a word and they were almost home. Lately she had been worrying about Bliss. Ever since the attempted shooting of that South African, he had been unusually agitated. His stomach was bothering him again and he had difficulty falling asleep at night. She often found him in his study just staring at the walls. Whereas before, he had shared his concerns with her, he now kept them to himself. It had also been over two weeks since they had made love. It's probably the nomination, she thought. She knew how much it meant to him and deluded herself into believing that once it was over, everything would be okay.

THREE

Andy was scheduled to present a paper at a symposium in Boston so Leslie decided to visit the State College where the President had spent his formative days as an undergraduate student.

"No way my lovely," Andy insisted. "It's just too dangerous, you could easily get into all kids of trouble and no one would be there to help."

"Bullshit!" Leslie was angry, remembering that she had left a husband who had insisted she couldn't even go to college. "I'm a grown woman or hadn't you noticed. I'd say I've been on my own more than a few years now, and I can handle myself quite well thank you. Besides, what can happen on a college campus?"

"You could get shot at for one thing," Andy replied.

"Nonsence, remember it was you they shot at anyway! Andy." she changed her approach, "if we're in this together, then we've got to have confidence in one another, and that means I'm your partner, not your playmate."

Andy knew better than to fight the battle of the sexes, and besides he knew that Leslie was right. He had been attracted to her because of her independence and he liked her that way.

"Okay, I can't stop you, but promise me you'll be extra careful. Whoever is responsible for the attempt on my life is no fool. He's bound to know about you and about us."

"Oh," Leslie chided him. "Are we that well known?"

"Absolutely," Andy replied. "Why there isn't a faculty

136

wives party where they don't fantasize about our relationship."

Leslie drove Andy to the airport. "You can fantasize all you like but stay away from those horny colleagues of yours, especially Mara, I hear tell she does her best research on her back...and please, be careful too."

Leslie was excited. The adrenalin raced through her body making her more acutely aware of every sensation. She looked forward to her investigation as enthusiastically as when she had been a student criminologist, perhaps more, because this was not a textbook assignment, it was the real thing.

She would have a legitimate reason for visiting the college as a professor herself, yet she also kept the ID that would identify her as a member of the press. She tried to recall what she had learned from Andy. It was his perspective they wanted. How did Bliss experience his college days? What did he often think about? Who were his friends? Who were his teachers? And of course the unspoken question, and the most important one.

She tried to picture the college as it must have been in the days immediately preceding the end of the war. In 1945 the school had primarily been a teachers college but with a growing emphasis upon the liberal arts. Like Bliss, most of the students were from a lower-middle class background, many of them from rural areas and small towns. They would be pimply-faced farmboys with the smell of fresh manure still on their boots, innocent blond and blue-eyed teenage girls whose parents were convinced that schoolteaching was a big step towards middle-class respectability and the only proper career for a lady. She remembered reading a study of "Middletown" which emphasized the girls having domineering mothers, whose educational level was higher than their fathers. They would be dissatisfied with their lives and would push their daughters into achieving their lost dreams.

Fraternities and sororities would be based upon snob appeal, and would be important vehicles for social mobility. Athletes would be popular too. Leslie wondered how a good-looking, husky, high school football player with an inquisitive nature would fit into smalltown college life.

She suspected the faculty would be traditional rather than innovative. They would be concerned with molding their students so that they could take their place as solid middle-class citizens in a war weary America. Inexpensive housing would be difficult to find because of the unexpected numbers of servicemen returning to school under the G.I. Bill. No doubt, there would be special places for students of different political persuasions to meet and discuss their emerging ideas about utopian societies, but there wouldn't be many radicals among the student body.

She tried to imagine the campus with old wooden buildings, inadequate laboratories, overcrowded classrooms and the new quonset huts which would be hastily constructed everywhere as makeshift offices and dormitories. There would be no graduate programs, no large government research grants and professors would not be forced to publish. The emphasis would be on good teaching. For one wistful moment, she almost wished she had her career during those times.

Leslie headed for the library and the yearbook for the class of '48. She was eager to learn all she could about a political science major named Bliss Mansfield.

"Bliss, maybe we made a mistake, I mean maybe we shouldn't have come."

"I know. Jerry, my stomach's all in knots and I feel like throwing up, but don't worry, it's going to be okay."

"But what if it's not. Maybe I'll flunk out. I was never good in school like you were. The only reason they let me in was to play football. I'm scared.

Bliss looked at his friend Jerry Westerdale, he really was scared. So am I thought Bliss, but I'm not going to let it get to me. I've worked too hard to get here in the first place.

"Jeez, just look at these classes, Freshman English, Math, Psychology, Earth Science and History. I went to the bookstore yesterday. They've got ten books for those courses. Does that mean I have to read all of them?"

"I guess so Jerry. Look, don't worry so much, we're roommates and I'll help you."

"Jeez, Bliss, thanks, sometimes I don't even know what I'm doing here."

Bliss, and hundreds of other freshmen were suffering from the initial stages of what some anthropologists would later refer to as culture shock. Away from home for the first time, lonely, facing new responsibilities and living in strange dormitories, they would be absolutely terrified by the mysterious demands that would be made upon their fledgling intellect. A few would succumb and leave before the start of classes. Others would drop out during the semester, but most of them would survive that first year, and if they made it through the next one, would four years later receive baccalureate degrees.

Bliss walked into the classroom and not wishing to be noticed took a seat in the back, which, of course, made him all the more conspicuous because there were only twelve students in the room. I must be in the wrong class he thought, but before he could leave, a thin, almost to the point of being emaciated, young man, his hair flying in every direction and wearing a three-piece rumpled and stained herringbone suit, closed the door and strode imperiously to the blackboard. "Professor A. Markham" he wrote on the board.

"This is *my* seminar in political philosophy, we will read one book each week. You will write six papers and there will be three exams and a final. Now, what do I mean by political philosophy?"

An uncomfortable silence spread throughout the room. Professor Markham paced back and forth, like a tiger stalking his prey. He looked angry. "Well, if you can't answer the question what are you doing in my class?"

The accusation was more than he could stand and without quite knowing why, Bliss raised his hand.

"Yes. The young man in the back."

"Sir, a philosophy is a way of life, so a political philosophy must be a belief in a particular system of government."

"What do you mean, 'a way of life'. Where I grew up basketball was called a 'way of life'. Is basketball a philosophy?" The class snickered.

Bliss refused to give in. "Well, in a way it is. The principles behind basketball, the responses, the emotions during the game, are all based upon particular concepts, abstract philosophical ones. They give basketball a special meaning and make it more than just a game."

The professor quickly replied. "what do you mean by abstract concepts?"

"Something that's not tangible, that goes beyond the mundane. It need not necessarily be even conscious." Bliss tried to remember what Mrs. Goldsmith had said. "Abstractions are relative to context and therefore cannot be right or wrong."

"Any other brilliant attempts to answer the question?" the professor sarcastically asked. Once again there was no response. "Next week you will read in its entirety, Saint Augustine's City of God. Perhaps then we will know what aphilosophy is. Class is dismissed."

"You, the young man in the back," he pointed a boney finger at Bliss. "Come here, please." Uh-uh, Bliss thought I'm really in for it now. He slowly measured his steps to the front of the room while the other students quickly made for the door.

"I don't believe I know you young man, let me see your class card." Bliss wasn't sure what he meant so he handed him his registration packet.

"Why you're only a freshman. This is an upper-division seminar. You don't even belong in this class."

Bliss turned a livid shade of green. "I know Professor Markham, I realized my mistake and was about to leave when you closed the door."

The teacher stared at him and then smiled. "Go to the Registrar's office and ask them for an add card." He scribbled something on a piece of paper. "Here, be sure to give them this, that is if you want to take the class. Do you?"

"Oh boy, yessir." He was ecstatic and ran all the way to the Registrar's office.

Bliss read and wrote and kept on reading, often till the wee hours of the morning. Professor Markham became his mentor and guided him quickly through the Greeks and the Romans, around Marxism, Imperialism and Capitalism, underneath Atheism, Deism, Bhuddism, Shinto, Christianity and Judiasm, across Europe, Asia and Africa, into art, music and literature, and past philosophy, sociology and political science.

Bliss finished the required texts and was sent to the library to read further. He found obscure pamphlets buried in the stacks and brought them to his master. They spent long hours discussing, arguing and occasionally agreeing about philosophy, law, politics, nature and humankind. The brilliant, erratic professor and the bright, inquisitive student enjoyed a relationship that few scholars or students would understand. Together they searched for truth and the meaning of life and once in a while they thought they had found it.

Jocelyn McCallister was an exceptionally attractive dark-haired beauty. She stood no more than five-feet tall. Her deep black eyes were so overpowering that few people appreciated her pert nose and sensuous lips. She was always well dressed yet her wardrobe was always so proper and prim that she was easily noticed, even on a campus that was an exemplar Mid-Western morality. Her father was a fairly successful attorney while her mother tutored students in French and Spanish. They lived in a respectable yet inexpensive house three blocks from the campus.

She was the very youngest of four children. Her brother had been killed in France during the war, her two sisters were schoolteachers already married and starting their own families. She was her grandmother's darling and, as is the case for so many change-of-life babies, she was adored, pampered, overprotected and, many would claim, spoiled. Treated like a fragile princess most of her life, she grew up surprisingly with confidence and poise almost to the point of being arrogant. Ever since she had been a little girl she had displayed a curious and active imagination, never accepting answers on faith alone. A straight A student, she would soon inform her parents that becoming a schoolteacher left much to be desired. They would be momentarily shocked, but secretly pleased that she intended to pursue a graduate career in philosophy.

Socially she shied away from classmates, almost as if she preferred the company of professors and books. She was soft-spoken and articular. Unlike Bliss, who could easily become outwardly excited over a new idea, she maintained a complacent, almost serene, demeanor. If you didn't know her it would be difficult to realize that she was the best student in the junior class.

Jocelyn did not date. Confident as she was of her academic qualities, she was secretly terrified of men. On those occassions when a classmate would ask her out she would smile, thank him for his offer, and tactfully decline, claiming a real or imaginary, but always acceptable excuse. Her parents never suspected her real

142

reasons. They assumed that their daughter merely accepted the realities of race relations in America and being one of five Negro students at the college, preferred to leave well enough alone.

"Wowee, shit and shinola, what a woman," Jerry Westerdale was shouting. He stumbled drunkenly back to the rooming house, collapsed on the bed and buried his face in his pillow. Bliss tried to resume his reading but Jerry didn't care.

"She was black as the ace of spades with tits the size of watermelons. I could have humped her all night."

Bliss realized the futility of trying to study. "Want to tell me about it, conquering hero?"

"Yeah." Jerry was slurring his words. "It was after practice and the guys dared me to go down to 'Niggertown'. We all jumped into Scott's chevy and drove over the tracks to 'Mama's'. You know, she didn't want to let me in because I was drinking, but when I took out my wallet she changed her mind real quick."

Jerry continued to brag about his exploits with the colored whore, Viola. Bliss was, he had to admit, somewhat envious. His own romantic interludes usually ended with a good-night kiss, or on better nights, some clumsy attempts at passion in the back seat of a friend's car. He was not a virgin and unknown even to Ed Hall had enjoyed Norrie's multi-talented lips and thighs in back of the Elkton Eagle's all-purpose stadium. Yet, like many young men he believed in the romantic novels he read about and, simple as it may seem, was waiting for the girl of his dreams.

Jerry Westerdale, a borderline student, whose talent as an all-conference tackle kept him at school, obviously had other fantasies. His exaggerated exploits nevertheless amused Bliss who realized that Jerry would feel hurt if his best buddy would not listen to his boasts of conquest, be they what they were.

Bliss had never thought about either the sexology or

the psychology of inter-racial relationships. There were no blacks in Elkton and only a few at the college. He was intellectually incensed at the degradation of slavery and was too sensitive to join his peers in their limited attempts at ethnic humor, but the thought of dating a black girl just had not occurred to him.

Markham's seminar in international politics was a must for all serious political science seniors. The class was limited by the professor to what he considered the "brightest and the best." His reading list ran over five single-spaced typewritten pages. The books and articles were always placed on reserve in the library.

"What do you mean the books have already been checked out?" Bliss shouted angrily at the librarian.

"I mean exactly that, and if you have to shout at someone I would suggest the young lady sitting by the window. She checked them out less than ten minutes ago."

Bliss marched to the window table. Damn, he thought, she's sitting in my favorite place too. "Where do you get your nerve taking out all the books," he accused her. "Don't you know there are other students in the class. I have a right..."

She looked up at him, surprised by his bad manners. "You're shouting you know, and this is a library."

Bliss looked down and met her eyes. He suddenly felt very foolish, like a small boy who had just thrown a temper tantrum. "I'm sorry," he whispered. "Can I start over again?"

"Yes, of course you can," Jocelyn continued to look up at him.

"I'm Bliss Mansfield and I just made a fool of myself, will you..."

She interrupted him. "I'm Jocelyn McCallister, and the answer is yes, I forgive you. Would you like to share these books?"

He was still staring at her, such dark eyes and what

soft brown skin. She's beautiful, he thought. He started to sit down but his feet didn't get the message. His heel caught on the back of the chair and before he could regain his balance he fell over, sending her to the floor, and landing on top of her. He lay there unwilling to believe what had happened. His body pressed hard against her and he felt her warmth. And then they started to laugh. Their voices became louder and louder, echoing across the room and causing the other students to stop and stare at them. Bliss tried to apologize but he knew he sounded ridiculous. He helped her pick up the scattered books and papers.

"You must think I'm a clumsy oaf," he started.

"Yes, you are," she replied but her eyes were not angry, they were smiling at him.

"Can I buy you a cup of coffee," he offered.

"I'm sorry, I've got a class now, perhaps some other time." She gathered her belongings and quickly left.

"Tandy's Hut" was across the street from the behavioral sciences building. It was a third-rate coffee shop which had been closed down twice by the Board of Health. Coffee was five cents and refills free, so it was immensely popular with left-wing radical students who believed in dark seedy places and who also happened to be poor. Bliss wasn't a radical, at least not in the traditional sense. He was an A student, an honor ROTC Cadet, clean-shaven and modest. Yet, Tandy's provided one of the few places outside of Professor Markham's class, where one could freely discuss unpopular ideologies.

Jocelyn McCallister was also a noontine habituee. Her reasons had less to do with politics and more with convenience. Her classes ended at twelve and began at one. Tandy's was as good a place as any to spend the hour.

"Pardon me, Miss MacCallister, but may I buy you a cup of coffee?"

145

"Yes, Mr. Mansfield, you can, providing you don't trip and spill it all over me."

They both grinned. "I'll do my best ma'am."

She was wearing a red skirt and a white peasant blouse emphasizing the dark hair curling about her shoulders. Her eyes had told him she was apprehensive.

"Is this an accidental meeting Mr. Manfield?"

"No! First my name is Bliss, second I've followed you for a week and I owe you and apology and..."

"You don't owe me anything, Bliss." Her eyes were angry now.

"...and thirdly you're always interrupting me and putting words in my mouth. I just wanted to see you again."

"Did you need an excuse," she teased him. Control yourself, Jocelyn, you've never acted this way before.

"Yes," replied Bliss. "You're the most attractive young lady on this campus but you act so damn snotty. Look, just because you're black and I'm white doesn't mean..."

"Shhh, you're raising your voice again."

Bliss and Jocelyn did not go to Professor Markham's one o'clock class. Instead they walked up the hill, past the college, and sat on the grass overlooking the river and the woods. Their conversation was animated and excited. They spoke of philosophy and politics and it was almost dark before they started to talk about themselves.

"I'm a virgin and I'm afraid of men." She had never talked about these things.

"I spend all my time talking about politics because I'm too embarrassed to say what I really feel."

"How do you really feel, Bliss?"

There was a cool breeze but he was sweating. "I want to touch you." He put his hand on her hair, felt its silky texture and ran his fingers through her curls. He touched her nose, her cheeks, her lips. She quivered as he reached her sholders and let his hand fall to her breast. Her eyes were closed and her breath shallow as he unbottoned her

146

blouse. They were rising and falling rapidly, stretching against her brassiere. He unhooked the small snap and removed the white bra. Jocelyn's skin was like brown velvet. Pink nipples hardened to his touch. Her mouth was soft and yielding, her tongue on fire. She began to reach for him. He nervously crept under her skirt and slid his hand beneath her pants. She moaned as he placed his middle finger between her legs. He was gong to bury his face in her. She was so wet.

Suddenly she stopped him and pulled away. "No, I can't!" And then she was crying. "Bliss Mansfield, I've never done anything like this before. It's not right. I feel cheap and small."

They sat there for a long time thinking of the right words to say but neither Bliss nor Jocelyn knew them. She knew it would be pointless to see him again. He was too ashamed to ask.

"Look, I know we're different..." he began. No, that wasn't it, the color of her skin didn't have anything to do with it at all.

It was like she could read his thoughts. "That's nonsense and you know it, white man. We're talking about a relationship and you're trying to pass it off as a bad joke."

"Will I ever see you again?" He felt it was a foolish statement but it was the best he could do.

She smiled and looked right through him. "Never, never again, that is unless you're going to Professor Markham's party. You can pick me up at eight."

And then they were running, hand in hand, down the hill and laughing with the exuberance and freedom of young people who had just discovered that they were in love.

They saw each other constantly, talked for endless hours on the telephone, spent evenings studying in the library and went to sleep reliving the past twenty-four hours and dreaming of the ones to come. They were both serious and sensitive and their relationship was hardly a secret. There were those on campus who gagged at the sight of a white boy and a black girl walking together. To make matters worse, Jocelyn's father was a closet racist, who strongly opposed the relationship, although he had to admit that Bliss was as fine a young scholar as he had ever met. Bliss did not tell his parents about her. There were those who would never undertand and those who never could. At first Bliss and Jocelyn just didn't care.

Jerry was deeply troubled and nervously paced back and forth in the small room they shared. How can I tell Bliss, he kept asking himself. We've been friends and roomates ever since we were freshmen. Jerry's fraternity brothers had made it quite clear. Bliss was always welcome at parties; his girl friend was not. It didn't matter to him, Jerry thought, personally Bliss was Bliss and Jocelyn, Jocelyn. Who cared about color? She was so light skinned anyhow, he'd seen darker tans on white folk. Jerry liked her too, she never made him feel dumb and that meant a lot to him.

Bliss took the steps two at a time and burst into the room.

"Jerry, me buddy, I think it's about time you found a new roomate."

"Huh," was all the reply Jerry could muster.

"I've got a room crosstown, down by Riverhead," he grinned.

"Oh." Jerry understood. "So like you and Jocelyn can be...alone." Bliss merely smiled.

"Hey, I got something to tell you and I don't know how to do it, bein' we're friends and all."

Bliss became suddenly attentive. "Speak your mind, buddy."

Jerry kept looking at the floor. "It's about home-coming dance...uh...the other guys in the house...they uh...it's about you and Jocelyn, they fell...uh..."

148

"Go on," Bliss demanded.

"They don't want you comin' because she's colored. There, I said it."

His voice was calm concealing the rage inside. "How do *you* feel about it Jerry?"

"Aw, Bliss, it never made any difference to me."

Bliss believed him. Jerry wasn't a bigot, he doubted he could ever be one. But perhaps he was worse, a lackey, a messenger boy, and the message he carried was despicable. He was about to ask Jerry if he had protested the decision but it really wouldn't make any difference.

He had been invited to the homecoming dance at the house ever since they had rushed him in his freshman year. Even when Bliss made it clear that he didn't have the time for fraternity life, they continued to ask him to their affairs. Apparently a five-foot, one-hundred-and-two-pound, colored girl was a major threat to their collective sensibilities and reputations. Since he had been dating Jocelyn, he had learned about white and black prejudice first hand. From subtle hints to outright rejection, the refrain was a repeated and familiar melody. Bliss slowly learned to hate; not with the cool detachment of a growing intellectual but with the anguish and torment of his raw emotions. He also learned to despise the American system that perpetuated and condoned racism and bigotry. It made little difference to him whether it was based upon economic or ideological grounds; it was wrong and it should be stopped.

Yet as his relationships, his affair with Jocelyn, continued to grow and their personal commitments to each other deepened, he found he had little time to devote to causes. So he found himself living more and more in a very small world bounded on one side by Jocelyn's love and on the other by Anthony Markam's intellect.

The world that Bliss so treasured came to an unexpected end on the evening of May 13, 1948.

Bliss and Jocelyn were studying together in his

149

apartment. Jocelyn had cooked a spaghetti dinner and now they were finally finishing the cheap red wine. It was raining. Jocelyn had an early morning final exam and left the apartment at nine-thirty. The rain had stopped and because she wanted to save the money decided to walk the two blocks to the bus stop rather than call a taxi.

Riverhead was a deteriorating neighborhood bordered by the railroad tracks and the river from which it took its name. Students, derelicts, prostitutes and down-an-outers shared its inadequate apartments and dilapidated homes.

"Hey Vince, do you see what I see?"

"Yeah, get a load of the milk chocolate honey."

The third man, Carl, who had been drinking longer than his two buddies made the suggestion. "Why don't we invite her to a private party, just the four of us."

By the time Jocelyn saw the three white men, it was already too late.

"Want to come to a party, doll?" His breath reeked of cheap wine and she noticed that his teeth were crooked.

"Excuse me, you're in my way." She started to push past him.

"Hey you snotty bitch, just who do you think you are." With practised expertise he grabbed her arms and forced them behind her back. Vince covered her mouth with his hand so she couldn't scream. They brought her to a deserted basement.

Danny who had first noticed her had always wanted to do it with a nigger-gal and here was his chance. "You guys hold her, I'm gonna get me some black ass."

Jocelyn struggled and managed to bite her captor's hand. "Let me go, damn you, let me go."

But her demands only served to increase their anger. He hit her in the face with his knuckles. They gagged her with her own socks and ripped away her blouse. Carl started to fondle her breasts.

"You like that, you slut, come on don't pretend with

150

me, I know you like it." He dug his teeth into her nipples. She tried to scream.

They removed her pants and while two of them held her thighs apart the third rammed his cock deep inside her. When the third man had finished raping her they removed the gag.

"Leave me alone, oh please, please, just leave me alone." She was crying and she was frightened.

"Hey Carl, think we ought to let her go?"

"Sure, but after the party." He was smiling. He took out a pocket knife.

"See this cunt, you do what I tell you or I'm going to open you up, understand?"

She shook her head, unable to speak.

"Get down on your knees." With one hand he grabbed her hair, the other opened his zipper. His penis was red and swollen. "Now sweetheart, you just open your mouth and suck me off."

She did as she was told but when he came in her mouth she gagged twice and then vomited all over him. Carl rammed his boot into her nose and she started to bleed. They made her kneel down and face the floor while Vince forced the neck of a beer bottle into her anus. Fortunately she had passed out and could no longer feel the pain.

"You nigga-cunt, that'l teach you a lesson. Shit, she puked all over my pants."

"Let's get outta here."

Hours later, bleeding and numb from the pain she made her way to the street and hailed a taxi.

"Look Miss, I know its none of my business but I think you should go to a hospital."

"No. Take me home."

"Okay, but you ought to see a doctor."

She literally crawled to the door and once inside went straight to her father's study where he kept the loaded .45. She shoved the muzzle back against the roof of her mouth and pulled the trigger.

FOUR

Mercedes McCallister Brown was sobbing hysterically.

"I'm sorry, I can't stop crying. I know it's been thirty years, but I remember my little sister's face, it wasn't a face anymore." She buried her eyes in her hands and sat there unable to control herself.

Leslie fought to keep the tears out of her eyes but it was a losing battle. The colorless liquid ran down her cheeks and stained her blouse. She found herself crying for a girl she never knew and for her tragic suicide. They seemed somehow related to her own fears.

"I saw Bliss only once after the funeral," Mercedes was saying. "He was in the Army then and he came back on the anniversary of her death. We saw him at the cemetery. I tried to comfort him but it was like he didn't see me. He just stood over by her grave and I swear he was talking to her. It was real spooky. He didn't cry. He just stared at the headstone and talked and talked. None of us ever saw him again."

Dr. Leslie Pace did not ordinarily drink in strange bars, and certainly not at two in the afternoon.

"A double scotch please."

"You sure you're all right lady?"

"I'll be okay." She hurried her first drink and ordered another. The bartender was concerned but he said nothing.

Why did she do it? At first it made no sense at all but then you had to know Jocelyn. She was terrified of men. Could she have faced Bliss afterwards? Was her shame so deep? It didn't seem logical, not for today's woman. But

152

1948 was a very long time ago and Jocelyn McCallister was a silent, sensitive, introspective girl. Her suicide would have been proper for a tragic Victorian heroine.

Oh, stop it Leslie, she thought to herself. You're becoming morbid and that kind of thinking can't help you or her. There were tears again in her eyes.

What about Bliss. God, how would anyone react to such horror. Leslie was calmer now, more rational. He had to deal with it some way. I suppose he could have blamed the individuals who were responsible for raping her, although they never caught them. That would be the sensible thing to do. Perhaps he turned to the church for comfort and solace. Wasn't he a Catholic? Maybe he just refused to face the truth and made believe it never happened, even pretended that Jocelyn wasn't real.

But Leslie knew better. Bliss would blame society. He would blame everyone, Jerry, Jocelyn's father, his parents, Sheriff Miller, the college, Elkton, maybe even Markham. Bliss was a political philosopher. He would find fault with the system that allowed it all to happen, the rotten, hypocritical, bigoted, racist, exploiting, sick American way of life.

He would turn inward, trust no one except himself. He would internalize his hate, his rage, his hurt. Yes, Leslie thought, he would make a superb soldier, he would enjoy the killing.

Detective-Sergeant Burton Carney was sweating in the squad room at Manhattan South. He was also remembering the description of a potential assassin on a university campus. He went to the files and retrieved the news clippings of a presumed gangland execution. It was probably only a coincidence but...He picked up the phone.

Director of Security Ron Mabra was starting on his second pack of cigarettes and it was only one-thirty in the afternoon.

"Let me speak to Chief Mabra please, this is Detective Carney from New York."

"Burt, is that you? This is Ron, what's up?"

"Remember the 'want' you sent out, it's a long shot but we've got a body here...fits your description. Interested?"

"Go on."

"Caucasian, about 30, six feet, very muscular, biceps like a weightlifter. He's got short hair but he was wearing a long black hairpiece."

Ron was interested. "Can you tell me more?"

"He's a Family man, name's Dominic Vereste, strictly a local boy. That's what doesn't figure. Why would he want to kill a South African or anyone else at your university?"

"Could be free lancing?"

"Could be, but whoever hired him would have to have connections to organized crime, and it would cost plenty too. The syndicate guns usually stick close to home. You got any of that out your way?"

"Negative. I already checked with the city and state authorities. We don't have any known Mafia in the area, and there's no connection with New York. Burt, could you do me a favor?"

"Is it department business?"

"It might be connected to the shooting. Could you get me a rundown on an Andrew Marcus Crane. He's an anthropologist, teaches out here. He's the one the gunman shot. I'll send you the details.

"Can do. Listen, are you still planning to visit?"

"You couldn't stop me now. I've got vacation time coming. I'll see you then. Listen, one more thing. How did Vereste get it?"

"Hands tied behind the back, single bullet in the forehead; a typical execution."

Mabra hung up the phone. Now he was confused more than ever. Neither Spaacklund nor Crane had any known relationship to the New York underworld, although Crane had been born in Brooklyn.

The Chief had convinced himself that Crane was indeed the intended target and that the demonstration staged by White and Rawlins was used as a diversion, so he had started on his own time, a private investigation of Professor Andrew Crane. But he came up with nothing. Crane had a normal childhood, an undistinguished high school career, except for his football prowess. He had served in Korea, received an honorable discharge, married, returned to college, went on to graduate school at Cornell, and after receiving his Ph.D., taught at SUNY Binghampton and then Columbia University. He had been to Taiwan and Hong Kong as a graduate student, later as a professional, and had joined the university staff back in '73.

His reputation as a professional was first rate. He had received his share of government grants, published numerous articles and written a book based upon his research in Taiwan. He was often sarcastic, but well-liked by both colleagues and students. He was an exceptionally fine tennis player, a talented skier; he lived in the country by a lake and had been having an affair with a Professor Leslie Pace since the fall semester.

Motive, where was the motive? Why would anyone go to so much trouble to have him killed? The nature of the attempt on his life seemed to rule out angry husbands, jealous boyfriends, disgruntled colleagues and failing students. The Chief had discovered that his wife had been fatally injured in an auto accident in '71. From '71 through '72, Crane had been missing. That is, he had not returned to Columbia. Mabra concluded that he had grieved for his wife, traveled about, and took the time to readjust to being single again. But he was curious. Maybe Burt would come up with something.

Andy sat back in the comfortable reclining seats of the 747, loosened his seat belt, lit up a cigarette and ordered his second boubon from the leggy stewardess with the plastic smile.

He was worried about Leslie. No, not really worried, concerned. Ever since their trip to the president's hometown he had continually looked in the rear view mirror for signs of a car following them. In Elkton and at the motel he anxiously searched for a suspicious stranger with a trench coat and dark glasses to record their movements and, to report back, in a foreign accent to his superior via shortwave radio codes.

He knew he was being melodramatic, but if the attempt on his life had been real, why was he now being left alone? the circumstances hadn't changed, or had they? He still knew about Korea, but did the President's recent prominence as a front runner for the Senate race mean 'hands off' for now. In their trip to Elkton they didn't find any damaging evidence. In fact, he agreed with Leslie and sympathized with the president in his attempts to understand the complexities of "small-town adult justice." It would be better to forget it, he thought. He would feel better after Leslie's call tonight.

Boston was hot and muggy. When he arrived at the Sheraton-Boston, he went straight to the bar. "Bourbon and water please."

"Andy Crane, of all people, why what a pleasant surprise."

Andy turned around. Mara was stunning. Her long blond hair curled about her slim figure, a skin-tight silk T-shirt outlined her full breasts and the muscles in her flat stomach. Expensive designer jeans emphasized her hips, her thighs and the crease between her legs. You could see she was wearing a bra but you couldn't tell about her pants. Her blue eyes sparkled with the hint of mischievous pleasures. If Dr. Mara Franklin had not become an anthropologist, he thought, she would have been a successful hooker.

"Good evening Ms. Sex Goddess. Mara, you are one beautiful woman. All I have to do is look at you and I get a hard-on."

Mara chose to ignore the remark. "Aren't you going to buy me a drink, tennis bum? Where's your girlfriend?"

Andy and Mara had been graduate students in Cornell's East Asia program. Although they were both good looking and sensual people their relationship was one of colleagues, not of lovers. Their one attempt at sexual satisfaction had occurred in Mara's professor's office at two on top of his desk. Andy remembered knocking his name plate on the floor during their gyrations. But it was only an athltetic contest. There had been no tenderness and no regrets. Mara had completed her fieldwork in Tokyo and had produced a monograph of some significance analyzing Japanese character and its effect upon changing family relationships. In the tradition of Margret Mead, her first two husbands had been anthropologists. She was now separated and currently an associate professor at Brandeis.

"Have you seen Jim lately?" she asked, as they moved from the bar to a more comfortable table. Andy watched the other men follow her movements. They exchanged professional gossip for an hour or two before parting.

Andy ate roast beef and cheesecake alone at Ken's Pub on Boylston Street and considered his other reason for coming to Boston, well, actually to Cambridge, just across the Charles. He had received an offer of employment from Harvard.

There are basically three routes to acquire such an academic position. The first two, a recommendation by the head of a student's dissertation committee and competition on the open "meat market" were pretty well restricted to new and junior colleagues. Persons of Andy's rank and stature would be contacted personally, although a letter of such serious inquiry, similar to the one Andy had received was not that unusual. But offering Andy a permanent position was.

He was satisfied with his present position. His

university was nationally known and his department noted for its scholars. Moreover, he had never even hinted that he was unhappy or even available for employment elsewhere. Andy had friends on the Harvard faculty. If they were seriously going to offer him a position they would have certainly told him long before this.

Then again, Andy was not someone to overestimate his worth. If the offer had come when his book was first released that would be something else. He recalled that Harvard University Press hadn't even been interested in it. Nor was Andy successful enough to be a grand old man whose services were sought everywhere. It was also unlikely that Harvard or any other institution would hire an associate professor outright, without at least the formality of an interview. Yet the letter he received was an offer, not an invitation. Finally, Harvard already had an outstanding China scholar in the Department of Social Relations.

The offer might be legitimate but the timing and the circumstances were all wrong. Yet someone had seen to it that he was promised a position; someone with a lot of influence, enough probably to override or convince the Harvard admistration. He thought of President Bliss Mansfield. He concluded he wasn't for sale.

FIVE

Colonel Bruce E. Jones was a forty-eight-year-old Military Intelligence career officer, serving what he hoped would be his last tour of duty at the Pentagon. He was the recipient of a Silver Star, had been twice wounded in action and had received a battlefield commission. His hair was prematurely gray and he wore thick glasses. Out of uniform he resembled a college professor more than a professional soldier. At twenty-one he had married Sally Gaines and next month they would celebrate their 27th anniversary with their two sons, Brad a second-year cadet at West Point, and Martin, a freshman at M.I.T.

Andy had known Bruce ever since he was an enlisted man in Korea. They had kept in touch with occasional visits and letters and were as close as two men separated by geography and different careers could be.

"Andy, you son-of-a..." Bruce was waiting at the arrival gate and greeted him with a welcome smile.

"It's been too long, ole buddy." He was thinking it really was good seeing him again. "I'd like you to meet Leslie Pace my colleage and..."

"Yes, it's written all over your faces," Bruce replied. "Leslie, I'm delighted to have the opportunity." He embraced her with an affectionate bear hug. What a strikingly beautiful woman, he thought. He was almost glad Sally was out of town visiting her mother.

The drive from Dulles was a pleasant one as they squeezed into Bruce's MG and headed out towards Springfield. His suburban Virginia home had cost $70,000.00 and he was lucky by Washington standards to have obtained such a good buy.

Andy and Leslie relaxed in the den filled with mementos and photographs depicting his military career and family life. Andy was thinking how much you could tell about a person, just by the kinds of clutter they save and display, when Bruce returned from the bar with cold drinks.

"Bottoms up, me buckos. How long can you stay?"

Andy exchanged glances with Leslie. "I really don't know. It depends upon what we can accomplish."

"Well, you're welcome as long as you like." He had noticed their concern. "You're not in any trouble, are you?"

"I think we are," Andy answered. They told him the entire story.

Bruce thought for a moment. If anyone else had told him such a cock-and-bull nonsense he would assume they were nuts. But Andy and Leslie were serious and he had too much respect for their friendship. He had followed Andy's career, particularly since Elaine's tragic death. Andy often joked about important matters and could be irreverent and amusing when it suited him. But he was a good anthropologist and field investigator. He wasn't joking now.

"You two wouldn't be putting me on, would you? Your story sounds like *The Day of the Jackal* and *The Manchurian Candidate* combined."

"I wish it were only that simple. If you take the events separately they don't seem to mean very much, but all together, well, that's a different matter."

"Bruce," Leslie added. "When Andy first told me about Korea I thought he might be hallucinating, but now it all makes sense to me." She couldn't forget Jocelyn. "We thought about going to the authorities but we really have no evidence. Will you help us?"

Bruce knew he couldn't refuse and grinned. "What are friends for?"

That evening they dined at Le Bistro Francais and enjoyed the posh atmosphere of Georgetown's night life at "F. Scott's." Andy was surprised when the cocktail waitress informed him that gentlemen must wear their jackets at all times and Leslie was impressed by the good-looking, well-dressed men and their bejeweled and dazzling companions. Bruce was not impressed with the check. It had been a long time since he and Sally had gone "clubbing."

The early morning light shone through the bay window and was reflected off the brass buttons on Bruce's uniform. The friendly, even shy man they had dined with last night had been transformed into a formidable member of the military establishment.

"I've got to go to work this morning, but meet me at the river entrance about noon and maybe I'll have something to show you. You can use Sally's car. It's in the garage and the keys are here on the table."

While Andy and Leslie gawked at the Capitol and wandered about the Smithsonian's aerospace museum, Colonel Bruce Jones rode the cart through the narrow corridors to his Pentagon office. The Pentagon complex reminded him of a resort he had once worked at as a young man. He had been the children's busboy, one step below cook's helper. He chuckled to himself as he remembered the familiar story. There were these two lions that had escaped from the Washington zoo. They decided to separate and meet one year later. When a year had passed the first lion was emaciated and tired, his name was falling out and he was in poor spirits. He envied his friend who was fat with such a sleek coat. He told him about living in alleys and eating scraps from garbage cans and wondered how the second lion could look so good. "Oh," he replied, "I went to the Pentagon. Every morning I would eat a General for breakfast and they haven't missed any yet."

Bruce was at the zenith of his career. He could count on

retiring as full colonel. The promotion and the stars went to the men with the West Point rings, and even for them they were mighty hard to come by these days.

"'Good morning Evan," he said to the Master Sergeant at the records room.

"Morning, Colonel, how you doin' today?"

"Surviving, Sergeant, just surviving. I want the records on a Captain Bliss Mansfield. He was honorably discharged in about '54. Field Artillery, I think; served in Korea."

"Sure thing, Sir."

Forty minutes later M/Sgt. McMasters brought him the file and he signed the receipt. The request was not an unusual one. As a senior intelligence officer Bruce had access to service personnel files and routinely checked them out.

When he returned to his office, the Sergeant picked up the phone and dialed a number in Langeley, Virginia. Two months earlier he had been instructed to report anyone requesting information about a Captain Mansfield. Across the river, the man with the deep tan and the pleasant smile thanked the Sergeant and asked to keep him advised should Colonel Jones request any additional files.

At noon, Bruce met Andy and Leslie and after a stand-up luncheon at an Oyster bar, gave them a tour of the Pentagon and returned with them to his home.

The file was spread on the table before them.

"OK, after he was commissioned he went to Fort Sill for training as a Field Artillery Officer. When the war broke out he was sent to Korea with the 58th Field, supporting the 65th Infantry from Puerto Rico. Hmm, in March 1952 he was declared 'missing in action'...later in September he was assigned temporary duty at the UN compound at Chejudo..."

"Wait a minute Bruce, missing in action, you mean they didn't know where he was?"

"That's not so unusual, we were moving around quite a bit then. Sometimes a man listed as MIA might be with another unit, or hiding out in the hills stranded behind enemy lines and just waiting for the opportunity to get back to his own forces. He could have even been captured by the enemy. Hell, we thought people in my outfit were dead and a week later they would turn up."

"But Bruce," Leslie asked. "This wasn't just days or weeks, this was, let me see, almost seven months."

"Well I guess that is unusual, but not impossible."

"Could he have been captured and been held at a POW camp?" Andy was thinking about brainwashing and other means to coerce American soldiers to become turncoats, like the reports he had read when he was in Taegu.

"There's no indication that he was ever a POW and we kept pretty accurate records on prisoners. Still, it could be possible, but I doubt it."

"Then what was he doing," Andy insisted. "We've got to know. Maybe I'm wrong. God, I hope I am, but I think something must have happened to him, something important, enough to make him change the course of his life."

"Are you sure you're not overreacting?" Bruce challenged him.

"Perhaps, but I don't think so. That man is going to be a United States Senator, and frankly, those missing months scare me."

Bruce was becoming concerned too. He was fairly certain that Mansfield would be investigated before he took his seat in Congress bu there would be no reason for anyone to look so closely at his military service. His record was similar to those of many young officers who had served during the Korean war.

Bruce made the suggestion. "The only way we're going to find out more about 'your man' is to go over his military career with a fine toothcomb. We'll have to

163

locate people who actually served with him and that won't be easy, twenty-five years have passed since that time, people get lost...also a lot of them would prefer to forget those days. But we know the units he served with and if we're lucky we might find someone."

"What can we do to help?" Andy asked.

"Nothing right now. Let me check it out, I'm supposed to be the intelligence officer around here."

"Bruce," Leslie cautioned. "Please be careful."

SIX

Second-Lietenant Bliss Mansfield was stationed at Fort Sill near Lawton, Oklahoma. The base being primarily an artillery school, the area was flat for miles around. Mansfield completed training in the use of the 105mm. howitzer, the basic artillery-infantry weapon. He also leaned about the 155mm. "long tom," as well as the eight-inch guns with the 360 lb. shells that could fire over twenty miles.

Bliss was a deeply disturbed young man, perhaps a borderline psychotic. He was so obsessed with Jocelyn's rape and suicide that he thought of little else while he was awake. At night he dreamed about revenge. One nightmare in particular kept occurring. He had caught the rapist and was cutting off his testicles with a butcher knife. But each time he killed him, two more would appear to take his place and their faces would always change; they would look like Jerry, like his father, like Jocelyn's father, Sheriff-Miller, Professor Markham, his Battery Commander and even the President of the United States.

He welcomed the military life. It was ordered and directed. He had little time to think and someone was always telling him what to do. He liked that.

But nobody really knew him. His aloofness and icy complacency was interpreted as the mark of a calculating leader. Exacting precision and order, instead of being considered compulsive, were an indication of a fine officer. Once he went into a Negro bar near Lawton and when the bartender hesitated about serving him, Bliss beat him senseless; but the incident was never reported to the Military Police.

The day he received his orders to Korea, he actually smiled.

Each infantry division is made up of three infantry regiments. Each regiment is supported by a battalion of field artillery consisting of three firing batteries. As a junior officer, Bliss was assigned to "Charlie" battery, in support of "Love" company as a forward observer. He would take his jeep and trailer, along with three men to the top of the ridge, dig in, and run wires back to the battalion. Then he would mark off every access leading up to his position with circles, or as they were more commonly called, "goose eggs," defined as pre-arranged artillery concentrations, selected in advance and marked on a map indicating potential targets. He could now communicate their positions by radio, phone, or walkie-talkie to the battery.

When the enemy was sighted, he would call upon his howitzers and other fire power. If there were too many enemy soldiers, and if they were threatening to over-run him, he was instructed to retreat and take up another position. If he was exceptionally heroic, or stupid, depending upon your perspective, he could call the fire upon himself. It was rumored that the latter was a "surefire" way of winning a Congressional Medal of Honor. Such awards were generally made posthumously.

Colonel Jones was having his difficulties locating persons who remembered a Lieutenant Mansfield who had served in Korea over a quarter of a century ago. He was also having trouble getting "jackets" on those men who might have helped him.

"I'm sorry, Sir," M/Sgt. McMasters had told him. "But I have instructions not to release files to personnel who have received orders for overseas assignments."

"That's nonsense, Sergeant, I've no such orders."

McMasters showed him a paper that had just come from the Army Security Agency. "That's you, isn't it

Colonel."

Bruce didn't believe it. He phoned General Johnson's office.

"Yes sir," the WAC SP 6 informed him. "The orders came down late yesterday, you're to leave next week with an M.I. team for Kabul, Afghanistan."

This is ridiculous, Bruce thought. What the hell do I know about Afghanistan? He read the orders and went back to his office. He read them again.

Bruce angrily left the Pentagon and went to a pay phone outside the building. For all I know, my fucking phone's tapped, he muttered to himself. He called a friend at Bethesda and hailed a taxi.

Colonel Fredrick Munoz was a wiry, dark-skinned man who had been a CO with the 65th Infantry from Puerto Rico.

"Mansfield, Bliss Mansfield, yeah I've heard the name. Isn't he the University President who's been in the papers?"

"Right, but he was also a forward observer with the 58th Field back in March of '52." Bruce lied, "I'm doing some work for the JAG. Did you know him?"

Fredrick thought for a moment. "Well, I don't think I recall the name. A forward observer you say. I'm still not sure. Let's see, March, we must have been around Kumwah, The CCF over-ran our positions lots of times." He thought for a while. "Hey, I know who can tell you, Jim Eastlick, he was with the 58th."

Major J.C. Eastlick (US retired) was writing his memoirs in his Victorian study overlooking the Hudson, when he received the call from Colonel Jones.

"Yes, yes I remember him, moody young fella, always wanting to be alone, fine officer though. You really should talk to Eddie Fishbein, he's a lawyer in Trenton now, but he spent a lot of time with Mansfield up on the ridges until he was captured. Spent four months in a camp up by the Yalu. He's been helping me write my

167

memoirs."

Bruce thanked him, he didn't feel like going back to his office so he went home and told Andy and Leslie about Fishbein and Afghanistan.

"I don't like it, Bruce, I don't like it a bit. Yesterday you start to ask questions about Mansfield, and before the day is over you get these crazy orders."

"I know, Andy, it smells. But I'm a soldier and orders and orders."

"Have you ever been to Afghanistan before?" asked Leslie.

"No. But once I served with a team in Teheran. That was over fifteen years ago."

"How long will you be away?"

"Oh, a week, maybe two at the most."

"What will you do there?"

"Sorry, can't talk about that."

"Is it dangerous?"

He laughed. "No. Please excuse me, I've got to phone Sally and give her the news."

Andy called Ed Fishbein that afternoon and made plans for himself and Leslie to fly to New Jersey. They rented a car at the airport and drove to a suburban apartment complex just outside the city limits.

Ed Fishbein was a successful lawyer about Andy's age. He had been recently divorced and, Leslie thought, judging from the numbers of nubile young women sunning themselves by the swimming pool, was enjoying the rewards of bachelor living. Ed was born to Yiddish-speaking immigrant parents. He had grown up in Newark and ran away to enlist the day he turned eighteen.

Andy used his press card and introduced Leslie as his photographer. They were doing an in-depth background on Bliss. At first Eddie was reluctant, but after he and Andy had exchanged a few war stories and more than a few beers, he relaxed.

The two "newspersons" listened attentively to his

unusual and frightening story.

The five soldiers shivered in the frigid evening air. A full moon illuminated their positions but cast eerie shadows on the valley below. They had been under heavy attack for the past three days and were starting their dinner of cold beans as they settled in for the long night ahead.

"Might as well eat while you got the chance," S/Sgt. Killebew muttered. "You know damn well these fucking Chinks will be back again."

Pfc. Fishbein nodded his agreement. He had been wounded two weeks ago and the pains in his leg hadn't let up. Cpl. Reilly and Pfc Stoltz checked the radio equipment for the third time in an hour and stared out into the wet darkness.

"Shit," Reilly complained. "He's a weird one, the Lieutenant. I think he really likes the night." He glanced at Bliss sitting silently less than ten yards away.

"Maybe, but he's got guts. Been here over a year and he's never cracked. It's almost like he's fighting his own private war."

"You're right, Stoltz," Reilly agreed. "But I think the war's in his head." He wasn't really sure why he did it, but Reilly touched his crucifix and felt better.

Bliss walked out to the MLR and looked down at the valley but it was too early to detect any movement. There used to be a village here he thought, with thatched roofs and mud walls and trees. The farmers would be smoking their long pipes while the women planted the seedlings. Children would be playing, they would laugh and run. All that's left is a few bombed-out huts and the rice paddies, most of the villagers left when the shelling began.

They first heard the bugles, shattering the stillness of the night with their awesome wail. It sounded like a hundred banshees suddenly released from the depths of hell.

169

At 2300 they came charging. You couldn't tell how many they were but you could hear them stumbling over the beer cans filled with rocks hanging from the barbed wire. The searchlights came on and now you could see them. They appeared fat because of the heavy quilted uniforms they wore. Their round faces glistened, exposed by the flares. They weren't wearing helmets, only soft baseball caps and tennis shoes or thongs on their feet. They swarmed forward like a human tidal wave, screaming as they rushed to their death ready to fire their PPSH 41 "burp guns" and 1944 vintage, bolt-action Russian carbines.

Bliss got on the Army field phone. "Fox Oboe Love, fire mission, one-thousand CCF in the attack."

"Where?"

"At corrdinates four-two-zero-five, three-two-seven-zero."

"Adjusting two pieces." You could hear the bellowing of the guns.

"On the way...splash."

Bliss replied, "splash, wait." The ground literally blew up, the blast from the explosion lit the sky. Men died bursting into flame, but there was no noise. And then, all of a sudden, a roar of crashing thunder and the sound caught up with the light.

"Drop 400." Again the roar of guns.

"Add 200."

"Wait...on the way."

Bliss gave the final command, "add 50, fire for effect."

Still they kept coming. In the trenches the infantry nervously waited. To the left, twin 40mm guns and on the right, three quad 50's mounted on half tracks. Bliss waited until they were 500 yards away.

"Now!" The ridge mortars coughed, throwing their shells in a high arc, the guns blasted the night. They came leaping into the path of .50 caliber machine guns and hand grenades. Tracer bullets flew across the dark. Theirs were blue and ours red. They were being massacred but still they came, wave after wave, breaking through the perimeter. The fighting was hand-to-hand. M-l's were being used as clubs and men were running everywhere. Cpl. Reilly's neck was ripped open. He felt the sticky blood drip onto his fingers before he died.

It was quiet in the valley. They could still hear the sounds of the battle as they moved cautiously through the paddy fields.

"Sergeant, check that building." Bliss pointed to the one remaining structure in the village. "Stoltz, you and Fishbein, come with me."

They didn't see them waiting in the shadows. Pfc. Fishbein stuck his M-l in the enemy's belly and fired point blank into his guts. He turned and screamed as a second man's rifle butt slammed into his bad leg. Stoltz yelled to him and he crawled behind a rock. His head was throbbing with pain and he had trouble focusing his eyes. Through the haze he could see the Sergeant.

Killebrew was standing by the open door of the bombed out hut. An old woman and two children, they couldn't have been more than four years old, were facing him. They were horrified. The old woman was trying to tell him something but the Sergeant wasn't listening. He raised his rifle and deliberately pointed it at the woman's head. He fired. Then at the little girl. He fired again.

Bliss heard the shooting and turned around. He couldn't believe it. The woman and the girl were lying on the ground, blood running from their foreheads and staining the dark hair. He continued to stare at them. He thought he saw the woman smile. It was Jocelyn's face. And the little girl, she was Kathy Merino. He started talking to himself.

"I'm coming darling, don't worry, everything's going to be all right."

He heard her say, "Hurry Bliss, oh please hurry." He

171

raised his .45 and shot the killer twice in the back. Then he passed out.

Lt. Hwang was shocked. He had seen an American officer shoot his sergeant in the back. He must tell the Major about it when they returned with the prisoners.

Eddie continued with his story. "They took Stoltz and me and the Lieutenant with them. It was dawn when we reached what was left of their Army, I think it was the 15th CCF. Anyway, I spent four months in one of their POW camps and that was something else."

Leslie interrupted him. "What happened to Lieutenant Mansfield?"

"They took him with us, they must have known he was the forward observer and he'd know where all the guns were."

"Did you see the Lieutenant again?" asked Andy.

"No, that's the strange part. They'd keep the officers and enlisted men separate, but we'd see them occasionally so we knew who they were. When we were finally realeased I looked for him but couldn't find him. I talked to a captain later, but he had never heard of him. Maybe he escaped?"

"Did you report the shooting incident with the Sergeant?"

"Nope. I figured he got what he deserved. If it was me, I'd a shot him too." He poured himself another beer.

"What happened to Stoltz?"

"I think he died. One day they took him out to interrogation and we never saw him again."

They had taped his interview. Leslie took a few photographs to make it seem legitimate. They thanked him and left.

SEVEN

They were silent as they drove towards the airport.

"He's wrong you know. No American ever escaped from a Chinese POW camp."

"Do you think he's lying?" asked Leslie.

"He's got nothing to hide. He probably doesn't know."

"What do you think happened to Bliss?"

"We can assume that he was captured. Perhaps they took him to another camp. Yet, there's no record of his ever having been a POW. Then, about seven months later, he mysteriously reappears and is assigned to detached duty at Chejudo. What's a field artillery offier doing at a United Nations prison camp?"

"I wonder where Bliss told them he was all that time?" Leslie added.

"Pull over," Andy told her. "I've just got an idea and I have to get to a phone."

Ten minutes later he returned. "What about if we drive to New York. We can visit with your parents for a few days?"

"Fantastic, now what's your real reason?"

"I just spoke with a former colleague of mine at Columbia. He used to do some research with the government on returning POW's. Maybe he'll be able to provide some answers."

As they headed up the highway towards New York, Leslie couldn't help wondering how her parents, Simon and Beatrice Pace of Rye, New York would react to meeting Andy Crane, formerly of Brooklyn.

Simon was going over some contracts when Leslie called. He was elated. It had been almost a year since he had seen his "little girl", and with Belinda now living in Marin County, he felt out of touch with his family. He re-lit his pipe and pictured Leslie as she was at sixteen, tanned, freckled, hair flying in the wind. He remembered giving her the keys to her first car and how adorable she looked when she smiled at him.

Simon, you're getting old, he thought to himself. Sixty-six next month and your daughter is a thirty-five-year-old woman, not a child. I've got to call Beatrice and tell her. Perhaps she can come back from Sausalito in time to see Leslie. She must have had enough of Belinda's children by now. But I think I had better wait till Leslie gets here.

"Sarah," he called upstairs. "Prepare Leslie's room, she's coming home tonight." What about her young man? Best not to take chances, "...and prepare the guest quarters for her friend." He kept thinking, it's too bad Beatrice isn't here, but then I'll have her all to myself. He was a very happy man.

They arrived a little past midnight, tired from the long day's drive, and after a quiet nightcap with Mr. Pace went to their separate rooms and fell, exhausted, into bed.

It was only seven-thirty in the morning but Andy couldn't sleep any longer. He showered vigorously. He was impressed with his "guest suite." The bedroom itself was twice as large as any room he had ever lived in. He was reminded of the small stuffy room he slept in when he was a child. There was no air-conditioning and only one window. He would position two fans, one at his head and the other by his feet and keep them on all night.

He knew Leslie's parents were wealthy but he was not prepared for the opulence of it all. He had presumed that their home would be garishly decorated and hideous. Well, he was certainly wrong. The decor and period furniture were stylishly correct and, all in all, rather pleasant to look at.

Simon was having breakfast on the patio. He motioned Andy to join him, studying his daughter's beau. So he's an anthropologist, he thought, looks more like a tennis player, lean, muscular and quite handsome although he might do with a haircut. He compared Andy to his son-in-law, Michael, thin, with a receding hairline, thick glasses, a drooping mustache and all those allergies.

Andy was impressed with him as well. I hope I look like that when I'm in my sixties, the man keeps himself fit, and I couldn't help noticing the books in his library. I wonder if he plays...

"Excuse me sir, but do you play tennis?"

He must have been reading my mind. "Yes, when I can arrange the time." Should I ask him? Why not?

"I was just getting ready to go to the club today. Would you care to join me; that is if it's okay with Leslie?"

"I'd be glad to join you, but I'm afraid I don't have any equipment with me."

"That's quite all right. I think we can find you some clothes and a racquet." He changed the subject.

"Andy, do you mind if I ask you about your relationship with my daughter. I'm afraid I'm just an old-fashioned father."

I like the man, Andy thought. "Just between you and me, I love her."

Simon was pleased with his answer. He decided wisely not to pursue the matter further. They chatted amiably about anthropology, China and the university until Leslie joined them. She kissed both men good morning and spoke with her mother promising to stay a few days. Mrs. Pace was flying back from the coast and couldn't bear to miss her.

The club was nestled between short rises, New Yorkers called them hills. White stucco walls and natural wood for the English Tudor buildings, trimmed hedges lining the path to the golf greens; all of it enhanced the club's claim   to eminence. It reminded Andy of a John O'Hara scenario from "On the Terrace."

Andy was paired with Simon against two men, more his own age; Kurt, a Wall Street broker and Christopher a promising tax attorney. Whatever misgivings Andy may have held about his deprived boyhood, tennis was his game and the green hardcourt his arena. Andy and Simon easily won, 6-3, 6-1. Christopher was awed, Kurt substantially impressed and Simon genuinely surprised. Andy dominated play in the backcourt and at the net. His service was terrifying.

Leslie and Andy engaged in a leisurely lunch on the clubhouse deck overlooking the swimming pools.

"Andy, what do you think of Dad?"

He was serious now. "I wish my own father could have been more like him." Andy's father had died when he was twenty-four. He had been an alcoholic.

"Do you have to go?"

"I told John, I'd see him this afternoon. What time is dinner?"

"Mom won't come in till eight. We'll just have a light snack."

John Slovik was a sociologist, a Yale graduate, he had taught at Columbia for fifteen years and had a reputation of international dimensions. He was particularly interested in small group interaction, social dynamics and the re-socialization process. Five years ago he had written a book about American POW's during the Korean crisis.

"You're looking well Andy. Seems the country agrees with your life-style, yes?"

Remembering Bruce's assignment to Afghanistan, Andy decided to be cautious. "I'm doing some research with emigrants from China, the People's Republic that is, particularly the re-education that takes place in the rural villages. You've done work with returning POW's and I was hoping you could tell me something about their indoctrination methods."

176

John was interested. "You've read my book, of course?"

"Of course," Andy lied.

"Well, then..."

"John, first off what were the camps like?"

"Physically, the food and housing were bad but not unbearable. They were usually native villages which had been evacuated; thatched huts, mud walls, pretty crowded conditions though. The rooms themselves were small and the prisoners would sleep on the floors. It really got cold in the winter. For most of the Americans, well... it was rough, even those who lived in poverty here weren't used to the nutritional and health differences. Are you interested in the medical etiology?"

"Not particularly, it's the prisoners themselves. Could they be brainwashed?"

"I don't think so. The Army thought of brainwashing as a process that produces an obvious alteration of character, in other words a completely changed person. Given the techniques the Chinese used, repetition, harassment and humiliation, it couldn't happen. Oh, not that it's impossible. Using the proper drugs, hypnosis, torture and sensory deprivation we can turn a man into a vegetable, but the Chinese weren't interested in that. They, well they wanted to present, strange as it seems, a 'good-guy' image. You know, 'friends of the people,' the enemies of the 'imperialistic war-mongering robber barons'."

"But they did produce traitors, 'turncoats' I think they were called."

"Yes, indeed. Spies is a better term. Those men were well indoctrinated. They could spout chapter and verse from the Communist manifesto on up. They were also well prepared for their assignments, had elaborate codes and explicit instructions on how to reach contacts. Some of them were told to wait as long as five years before pursuing their 'activities.' "

"What kind of activities, John?"

"Most of that's privileged information, but you can imagine some assignments; sabotage, recruitment, disruption of almost anything."

"Could it include assassination and murder?"

"Well, not really, but of course anything is possible. I think you've been reading too many spy stories. Did you know that not all of the men have been accounted for?"

"You mean they could still be walking around free, carrying out their assignments?"

"Sure."

Andy wasn't really surprised, but nevertheless it bothered him.

"What kind of men were recruited, or turned traitor?"

"We honestly don't know. We have enough data on all kinds of collaborators but there's nothing statistically speaking, in thier heredity, environment, rearing, education, occupation, family background, race or religion that explains their conduct as a prisoner. I think the critical variable is the relationship between the individual 'political instructor' and each prisoner.'

"Come on John, you've got to know more than that."

"Okay, the Chicoms would divide the prisoners into two basic groups; reactionaries and progressives. They'd leave the reactionaries pretty much alone, it was the others that really interested them. There were, of course, men who couldn't stand the least amount of stress, they'd collaborate even under the threat of punishment. Then there were the opportunists; they would inform on their own for power or privileges and they weren't very nice poeple. Another type would go along with them, just following the path of least resistance; and then, of course, there was a very small group who would actually embrace Communism."

"Why?"

"Why? Who knows, perhaps they were uncertain of themselves, willing to become part of any movement that would offer them an opportunity different from what they had before."

Andy decided to take a chance. "How about someone who was well-educated, politcally astute, I mean really informed? Someone who had recently suffered a great loss, like the death of a loved one, and who blamed the American system for it all."

"It's possible." He added with a grin. "I guess they could even recruit me if they promised I wouldn't have to teach undergraduates."

"I'm serious, John."

"Hmm, so I see. From what I've learned the most likely candidates, that is the best 'progressives', were usually between 18 and 24, with superior intelligence, but little formal education and little social or political maturity, generally from a lower income group though rarely a minority."

Andy continued to listen while John spoke about the typical life-styles of prisoners, how indoctrination worked, why Americans, unlike the Turks, had a poor morale and almost no *esprit de corps.* He thanked John and they exchanged some small talk. Andy looked at his watch and said he was sorry but that he had to go.

As he drove at a leisurely pace along the old Boston Post Road he thought about what he had learned. John's knowledge of POW life was pretty extensive, but John was a sociologist dealing with statistical regularities and predictive behavior for catgories of prisoners. He couldn't answer the one question that Andy had to know. Did Bliss Mansfield return from a Chinese camp a Communist sympathizer, agent, spy, saboteur or worse? John had told him that given the proper circumstances anyone could be brainwashed. What were those circumstances as far as Mansfield was concerned? Bliss really didn't fit the category for the 'progressives'—he was well educated and politically astute. He couldn't imagine the president swallowing the party line.

Andy didn't want to be too specific. John Slovik had a naturally suspicious mind and Andy didn't want him knowing too much. If only I knew how the president had spent those seven months.

Beatrice Eddington Pace was a patrician, a walking advertisement for careful grooming, designer wardrobes, expensive jewelry and lots of leisure time. She wasn't really a "cold" woman, but the desire to protect her daughter from the scheming of less well-born men made her wary of Andy.

"So nice to meet you at last Dr. Crane, I've heard so little about you. I'm afraid my daughter doesn't confide in her mother anymore."

Andy thought, defensive bitch isn't she, but he wasn't angry. The women in Taiwanese villages weren't much different. He recalled the day one meddlesome old crone was so upset when Andy wanted to talk to her unmarried daughter, that she chased after him with a stick.

"It's a pleasure to meet you ma'am. I'm afraid I have the advantage, Leslie's always talking about you. She's very proud of her mother."

Disarmed for the moment, Beatrice could only reply, "Ohhh."

She relaxed considerably over cocktails and when she learned that Andy was a respected scholar, a widower, and a tennis player, she even forgave him his background—well, almost.

"You say you grew up in Brooklyn. Simon, do we know any Cranes from Brooklyn. That is your real name, isn't it?"

Simon nuged her under the table with his foot as if to tell her to keep her mouth closed. "No dear, Andy tells me his parents have been deceased for some time now."

"I'm sorry Andy." She patted his hand and was genuinely sympathetic.

The next day Leslie drove into the city to shop with her

mother. Andy declined the invitation preferring to relax. He did just that, sitting out on the patio and sun-bathing in the pre-summer heat. Simon had gone to his office, so he was alone save for Sarah, the housekeeper, who Andy felt was keeping a watchful eye on him lest he steal the silverware. He went swimming about noon, had a light salad for lunch and lay awake making future plans.

Well, let's assume that the president was at least involved with the Chicoms in some way. Perhaps they had seen him shoot the sergeant and had blackmailed him into helping them. Let's also assume that Bliss had been the man he had heard in the village that night, and that he had helped the Chinese soldier named Sung to escape. That would implicate him even deeper. But would it end there? No! The phone conversation he had overheard strongly suggested that Mansfield soon to be perhaps a Senator, was still very much involved.

A cool breeze moved in from the water. Wait a moment! Now if Bliss was an agent, what was his mission? A U.S. Senator taking orders from Peking? What if he isn't the only one? Could there be others? He started to imagine the designs of a grand conspiracy, but dismissed the thought as being somewhat ridiculous and overly melodramatic.

OK, let's say I am a high-ranking Chinese official. We capture Bliss, convince him somehow to aid our cause. Given Mansfield's preoccupation with Jocelyn's death that might not be so difficult. Then I plan to send him back to the states, but an emergency situation develops and Bliss is used to free Sung. Okay, now he returns to America and starts to build a future. If his future is going to be that important, then i wouldn't leave it to chance. I would help him. Just a little help, in the right places and at the right time.

I don't think we're finished with Bliss Mansfield yet. Crane recalled the president's biography. He had completed his graduate work at the University of Chicago. They would start there.

181

EIGHT

On Monday, July 27, 1953, Lieutenant-General William H. Harrison of the United Nations Command and Nam II of North Korea entered the wooden building the Communists had erected in Panmunjon. At 1001 hours they signed the first of eighteen documents prepared by each side. It took them twelve minutes. Then each man got up and left the building without speaking. It was called a cease-fire.

General Kao Hai-yuan had known long before July that the fighting had to end. He had predicted their failure when the "Imman Gum," the North Korean People's Army first invaded the south. Thus the "committee" was established four months later, when China entered the war.

By 1953 five American soldiers had been selected. They were all college-educated men who were so disillusioned with their country that they were willingly recruited. Their backgrounds were thoroughly investigated, for they had been chosen with a very special purpose in mind. They would all return to the United States, establish themselves in their community and in time rise to positions of national power and influence.

All the men were ambitious, capable and dedicated; without doubt, they would be successful. Their careers would be carefully watched and they would be quietly "assisted" when necessary, often without them realizing. The "committee" saw to it that they would not know each other. Their names would never be used and they were known only by their codes; "apple-blossom," "sleeping giant," "quiet turtle," "beautiful flower," and "wise uncle." Their loyalty was of course assured. Should they question their commitments, their careers could easily be destroyed and, if necessary, their lives ended.

They would accomplish what the Chinese soldiers could not do in 1950. They would win the Korean War.

Dr. Slovik may have been a sociological expert on POW's, but he wasn't even aware of the existence of "Camp 10" nor for that matter were most Chinese. It was ironically called Camp 10 after the Korean reference to a "Number ten G.I." the term most frequently used to describe a despicable American soldier.

True, it was a prison camp, but an unusual one. It never held more than six prisoners during the three years it was operational. The entire staff, including the guards, twenty persons in all, were political indoctrination specialists. Its commandant wa a Chinese general who held a Ph.D. in Psychology from Cambridge. It wasn't located on the Yalu or in Manchuria. Instead, it was isolated in the rugged mountains of China's westernmost province. The Chairman of the People's Republic knew of its location, but even he wasn't sure what transpired behind its walls.

Bliss was brought in by helicopter in the early hours of the morning. He had been drugged, so he slept throughout the journey. Two men, dressed in peasant clothing took him to a small cottage. There was a room with an American queen-sized bed, a nightstand, electric light, and in the center a pot-bellied wood burning stove. Two sets of clean clothes hung from a rack on the wall. A smaller room contained a washbasin, towels, open-hole toilet, a razor, soap, talcum powder and a mirror. In the largest room a bookcase ran the length of the wall filled with magazines, books, Chinese-language primers and newspapers in English and Chinese. A writing table filled another wall and held paper, pencils, an ashtray and a casette tape-recorder. An oversized, worn but comfortable chair sat in another corner. The rooms were immaculate and smelled of fresh deodorant. It was to be his home for the next seven months.

From the window he could see three other buildings in the compound surrounded by a barbed wire electrically charged fence. The terrain was desolate and the camp obviously isolated. It was at least 6,000 feet above sea level and, Bliss guessed, situated in part of a formidable mountain chain.

For the first three days Bliss was completely alone and saw no one with the exception of the guard who brought him meals of soup, rice, vegetables and tea twice a day. It took them that long to gather the necessary background information. On the fourth day there was a knock on his door.

Surprised, Bliss could only reply, "come in."

A large man with a receding hairling and a comfortably protruding gut entered. "Do you mind if I smoke?"

Bliss was amazed. I am a prisoner in this man's camp, he thought, and he knocks before entering and asks if I mind if he smokes. I don't believe it. He replied, "Of course, suit yourself."

"Thank you." He brought out a pack of British Players, made a ritual of withdrawing a cigarette, struck a wooden match on the heel of his boot, inhaled deeply and blew the smoke out through his nose as he stood there watching the Lieutenant.

"May I have one?" He hesitated before asking.

"Oh, please forgive me, I didn't know you smoked." He offered Bliss a cigarette.

Bliss accepted the gift and glanced suspiciously at the ashtray on his table. The portly gentleman continued.

"I'm afraid I must also apologize for my bad manners. I have not introduced myself. I am Kao Hai-yuan of the People's Republic of China. May I sit down?"

Bliss nodded affirmatively while the general lowered his bulk into the comfortable chair. "Where are we?" Bliss asked.

The gentleman smiled. "In a prisoner of war camp."

Bliss was nervous but decided to press his luck. "Are we in Manchuria?"

The gentleman was silent. He continued to smile. He took a small pad and pencil from his jacket. "I am required to ask your name, rank, serial number and date of birth."

Bliss answered his request. The Chinese General continued to smile at him.

"Any other questions?" Bliss asked. He was confused. Having heard about POW camps and the treatment and interrogation of prisoners, what was happening here made no sense at all.

"Questions such as..." His Chinese captor gave him a quizzical look but maintained silence.

Bliss blurted it out. "My unit?"

"Oh, we already know that."

"My hometown?"

"Yes, we know that also."

"What is it?"

"Elkton."

"My mother's maiden name?"

"Agatha Crowley."

Bliss was speechless. He had not been prepared for this at all.

The General opened the door. "I will be seeing you again. There is one thing though...I am curious as to why you shot your Sergeant in the back." Without waiting for a reply he turned around and left. Bliss noticed that he had accidentally on purpose, left his cigarettes on the table.

General Kao held a meeting with his staff. "He is now bewildered. The reversal of roles, my refusal to ask questions and his luxurious accommodations have unnerved him. He does not know what to make of it nor what to expect from us. I want no contact with the prisoner for the next week. Is the video camera working?"

"Yes Comrade General. How long do you think it will take him to find the device?"

"Not long, a day or so." He addressed Liu. "In one week you will ask him to help with the latrine." Liu nodded.

"Do you think he will try to escape?" Captain Chan asked.

"I don't really know, perhaps yes, perhaps no," the General replied. "He is a very interesting man."

The General was correct, Bliss was indeed unnerved. Nevertheless he created a routine for himself. He would wake up at what he imagined was dawn, do calisthenics and exercise by running in place, then he would wash and shave. After the first meal he would mark the event on a calendar he had fashioned. He discovered the hidden camera the first day, but made no attempt to remove it. During the following days he would alternate between reading and sleeping, and wait for the second meal. He watched the shadows and tried to estimate the time from the position of the sun. He often sat looking out the window but never saw anyone moving within the compound. As far as he knew, he was the only prisoner in the camp. He thought about escaping but both the window and the door were firmly secured. Without knowing where he was and unable to speak the language, escaping seemed futile.

He knew his position was an unusual one. Anyone who had taken the trouble to learn his mother's maiden name would have surely known he was a forward observer yet they had made no attempt to interrogate him. On the third day he started a project to learn Chinese from the Yale primer that had been provided. On the sixth day he fantasized and talked to himself. That night he cried himself to sleep.

After the first meal of the seventh day, Lieutenant Liu

entered the room and bid him a good morning. "If you would like, Lieutenant Mansfield, we would like your assistance. We are building a latrine. Would you care to help us?"

Bliss was stunned, his captor's behavior never ceased to amaze him, but the opportunity to get outside the cottage and the need for human companionship was overwhelming.

All in all, six men were constructing the latrine. Bliss was given a shovel and helped to dig the trench. At noon the men took a break and shared their tea and rice-cakes with him. Bliss' suspicion that his situation was unique was confirmed. All the men spoke fluent English. They were polite but did not ask questions. In the afternoon Bliss noticed that the men were unsure how to proceed and he volunteered his help. In an hour he was explaining procedure and giving orders. The Chinese listened attentively to him.

At about 1600 hours General Kao inspected their progress and spoke with Lieutenant Liu. He walked over to where Bliss was sitting. "Thank you for helping us Lieutenant. As a reward may I offer you dinner in my quarters? You will be my guest."

Bliss eagerly accepted. He had been instructed to learn all he could about the enemy, and chose to view this invitation as such an opportunity. Besides, he was anxious to speak with the General.

He scrubbed himself and changed into fresh clothes. Lieutenant Liu escorted him to the General's hut.

"I apologize for the humble fare."

"No need to General, this is absolutely delicious."

They made small talk about the latrine construction, Bliss' facilities and other inconsequential matters. When they had finished with dinner, the General produced a bottle of chilled white wine, offered Bliss a cigarette and announced in a pleasant voice. "Lieutenant, I think we should talk now."

The conversation Bliss later recalled was as unexpected as the events of the previous week.

"You are an astute and politically sophisticated man. I will not try to belittle your stature by insulting your intelligence. We want you to help us and to do it willingly."

"I am a Lieutenant in the United States Army, my serial number is..."

He was interrupted. "That is quite unnecessary." The general's tone was commanding but not angry. "We know all about you, let me tell you about yourself."

General Kao's monologue was an amazing piece of research. He knew everything, including his relationship with Jocelyn. The General told him things he had forgotten, things he never remembered and things he had wanted to forget. Then he spoke briefly about the problems America would have to face in the future. When he was finished Bliss replied.

"And do you think Communism will solve these problems?"

"No I do not," the General responded. "Communism, Chinese, Russian or American style is merely a political philosophy. I can tell you that it will work in China. I do not know about America. Ideologies are useless without men to support them, intelligent men who can manipulate others and plan their destinies. Men who are sensitive and introspective, men who can become leaders. Are we such men Lieutenant Mansfield?"

They continued the discussion until the wee hours of the morning. Bliss knew that what he was doing was against the code of conduct for prisoners, but he was so impressed with the General's honesty, commitment and intellect that he could not help himself. He was also extremely anxious to talk to someone about Jocelyn. When Bliss spoke about her suicide, there were tears in the General's eyes.

The third week Bliss began seriously studying Chinese.

For the next six months he learned about China and the Chinese people and about life, reality and dreams. He was also instructed in the techniques of espionage.

It was hard to say when Bliss was converted or that he was even converted at all. While it is true that he harbored a deep resentment towards American racism, he mistrusted any ideology, and he really believed in the people and the brief history of the American Republic. Perhaps Professor Slovik was correct when he suggested that the relationship between the political officer and the prisoner was the essential variable. Bliss Mansfield and Kao Hai-yuan became friends, good friends, sharing dreams that superseded philosophies and countries. In their own way they were committed to a better world and to a large extent believed in each other. Bliss saw the General as the wise father he had always wanted and the General regarded Bliss as the son he never had.

When the time came to take leave of each other, General Kao and Lieutenant Mansfield embraced publicly and said their good-byes. Bliss was returned to a point about ten miles from where he had been captured. He was to make his way back to the American forces.

It was dusk, a time when the shadows played tricks on men's eyes.

"Halt, who goes there?" A figure had emerged out of the brush and had startled Private Olivera. He was an American dressed in native clothes with his hands on top of his head.

Forgetting protocol the private exclaimed, "who the hell are you?"

"My name is Lieutenant Bliss Mansfield. I was with the 58th Field. We were overrun and I've been hiding out in the hills."

"Jeez, that must have been months ago. Just stand where you are, sir, and please don't make a move or I'll have to shoot you."

"I'm Captain Livingston and this is Captain Hurd, Lieutenant. We're from Military Intelligence for this sector. We heard your story from the private but we'd like to hear it again."

Bliss grinned. "You mean you don't believe me."

"Frankly it's the most absurd tale I've ever heard."

"I don't blame you, half the time I don't believe it myself. Can I have a cigarette first?"

"Help yourself."

"Seven months ago I was forward observer to the 65th's Love Company. We were attacked and the Chicoms overran our position. I made it down to the valley with three of my men but it was crawling with enemy. We were captured."

"Excuse me for interrupting Lieutenant, but do you remember the names of the men?"

Bliss remembered. "Yes, S/Sgt. Killebrew, Pfc. Stoltz and Pfc. Fishbein. Cpl. Reilly was killed during the initial attack."

Both Captains glanced at the papers on their desk and nodded silently to each other. "Please go on."

"The first night we traveled over ten miles. We were all dog-tired. Stoltz attracted the guard's attention and I escaped."

"You escaped, just like that?"

"That's right, I just walked away. Well if you don't believe me ask Stoltz."

"Pfc. Stoltz is dead Lieutenant."

"Oh."

"Please continue."

"I made my way to a village where I found a Korean couple who were willing to help me. The man spoke some English. They hid me from the CCF in the mountains. I don't know how long I stayed there, but later I fought with an ROK unit."

The Captains spoke to each other. Captain Hurd left

190

the room and Captain Livingston offered the Lieutenant another cigarette. "Lieutenant we are naturally going to have to check out your story. It is very important that you remember the village and the names of the couple and of the ROK unit's commanding officer."

"Yes sir."

Both the Korean couple and the ROK Army officer verified his story. There was no reason to investigate further.

In September of 1952 the truce talks were deadlocked on the matter of POW repatriation. Everyone was tired of the long and bitter war. The battle-weary Lieutenant was debriefed and sent to the rear for a well-deserved rest. He was attached for temporary duty with the United Nation's forces at Chejedo.

In New York City, Chief Mabra, Detective-Sergeant Carney and Stephen Costa, a former CIA agent and a friend of Carney's made another discovery about Professor Andrew M. Crane.

NINE

Ron Mabra had known it all the time. Crane was the intended victim. Only he didn't know why. His combined vacation-investigation to Burt Carney in New York had paid off. Carney helped him trace Crane's movements after the tragic automobile accident that had killed his wife in late October of 1970.

There was really no reason for the accident. The West Side Highway was jammed during the rush hour traffic. Elaine Bravermann Crane was on her way to meet Andy. She had stopped at Brentanos to pick up the best-seller she had been patiently waiting for, and was in a hurry. She didn't see the car jump the divider and by the time she had hit her brakes it was too late to prevent the car directly behind her from a rear-end collision. The force of the crash sent her head through the windshield. Her neck was broken immediately. She felt no pain. They buried her three days later in Mt. Hebron cemetary on Long Island. The funeral was a quiet family affair where everyone cried a great deal. For the first time in seventeen years Andy returned to an empty house.

From the information Sergeant Carney had managed to obtain, he learned that Andy had left his position at Columbia, and sold his duplex in Brooklyn Heights. Then he had flown to San Francisco, spent a week at the Jack Tar Hotel and the next six months at Squaw Valley, skiing, drinking, forgetting and remembering.

Stephen Costa had worked for the Company for the better part of twenty years. He was never comfortable with the clandestine intrigue that characterized the CIA's involvement in foreign and domestic affairs. He knew his opinion carried little weight. He nevertheless kept his feelings to himself when he was assigned to operation "Dragon Lady," the code given to an important Chinese Communist defector. She had been snatched from the Chicoms in an East African Republic, debriefed at Langley and, while she was awaiting a new identity, was being kept under wraps at the Squaw Valley Lodge at Lake Tahoe in California. It was there that she met Andy Crane.

Costa explained. "She must have been an important defector because there was an attempt made on her life. The assassin missed his target and took out Agent Stan Burris who was assigned to protect her. The Company assumed incorrectly that Andy was the hired killer and sent another man to 'sanction him.' That was the CIA's way of evening the score. Unfortunately for Langley, he didn't succeed. Crane killed him in self-defense and in the confusion the Chinese defector vanished.

"Jesus H. Christ!" exclaimed Ron.

"We had a problem. To bring Crane to trial, we would have to admit to the attempt on his life, and we couldn't do that. I don't think Crane knew who the girl was, so we couldn't go public without disclosing the operation and, of course, revealing our ineptitude. Anyway, there was no reason to eliminate Crane. We don't go around shooting civilians. We made up a cover-story, the usual attempted-burglar-surprised-by-a-guest, and the local authorities bought it."

"Who was responsible for the operation?" Mabra asked.

"Lawrence, Malcom Johnson Lawrence."

"Good God," Carney interrupted. "He's the Deputy Director."

"Right, and no one wants to fuck around with him, he's a big wheel now."

Mabra thought for a moment. Then he asked Costa, "Could lawrence have waited all these years and then gone after Crane?"

"It's been done before."

"But you said Crane doesn't know anything."

Costa replied. "Yeah, but maybe Lawrence isn't so sure, and he's just covering his tracks now that he's a honcho. You've got to understand the way the Company operates. Everyone's afraid. If someone could prove that Lawrence screwed up, then he's in real trouble. There are a lot of psychos back in Virginia."

"Well, it fits," Mabra concluded. "The attempt on Crane's life has the markings of a professional job—real smart if you ask me, getting a mob-pro from New York, and then killing him so he couldn't talk. What are we going to do about it?"

"Not we," said Costa. "It's your baby. Just leave me out. I want to enjoy my retirement."

"Actually we've got no proof, Ron. If Steve won't testify then we've got no case, just hearsay and a lot of coincidences. I'd like to help. Vereste's murder is still within my jurisdiction and I hate to leave it unsolved, but I don't want to mess with the CIA. If Lawrence tried to silence Crane, there's no telling what he might do to anyone who starts to make waves."

Chief Mabra was a practical man and he had reached what he considered a practical decision. "Listen, I'm going to write this all up, everything we know and what we suspect. I'm going to put the report in a safe-deposit box and give you the extra key, Burt. First I'm going to warn Crane. If he's a sitting duck he ought to know it. Then I'm going to make some inquiries about Deputy-Director Lawrence. Can I count on both of you if I get some solid, no-nonsence evidence?"

Carney gave his consent and Costa reluctantly agreed. If the Chief could prove Lawrence was involved in the attempted shooting of the Professor or in Vereste's death, they would support him.

The past seven months took on the elusive quality of a nightmare. At first Bliss refused to believe they had ever happened. Gradually he came to accpet his decision. It became one young man's valiant struggle to destroy once and for all the sickening corruption and hatred that was responsible for Jocelyn's shocking suicide. His allegiance was to a cause; a private pact with his friend General Kao rather than to an international Communist conspiracy. Of course, he thought, the Army wouldn't see it that way. To them he would merely be a traitor, a candidate for a court-martial and a firing squad. He had to be careful.

His duties at the United Nations's compound were perfunctory. He was just biding his time waiting for "short-timers" orders stateside. He would rise about seven each morning, breakfast at the Officer's Mess and spend most of the day shuffling papers. Occasionally he would be asked to accompany the Military Police when they transported a prisoner from one installation to another.

He would spend his evenings drinking at the Officer's Club, watching old movies and writing letters to his mother. Once, he started to write to Jocelyn's parents but found he had nothing to say. He also spent his leisure hours studying Chinese.

General Kao was angry.

"General, you must forgive my presumptuous behavior but we have our problems as well."

"Then get on with it, I have work to do." These political cadre had always bothered him, this one in particular with his "official airs", and overblown sense of importance.

"As you well know, during the conflict it is not uncommon for intelligence officers to travel with the remaining North Korean People's Army units disguised as footsoldiers. One such officer was captured when his Korean unit surrendered to the Americans. He was taken to a compound outside of Taegu, and is scheduled to be brought elsewhere for more intensive interrogation."

The General was now impatient as well. "What does this have to do with me?"

The officer smiled revealing his white teeth. "Captain Sung is no ordinary man. He was the People's Republic General Command Staff and is a cousin of the Chairman himself. We know you have a 'man' here and request your assistance."

A request indeed. More like a command, he thought. The General was disgusted. How Confucian, to risk a high priority agent and months of intensive training for a distant kinsman of the Chairman. China might have made a great leap forward but the older system of family loyalties was very much alive. In his opinion it would be extremely foolish to use "the sleeping giant" for such an operation. Unfortunately the General did not have a choice.

Lieutenant Mansfield was walking to his quarters when he was approached by a KATUSA, a Korean attached to the U.S. Army.

"Lieutenant Mansfield?"

"Yes."

"I am sorry to disturb your evening but I have an important message from your 'tzufu'."

Bliss was alerted, the term "tzufu" literally means "lineage father", or "paternal grandfather", the code name for General Kao. The two men moved into the shadows of the BOQ.

"What is your message?"

The Korean told him. "...when you arrive at the compound, walk to the village, it is but a few minutes away. On the road is a Kimchi restaurant. The proprietor is a Mr. Kim. Tell him you come from your 'tzufu'. He will tell you what you must do."

It was a simple matter to volunteer to accompany the

two MP's to the Taegu compound. They left the next morning, stopping only once and arrived in the early evening. Mansfield checked in with the Duty Officer and pretended to be looking for some "local action." He was advised to visit the village.

Korean enclaves that develop around American compounds are unlike traditional Korean villages. While they appear similar in structure to others, their functions are notoriously specific. They exist to service the sexual desires of soldiers far from home and as an initial conduit for black market operations. This village was almost entirely populated by "girl-friends", Korean women who had established long term relationships with the soldier "boy-friends" doing their tour of duty, and by older women, referred to by G.I.'s as "Mama-sans". They were responsible for the exchange of cash for Post Exchange goods such as cigarettes, soap, radio s and almost any other American product.

A typical house in this enclave consisted of a courtyard arrangement surrounding three or four single rooms, which the girls called home. Some local Korean base-employees, "bar-girls," "street-girls," "suckahotchie-girls" and "Black G.I.-girls" also live there. The pecking order among these Korean women who catered to servicemen was very complex.

It had rained the night before, so the road leading to the village was muddy and made almost impassible by the trucks, jeeps, and bicycles that regularly travel it each day. Lieutenant Mansfield stayed close to its edge as he made his way to the small restaurant, owned and operated by Mr. Kim and his sons. He could smell the pungent aroma of the Kimchi stew long before he arrived. Mr. Kim must have been waiting for him. He was standing in the doorway and carefully scrutinized the American but remained silent.

"Mr. Kim?" Bliss asked.

"You are speaking to him."

Bliss moved closer. "I was told you have a message from my 'tzufu.' "

The man studied his face and whispered, "please come with me."

They walked down the road. Mr. Kim entered a courtyard and Bliss followed. When they were inside the room he spoke.

"We must hurry Lieutenant, Sung will be questioned in the morning. They do not know he is Chinese and they must not find out. You will have to see to it that he escapes."

"What should I do?"

"It's been all arranged. When the MP's take him to the interrogation center you will accompany them. They will have to drive through the village. Just after they pass the main road, there will be a diversion. A truck will pretend to break down and will block the road. At that time the compound will be attacked. You will have to see to it that the MP's cannot tell what happened."

Bliss did not believe his own words, "Will I have to kill them?"

"You must. I'll do my part. See to it that you do yours, Chun swei dzu jyu ren."

The prisoner was a small wiry man. Bliss thought he was about 30 but with Koreans or Chinese he could never be sure about their age. He wondered why they had gone to all this trouble. The prisoner did not appear to be particularly important, but he was sure the General had his reasons.

"You mind sitting in the back with the Korean, Lieutenant?"

"It'll be okay, Sergeant."

"Okay Mike let's go, I'm freezin' my butt off."

At 0320 hours they checked out of the compound and were driving through the village.

"God damn!" the Sergeant exclaimed. The road, really

198

an enlarged dirt path was blocked by a Korean truck. The hood was open and two civilians were standing there, just staring at it with a puzzled expression on their faces.

The Sergeant sounded his horn, and yelled, "get out of the way."

One of the Koreans shouted, "No can do, belt break. You help fix, maybe yes?"

The Sergeant asked Bliss. "Hey, Lieutenant, okay if Mike gives these guys a hand?"

"Sure."

Corporal Mike Effinger got out of the jeep, walked over to the truck and leaned over the hood. At precisely that moment a loud explosion was heard and orange smoke filled the sky. It was followed by more explosions. They seemed to be coming closer.

The Sergeant screamed, "Everybody out, Lieutenant, get the prisoner out." The men hit the side of the road just as a mortar shell sent the jeep bursting into flame. Bliss unholstered his .45 and shot the Sergeant. At the same time one of the Koreans raised a wrench and brought it down on Cpl. Effinger's head. You could hear his skull crack. They loaded the two M.P.'s on the truck and closed the hood.

Sung spoke for the first time. "Thank you, Lieutenant, I shall always remember this." Then he leapt aboard the moving truck and they were gone.

Bliss made his way cautiously back to the compound although the attack seemed to be over. He described how the prisoner and the two M.P.'s were killed when a shell struck the jeep. Two days later he returned to Chejedo and before the week was over, received orders back to America.

During the long trip home, Bliss realized he was now irrevocably committed. He had deliberately killed an American soldier.

TEN

When intellectual snobs from San Francisco and New York meet, they will argue the merits of their respective cities and, if they can agree on anything, it would be that the vast country between their two meccas is a cultural wasteland. The chances are, that they had never been to Chicago.

Andy and Leslie boarded United Airlines Flight 993 from Kennedy at 10:50 in the morning and arrived at O'Hare International, one hour and fifty minutes later.

"It's so good to be by ourselves again, Andy. I really missed just the two of us."

"You have a beautiful home, a delightful father, a...well a typically-concerned mother. Sometimes I can't understand why a Westchester country club princess gave it all up to become a professor."

"Oh yes you can, Mr. Anthropologist. The silver spoon can also be a deadly trap."

"So can a university."

"Perhaps, but here I make the decisions. Success depends upon my efforts and so does failure. I'm my own person and I like it that way."

"Really, are you? Many of the decisions you make are limited by budget and programming. Your success depends just as much upon the goodwill of your colleagues, and being your own person only means you have responsibilities to others. That's the reality of a university, only we don't like to think of it that way."

"My, my, but we're being pessimistic today, aren't we?"

"I guess so. I can't help thinking about Mansfield. Now there's a real decision maker, or so it would seem. But he's got obligations and commitments too. I'm worried about them, especially if they emanate from Peking. Imagine, a real Manchurian candidate."

"Andy, are you sure? I mean, what proof do we actually have?"

"Nothing substantial, nothing that would stand up in any court. At least not yet, and that's why we're here, to take another look at our president's climb to the top. I'm just willing to bet he's had some help."

What they learned about Bliss was disappointing. He was a good student; an above-average doctoral candidate. He excelled in political philosophy and frequented leftist coffee houses. Married to an attractive and intelligent woman, the daugther of a philosophy professor, he led a life style no different from other graduate students of his day. Their queries turned up no suspicious activities, no clandestine meetings with secret agents and no involvement with Communist causes. They were about to give up until they spoke with Professor David Nielsen.

Nielsen was a friendly man, cautious yet outgoing; a curious combination. Andy introduced himself as a reporter.

"That's nonsense young man. I know who you are, your name's Andrew Crane all right, but you're an anthropologist. This is you picture on the jacket, is it not?" He removed a copy of Andy's book from his shelf.

Leslie thought quickly, "I'm afraid it's my fault Dr. Nielsen. I'm a legislative attorney and we're looking into President Mansfield's background. It's quite normal for potential Senators. Dr. Crane's been helping me since he teaches at the President's school. I told him to say he's a reporter. It sounds more...shall we say, appropriate."

"Do you have any identification young lady?"

"Yes Sir." She produced a card indentifying her as "D. Parkins", a lawyer with the Department of Justice. She took the initiative.

"I'm Denise Parkins. President Mansfield was a doctoral candidate in Political Science, wasn't he?"

201

David Neilsen agreed. He was still not sure about them but decided to answer their questions. He had known Bliss only briefly, during his last year of schooling and really couldn't help them. They were totally unprepared for his next statement.

"Does Mansfield still keep up with his Chinese?"

Andy just stared at him. "Would you say that again, please?"

"I said, does Mansfield still study Chinese?"

"What makes you think he speaks Chinese?" Leslie, alias Denise asked.

"We had another student in the department. Actually he worked for me as a part-time translator. He said he wanted to make some extra money tutoring Mandarin. So I put up a notice on the bulletin board. Later, I asked him if he had found any takers. He said he did, Bliss Mansfield."

"Dr. Nielsen," Andy asked, "was the President learning Mandarin in connection with his dissertation?"

"No, not at all. I attended his defense. He was interested in foreign concepts of justice, but he didn't read Mandarin."

"Why do you think he would want to learn Chinese?" Andy continued.

"Did I say learn? I meant study. My student told me that his pupil was already quite proficient in Chinese. Is that odd?"

"No, I guess not," Andy replied. "Whatever happened to your translator?"

"He returned to Taiwan the next semester. He said he had pressing problems at home."

Not wishing to further tax Nielsen's curiosity, Andy tried to change the subject. "Does my book on your shelf also mean that you are interested in China?"

"Well, yes...in a way," the professor replied. "I'm very much into comparative justice, particularly non-western legal systems. Your ethnography goes into some fine detail about how Taiwanese villagers solve disputes. Your book, by the way, is very well written. I wish I could say the same for Mansfield's."

Once again, Andy and Leslie were stunned. Bliss' book had been a best seller in its field and they had assumed it was a good one.

Nielsen continued. "To tell you the truth I didn't like his book at all. It panders to popular themes rather than scholarship."

"But it was published by Alden and that's a respectable academic press, isn't it?" Leslie remembered.

"Yes, I even reviewed it for Alden, and as a matter of fact suggested that they not waste their time publishing it. I was also surprised when they gave the book such extensive publicity. Oh well, perhaps they knew something I didn't. And now you two, I don't know what your game really is, but I've got an appointment, so if you'll excuse me."

Alden was based in Chicago. Andy called them and pretended he had a manuscript. He explained that he was in town for the day and wondered if he might see an editor. His appointment was for nine o'clock the next morning.

It was turning out to be a good day after all. They drove to a grassy strip that fronts the lake, a beach and picnic area.

"Denise Parkins," Andy teased her. "If I didn't know better, I'd swear that you were a CIA agent. Where in God's name did you come up with that?"

"It's my ex-husband's, the 'D' is for Dexter and he really works for the Department of Justice. It's an old ID I found it back home."

"Suppose Nielsen would have asked you for a driver's license, what would you have done then?"

"I don't know...punt, I guess. People are usually impressed with credentials, they don't think about such things."

They spent the latter part of the afternoon and early evening driving around Lake Forrest, where Leslie gave him a Cook's tour of the North Shore's "gilded ghetto" of her childhood years before her parents had moved to Rye.

When Andy entered his office the coffee was already brewing and the fresh pastries were on the table. He graciously offered the professor a chair across from his desk. "I hear tell you have a manuscript for us Dr. Crane?"

Andy smiled. "Not quite. I have a prospectus to offer you, that is if we can agree on royalties, advances and publicity." Irvington expected as much and was prepared to make a reasonable offer.

"I'm particularly interested in publicity." He wasted no time coming directly to the point. "Like the pre-publication attention you got for the President of my university, Bliss Mansfield. You seemed to have turned a third-rate piece into a virtual best-seller."

Oh no, thought Irvington, he would have to bring that one up. The editor was basically a principled man, but a realistic one. Over-promoting a book of dubious quality could be beneficial but it was really taking a big chance. He had read the three outside reviewer's comments on Mansfield's manuscript. They were not overly optimistic. The one from Nielsen at Chicago was a blunt rejection. He had also discussed the book's potential in the non-academic or trade market, but no one had thought there was much hope. Deciding to reject the book, he was instructing his secretary to draft a formal "thank-you-but", when he received a call from his chief. The word had come down from the top. Publish it. Put your best people on re-write and do it yourself if necessary, but get the damn thing out. Claude was shocked. He had known that books were published because of friendship or pressure, but nothing like this had ever happened to him before. He tried to explain it to Andy.

"Look, professor, that damn book was a fluke. Somebody on the board must have wanted it real bad. They overrode my veto and everything. There is just no way I could get that kind of publicity for you, unless, of course, you really have a bestseller."

"You mean you actually rejected the book?"

"Absolutely, it was sophomoric, full of crap, pardon me, the standard jargon of dissertation." He decided against telling the professor about the special bonus he had received for publishing the book.

"I'm afraid I don't understand?"

"Neither do I, this is just between you and me, but I heard there was some fat-cat congressman who thought the book was terrific so.."

"Do you recall the congressman's name?"

"Wait a minute, it was Parsons. That's it Parsons. Say isn't he the one that just dropped out of the Senate race in favor of Mansfield? Now that's really odd."

Yes, Andy thought, it would indeed seem strange. "Let me ask you, when you promote a book like *Justice in America,* doesn't it cost a lot of money?"

"That's another thing," Irvington replied. "It should have but it didn't. We received a pre-publication order for some 5,000 copies."

"Is that unusual?"

"I'll say it is, and considering the book in question, it's more like a miracle."

"Who ordered the copies?"

"I'll never forget them. The name of the organization was the *American Reader.* They had an office on North Michigan, but when I tried to call them later, I found out they had moved and that there was no forwarding address. I asked around but nobody ever heard of them before. It's like their only function was to buy advance copies of the book."

Andy thought so too. But it was logical, it made sense

however only if you knew about the president. The book had catapulted Bliss Mansfield from an unknown junior professor to an author of prominence. It was also likely that Bliss wasn't even aware of the help he had received. The incident only served to confirm Andy's suspicions. Someone had gone to great lengths and considerably money to see that the president's star was rising.

"What now?" Leslie asked on the sidewalk outside the publishing office.

"I'm not sure," replied Andy. He was still thinking about his visit to the publisher. "Les, it's clear now that Bliss had outside help. In fact he couldn't get the book published without it. That means there's an organization with sufficient clout promoting his interests. Yet we haven't had a clue to who they really are, that is, outside of a 'Communist conspiracy'. That's what worries me more than anything."

"Andy, perhaps, just perhaps, Bliss isn't the only one involved. What about Congressman Parsons? That's twice his name has come up. The key to Bliss has to be the people helping him. Who are they? How many?" She shuddered. "How far does it go? While you were gone, I went back to the university and checked on that foreign student of Nielsen's. His name was also Sung. He was a graduate student from Taiwan, and returned home when Bliss graduated, at least that's what his records say. I made a xerox copy of them. It even lists his address in Taiwan."

Andy was proud of her. "I've got a friend in the U.S. Information Agency in Taipei. I think I'll write to him and see what he can find out about the mysterious Mr. Sung. Right now there's not much else we can do here. Why don't we go back home and get our heads together? We can borrow Ian's sailboat and relax in the sun while we get ready for Hawaii. Anyway I'm tired of living out of a suitcase."

"Does that mean we forget about ole Bliss?"

Andy hesitated. "No. Bliss came to the unversity as a dean. I'll bet we find our answers right on the campus."

Leslie didn't tell Andy about it, but she was going to call her ex-husband and ask him about Congressman Parsons.

Located in Chapultepec Park only thirty-five pesos by luxury cab from the Maria Isabel Hotel, is "Del Lago." It has all the class and cuisine Mexico can offer. World travelers would not be disappointed.

Immense glass windows three stories high front onto a lake with a lighted fountain display of "dancing waters". Red velvet chairs highlight the dimly lit interior where green plants grow to reach the cork ceiling. In the tiered cocktail lounge, wealthy Latin men escort women young enough to be their daughters while they enjoy the music of a strolling Mariachi band. Those who understand Spanish would appreciate the sexual overtones of the ballads. On a small dance floor, the music is quiet, couples cling to each other and the mood is devastatingly romantic. The traditional Mexico City dinner hour had started at nine and now it was almost eleven.

Chao Ping-ti, and the man with the deep tan and pleasant smile were sitting once again at a table apart from the crowd. The American nodded to the waiter. *"Dod cervezas, por favor."*

"Si Senor." A few moments later the waiter returned with their drinks.

Chao remarked. "Outside the hotels, beggar women are sleeping in the streets while here, rich men laugh with their mistresses. When the revolution comes there will be no rich men and no beggars. It will be sad but it will be good." The American was strangely silent. "Has my friend from Virginia no words tonight?"

"No, old man, I am thinking about a security chief from the university. You know, he is in Washington asking questions about me. He believes I am involved in the campus shooting but for all the wrong reasons."

"Yes, my friend. He is, how do you say it, barking up the wrong tree."

"I know, but he still worries me. And the man and the woman?"

"Ah, they are very good. They have been to his hometown and the college. When they went to Washington, they made inquiries about his Korean service, but you know that. They spoke to the lawyer in New Jersey. He told them about shooting the sergeant. I thought they would stop there but they came to Chicago and started asking about his book."

"Can they prove anything?"

"No, but they are closer than I thought. I am concerned."

"What will you do, my people cannot help now."

The Chinese gentleman changed the subject. "General Kao died last month. He was 81. I wish he could have lived to have seen his fruit blossom. Did you ever find the girl?"

"No, it's been over six years now, she hasn't surfaced anywhere."

Mr. Chao smiled. "It's strange indeed. If the professor knows where she is he would have the answer to his mystery. She is the key to all his problems."

"We watched him closely after the incident at Squaw Valley. We thought he might lead us to the girl but he doesn't know anymore than we do."

"Yes."

The man with the deep tan and the pleasant smile finished his drink. "Everything is on schedule, it won't be long now."

The Chinese gentleman nodded in agreement. After his friend had left he raised his glass in a silent salute to his departed comrade, Kao Hai-yuan and to a dream that had begun over a quarter of a century ago in a mountain camp in the new China.

PART III

PART III

me...Fine, how are you? Dex, we've been doing some research on Congressional leaders, yes, what can you tell me about Duane Parsons...yes, that's right, Well...

ONE

Leslie sat on the bed procrastinating. She had been staring at the phone for the past fifteen minutes and was uncomfortably nervous. Running a comb through her long hair she slowly walked to the desk. It had been so long, she thought. Memories have a funny way of playing tricks on your mind. She tried to picture Dexter, suave, sure of himself, damned commanding in his pinstripe suit. So arrogant, as if it were all my fault.

The last time she had spoken to him was in the lawyer's office. He reluctantly agreed to the divorce settlement but his eyes were still pleading with her. They seemed to be saying, "come back, let's try again. This is a mistake." For a moment she had felt like bursting into tears and hiding in his arms.

Carefully, she dialed his Washington office. "Mr. Dexter Parkins, please...Dr. Leslie Pace...Hello...yes, it's me...Fine, how are you? Dex, we've been doing some research on Congressional leaders, what can you tell me about Duane Parsons...yes, that's right. Well, everything—family, finances, voting patterns, trips abroad. No, I am serious. I wish you wouldn't say that...Yes. And the children. Uh-uh, I love the university. Maybe soon...I will. Good-bye."

She hung up the phone and suddenly felt good, very free, and very lucky. It was going to be a glorious day. She dressed hurriedly, gulped the coffee Andy had left on the warmer, grabbed a sugar doughnut and raced down the road headed out towards the Racquet Club. She was so delighted with herself and so preoccupied with her thoughts that she failed to notice the '75 blue Ford LTD follow her to the highway.

Andy went to his office earlier that morning. Mrs.

Koehler, the department secretary glared at him.

"Dr. Crane, where have you been, your mailbox is overflowing, I can't see where I'm going to put any more books."

Most of the mail was, as usual, superfluous. For book advertisements, two complimentary copies of an introductory text, two notices of upcoming conferences, three requests for copies of the paper he had presented in Boston, intra-university memos and a letter marked "urgent and personal." It bore a New York postmark.

Andy paused to re-read the brief note. So the Chief thinks I was the intended victim, not Spaacklund, and he knows about Squaw Valley and the CIA. Mabra's speculation intrigued him. For a moment he wanted to believe him. Just suppose the Chief is right. Then all those fantasies about Mansfield may be just that. No! If this Lawrence wanted to hit me he had plenty of better opportunities before. Besides he wouldn't have waited for six years. Still...

Andy arrived at the club by ten, having promised Marcy Darrin he would play tennis with her. She was the fifteen-year-old daughter of one of his colleagues and was playing in the sectionals. Rallying with Marcy was like playing with a young Chris Everett. It would be a tiring but challenging experience.

Damn it, Crane, keep the ball deep, he muttered under his breath. She can really put those short shots away, that's more like it...stroke, now to her forehand. He moved swiftly to the net and smashed her return out of play. She was leading three games to two.

"I'm sorry, Dr. Crane, but I have to go now. Can we play again?"

"Sure, Marcy, just give me some time to rest." He wiped the sweat from his forehead and watched her bounce as she ran off to greet three other beautiful, tanned, and slim teen-agers. He was admiring the bodies of these innocent vixens and thinking like a dirty old man when he glanced over at the next court and saw Eli Ricketts move onto the hardcourt with President Mansfield.

They were starting to warm up and Andy studied the President. His moves are good. He's an experienced player, but his timing's off, he hasn't played for a while. Still, look at his hustle. He's a fighter and I'll bet he's got staying power. For a moment Andy thought of inviting him and Ricketts to a set of doubles. He'd play with Marcy. As he sent the ball flying at Mansfield he would scream "Chun swei dzu jyu ren" and the President would confess everything. He returned to reality and looked again at the man. Who would ever believe it. A secret agent of a foreign power casually playing tennis with a state asemblyman. Was Ricketts involved too?

Bliss enjoyed the game. Ricketts was out of shape and gasping for breath. Bliss let up on his returns. Remember now, Mr. Senator-to-be, this is a social game. Make him feel like he's a worthy opponent. He's a big man at the Capitol and you need his support. He hit the next serve just out of Rickett's reach.

He had recognized Crane but he wasn't worried. The shooting and the demonstrations seemed like they happened such a long time ago. His people had told him they would take care of the anthropoligist. Perhaps they could bribe him. A professor's salary was never enough and Crane liked the good life. Maybe they would threaten him. It doesn't matter, they were the experts in these matters and would do whatever had to be done. He remembered what the man from Washington had told him. "It's our problem and we'll take care of it, just concentrate on your campaign. Make friends and say the right things. Once you're a Senator everything will be okay."

Bliss wondered about that too. What happens when I

become a Senator? Except for that Chinese POW in Korea they had made no demands whatsoever. He had acted like his own man and had made his own decisions. What's it going to be like when I take my seat in Washington? He thought back twenty-five years, and for the first time in a long while he wondered about his commitment.

When it came to mixed doubles, Leslie enjoyed a distinct advantage. Her male opponent might easily lose sight of the ball. He would be so busy looking at her body. When it came to his wife's turn she would be so angry at her husband that she would blow her shot as well.

Beauty aside, Leslie was a very competent player herself. Teamed with Andy they made a devastating couple. They had just destroyed the Ericksons 6-2, 6-0 and were enjoying a well-deserved seven-up when Leslie remembered her appointment.

"Darn, I almost forgot, I've got a meeting with Dean Meyers. It's about those general education tutorials." She glanced at her watch. "Oh, my God, Andy, I've got to run. I'm late already and David is always so persnickety."

Andy had decided not to tell her about the Chief's note. She didn't know about Squaw Valley and there was no reason to add to her worries, Mansfield was enough. "Okay, see you back at the house for dinner."

Ordinarily Leslie would drive to the campus on the State Highway but she was late and Andy had shown her a shortcut on the back roads. The gravel path twisted and turned but Leslie was an experienced driver and it would cut as much as ten minutes off her time. When she first noticed the blue Ford it was already too late.

It was coming up fast behind her. What the hell...she thought and looked at the speedometer, it registered fifty but the Ford was closing. She pressed the gas pedal to the floor and watched the needle rise, 55, 60, 70. Good God, the car was still there. Leslie remembered something she had seen on a T.V. movie. Quickly she put on her lights. The Ford slowed and she moved ahead.

The sign said "sharp curve 25 mph." She braked and felt the wheels skid. The Ford was gaining. He must be doing close to 80. The blue car slammed into her bumper. She felt the shock and momentarily lost control. Again it smashed into the back. He must be crazy she was thinking. A cold fear seized her body. No! He's not crazy, he's trying to kill me.

The road twisted for the last time just before it became a straightaway. She was doing 85 but the Ford was staying with her. Suddenly it raced ahead crashing against her door and forcing her from the road. She tried to control the car as she ripped through the barbed wire fence and plowed into the meadow. The car jerked twice and came to a dead stop.

She sat there, stunned, gripping the wheel and watching the two men leave their car and start walking slowly towards her. They were wearing boots and T-shirts. The older man was surely in his forties and had a tattoo on his right forearm but she couldn't make out the design. The younger man, not more than twenty, was holding something in his hand. It flashed brightly when the sun's rays hit it at just the right angle. They were closer now. The young one had long hair and his front teeth were crooked. He was smiling at her. She still couldn't move. Paralysed with a strange fear, she waited for them.

"Get out of the car Dr. Pace." It was the older man who spoke. Leslie knew she couldn't panic now. She moved her hand slowly towards the window and the door lock but he was too fast. The younger man grabbed her hand.

"We told you to get out. Now do as you're told."

Leslie obeyed his instructions and faced her enemies. "What do you want?"

They were looking at her. She knew the look. She had seen it before and she also knew what they wanted. It was probably useless but she had to try. "Take my money, it's in my purse."

They continued staring but remained silent.

Leslie was a brave woman but she was terrified of being raped. Her roommate at college had been attacked and molested. The man had used a broom handle and had ripped her insides apart. Uh-oh, I'm going to be...Her stomach heaved twice and then she vomited all over herself. The smell made her gag and she retched again. She lay there on the ground sobbing hysterically. Her leg had been cut and the blood was flowing freely, turning brown when it mixed with the earth. And still they stood there looking at her.

She cried, "please, please, don't hurt me. Please, I'm begging you."

The older man spoke. "Keep your nose in your own business. Do I make myself clear, Doctor?"

"Yes, yes, I'll do anything, just don't hurt me." She closed her eyes and sobbed like a baby waiting for them to take her. She didn't believe it. They went back to the car, got in and drove away. She sighed with relief and started to cry again.

Andy was finishing the last of twenty laps when he heard himself being paged—"please come to the phone." Inside of thirty minutes he was at the hospital.

"I'm Dr. Butler. Your friend's had quite a scare. We gave her a sedative and she's resting now."

"How badly is she hurt?"

"Physicaly she's just fine. Got a nasty cut on her leg from some barbed wire, and there are some superficial bruises. She also threw up all over her clothes but she's unharmed. Emotionally she's very upset."

"What happened?"

"I'm not sure. A telephone repairman out in Locust Valley brought her in. Apparently she had a car accident and went through a fence."

When Leslie woke up she put her arms around Andy's neck and wouldn't let go. "O: Andy, I was so scared. It was like a nightmare." She told him about the two men. "Andy, take me home please."

That evening they sat silently sipping brandies, watching the sky turn orange as the sun set over the lake. Their exciting adventure as amateur sleuths was over. It was no longer a game. Leslie was unharmed but the message was clear. Mind your own business, or the next time you won't be so lucky.

"It was a warning, Les. First they tried to kill me and when that failed they tried a bribe." He told her about the offer from Harvard.

"Now, they threaten you...and next time..."

"What are you going to do?"

"I don't have a choice, do I?"

Leslie sat up. "Oh yes you do. You can't stop. Andy, we must be getting close to something, though I wish I knew what it was. They took a big chance threatening my life. It would have been easier to kill me. But they didn't. That means they don't want any more suspicious homicides."

"Les, honey, I love you, I can't take risks with your life."

"Thank you Sir Galahad, but it's my life and my choice. Besides there are no guarantees even if we stop now. I don't want to spend the rest of my life looking in the rear-view mirror everytime I go for a drive."

Andy knew she was right. He wasn't about to live like a frightened rabbit either, but from now on they would have to be more careful.

He kept the pistol in the bedroom. It was a precaution against burglars. He unlocked the drawer, took out the snub-nosed .38, checked the chambers and felt the comforting fit of the cold steel as he released the safety.

Leslie was frightened but she said nothing. They had made their decision and there was no turning back.

TWO

For most students and faculty, the academic year had ended. Administrators, however, have a twelve-month contract, and although their summers were certainly less hectic, they too needed to celebrate the conclusion of the spring semester. Without exception they all looked forward to the president's annual summer barbecue.

Bliss ordinarily enjoyed the party. It was an opportunity to relax with the members of his staff, renew the ties and trust that bound them together, and because he was the host, to re-assert his right to moral and practical leadership. Today he was tired. The speeches, dinners, large and small political gatherings were exhausting. Jealous of the time it took from his wife and family and from his own peace of mind, he remembered he had been warned that a Senate campaign would be like that. Now he believed it.

They were standing by the edge of the rose garden.

"Bliss, how will we ever get along when you go to Washington? We need a strong personality in the number one slot and Jim Hadley's not the man." The speaker was Roger Alvarez, Dean of the Business College and the only Chicano to hold a high administrative post in the university.

The President appreciated his comment, but he also knew that Roger was bucking for a vice-presidency. "Why don't we cross that bridge when we come to it Roger, we owe Jim the chance to prove himself." He noticed Alex gesturing. "Excuse me, Roger I see my wife needs me."

"There's a special delivery for you, he says you'll have to sign for it."

Bliss did not like to be interrupted but he signed for the packet. Noticing no return address, he was curious. He went to his study and closed the door. There was a brief cover letter. "When you address the Labor Council you will come out as strongly opposed to a further U.S. military presence in Korea. The information you need is in the enclosed panphlet. Good luck, 'sleeping giant'." Bliss burned the letter and scattered the ashes. He sat down in his easy chair and started to read. He couldn't believe it.

Marty Green was only three years out of school but he already enjoyed a reputation as a good investigative reporter, so he resented being assigned to boring and innocuous events. He viewed Mansfield's speech to the State Labor Council as a wasted evening. He had been following the campaign since the attempted shooting of the South African. Hoping for more excitement from the educator, all he had seen thus far was the same old political rhetoric; law and order, honesty in government, fiscal responsibility and more bullshit. With virtually no opposition, Mansfield could have just as well read from the Declaration of Independence. Marty liked the President's decisiveness in handling the demonstration. He had followed the example set by Hayakawa who had successfully promoted campus unrest into his own Senate seat. Now, he hated to admit it, but Mansfield was turning into just another glib politician.

Freedom Hall was packed. Smith had gone out of his way to fill the large auditorium. It really wasn't that difficult. Mansfield was a favorite of the union bosses as well as the rank-and-file. The fried chicken tasted like a wet paper towel and now the men were settling down to lukewarm coffee and expensive cigars. Marty closed his eyes and was almost asleep when Mansfield was introduced.

Smith was saying. "It gives me great pleasure to introduce the next Senator from this great state, President Bliss Mansfield." There was a round of polite applause.

"Mr. Smith, ladies and gentlemen..."

Marty stiffled a yawn.

"...appreciate the contributions of labor to..."

He had heard it all before and started to daydream, picturing Angela, the fashion editor.

"...understand the problems of working people..."

It was becoming difficult to concentrate, his eyelids were getting heavier.

"...as well as foreign policy. I am going to strongly insist that the United States not only reduce its military presence in South Korea but that we withdraw our troops once and for all."

Marty was suddenly alert. He started to write. Is he crazy? That's one hell of a controversial issue and this is a labor crowd. They support the military. What does he want to do; throw away his chances? Marty thought, this man's no fool, he wouldn't be talking like that unless he's got something up his sleeve, something big. Playing a hunch, he motioned to one of the busboys.

"Hey man, wanna make a quick five. Call this number." He scribbled the TV affiliate's phone on a piece of paper.

"Tell them you're calling for Marty Green and to get a portable, that's a mini-camera, down to Freedom Hall and tell them to hurry."

"...have based not only my own campaign but my belief in the future of our country upon the ethics of honesty. A country is only free when its representatives, elected and appointed, can be trusted to exercise their best judgement for the benefit of the people they have sworn to serve."

Bliss lowered his voice but spoke firmly. "I deeply regret that this is no longer so."

He was now speaking softly but the audience was stilled. "In the past months certain members of the Congress have been accused of accepting favors from a certain Korean businessman, Mr. Tongsun Park, whom

we suspect was acting under orders from his President."
He paused. "At least that's what a former Director of the Korean CIA tells us. Those alleged favors ranged from gifts and gratuities to junkets and outright bribes."

He raised his voice. "Money! Cash! Dollars! Dough! All to insure positive and sympathetic votes for the continuance of American troops in South Korea." He paused again.

"Whether or not a real need exists...The charges against public officials have been up to now allegations, not proof of guilt. Congressman Parson's committee has been charged with the investigation. That is the equivalent of asking the fox to investigate security precautions in the chicken coop."

The audience laughed uncomfortably. Bliss continued.

"Last week I was informed as to the nature and extent of these alleged gifts and bribes. Since then my staff has been working overtime to get at the truth. I am saddened to have to report that the charges are substantiated and that they can be verified. Congressman Parsons has been on the Korean payroll for the past three years."

While the audience gasped. Marty kept writing. Bliss named dates, places, names, bank accounts and stock transfers. He didn't merely hint at what took place; he fully documented each charge. If what he said was indeed the truth, Green surmised, Parsons would be spending much of his retirement in a Federal prison.

Bliss named a U.S. Senator and two other Congressmen, once again documenting the extent of their payoffs. He raised his hands asking the audience for quiet.

"The Korean scandal however goes further than that. It reaches into the White House itself." He paused for effect.

"All the way up to the cabinet. Secretary of Defense William Pritchard has been a Korean lobbyist since the day he took the oath of office."

The crowd was shouting now and Marty had to strain his ears to hear the details. Good grief, he thought, this man even knows the numbers of his Swiss Bank account. This was sensational and he was glad he had called for a camera team. It would be on the eleven o'clock news and make the morning's headlines. I'd better be careful how I write this, Marty cautioned himself. Mansfield has made charges that if proven libelous would ruin his chances for local dogcatcher, to say nothing of his finances and his future. Yet somehow Marty knew that the evidence would check out.

The Appointments Secretary to the President of the United States was sitting quietly in his living room sipping coffee and thinking about his wife's slim body when he turned on the eleven o'clock news. Stepping out of the shower his wife heard him say. "Jesus Christ, the shit's hit the fan." He rushed to the telephone but the private line to the White House was already busy.

Senator Robert Wallis, driving home from a late dinner party knew he had had one too many for the road and was experiencing some difficulty keeping his eyes open when he turned to the late news. His car went out of control hitting a parkway guardrail, before it came to a dead stop. The Senator was badly shaken but much more concerned with getting to his safe deposit box when the bank opened in the morning.

Representative Duane Parsons did not get the news until the next day. He was still in Seoul where he had just completed a two-week tour of Korean and American military establishments. He was going to recommend an increased defense expenditure when an aide brought him a telegram. He sat there in the dark for quite a while and contemplated telling the entire story. Finally he walked across the lobby of the hotel and changed his flight reservations from Washington to Buenos Aires.

Secretary Pritchard had spent a beautiful day visiting

his daughter. He had been worried about Carole and the grand-children ever since her divorce from that hot-head lawyer she had married. He knew it wouldn't work the first day she brought him home. They were fighting even then, but like a wise parent not wishing to interfere, he said nothing. Carole had made a beautiful recovery. She went back to business school and was now working in a regional office of H.E.W. He had seen to that. Sean and Erin seemed to be taking their mother's new responsibilities in stride and appeared to be adjusting to a single-parent home.

They had gone out to dinner at Enrico's, and now with the kids in bed, were enjoying a late drink and re-discovering the special warmth of a father and daughter relationship. Carole spilled her drink when she heard the broadcast. Secretary Pritchard was badly distressed. He excused himself and stood in the darkness of the children's room watching their silent breathing as they huddled beneath protecting blankets. Over his daughter's protests he summoned his car and returned to the motel. He took a single piece of official stationary from his briefcase and placed it on the desk. Careful to dot his i's and cross his t's, he started to write a letter of resignation.

The calamity prompted investigations at all levels of government. The President appointed a blue-ribbon committee headed by former Ambassador Mitchell Potter. Bliss was selected as the seventh member.

The Justice Department and both houses of Congress started "independent" investigations. The Chair of the House Committee on Ethics had his phone disconnected, and the Korean Embassy resembled a medieval fortress under siege during the Crusades.

The reaction from the public was overwhelming. Letters ran ten to one calling for the withdrawal of American troops, and at the Pentagon, lights burned late into the night. General Jason Carterett flew to Korea to re-assess Korean armed strength and their ability to withstand a North Korean offensive. The President himself had made it quite clear to Carteret that he expected a full report within two weeks.

Deputy Director Lawrence of the CIA headed that agency's task force. All intelligence gathering activities were stepped up and extra men were assigned to "Operation Korea."

The President made a speech to the nation pre-empting the tenth re-run of "Gone with the Wind." While official protests were lodged at the United Nations, world leaders in London, Paris, Bonn, Tokyo, Seoul, Moscow and Peking held their breath. All leaves were cancelled for military personnel.

Within a week, the furor had died down. The United States was still re-evaluating its commitment to Park Chung-hee's republic, and the world returned to the business of famine, droughts, floods, over-population, pollution, guerilla warfare, prejudice, poverty and politics.

Senator Wallis maintained his innocence and threatened to sue Mansfield, but did no such thing. Congressman Parsons was presumably somewhere in Argentina and unavailable for comment. Secretary Pritchard and three other government employees handed in letters of resignation which were eagerly accepted. Tongsung Park was back in Korea and refused to return to America. For the first time since its inception, Reverend Moon's Unification Church suffered a decline in membership.

Mr. Chao finished his dinner at the Peninsula Hotel in Kowloon, gave a generous tip to the surprised waiter and had the doorman call the green Rolls Royce. He was smiling to himself. Phase One had been a tremendous success.

THREE

Chief Mabra was also having his troubles. With his vacation almost over he had very little time left, and thus far his investigation of the CIA Deputy Director was frustrating. He remembered Washington as being a city of insiders jealously guarding their secrets, but Langley was much worse. Oh, people were polite over the telephone, "Yessir," "I'm sorry, Sir," "No Sir," we don't ordinarily allow..." but records were classified or unavailable and appointments impossible at this time. Lawrence's past was guarded almost as fanatically as his present operations. All he had learned was that the Deputy had been an officer with the Counter-Intelligence Corps (CIC) in Korea during the United Nations police action. He had apparently been recruited there and had served as an operative and later station chief in Southeast Asia. He had been involved in covert operations during the early days of Vietnam and more recently, in Laos.

The Chief had spoken to the authorities in Squaw Valley, but they preferred to leave things as they were. It was a simple burglary. The guest had accidentally killed the intruder in self-defense and nobody ever heard of the CIA.

Mabra was finishing his dinner in the Hilton's coffee shop when he noticed the man speaking to the cashier and started heading over towards him.

"Greg, Greg Albers, is that you, you ole son-of-a...It must be at least ten years."

Greg had been a Lieutenant for the Los Angeles Police Department when Ron was a Sergeant. They had become fast friends during a particularly sticky and embarrassing investigation of police involvement in organized crime. Unlike Ron, Greg had kept in shape. His tight belt revealed a flat stomach and Ron noticed that he was wearing a shoulder holster. They shook hands and talked about earlier times.

"How's the campus life, ole buddy? Still makin' it with the co-eds?"

"What brings you to the capital, Ron?" They had adjourned to the bar and were enjoying a second round.

"Oh, nothing much, just playing tourist, celebrating being away from the wife and kids." Then he changed his mind and decided to tell Greg the truth. His Washington friend was silent for a few moments. He ordered another round and looked right at Ron.

"Mabra, I don't know if I should tell you this but I work for the Company, have ever since I left the force. Look, you be careful. Even I wouldn't want to mess around with Lawrence, at least not these days, he's busier than hell with this Korean Watergate thing."

"I need help, Greg. The Agency just closes doors in my face. I'd really appreciate whatever you can do."

Greg thought about it. "Okay, we're old friends and I guess I owe you a few." He lowered his voice. "Just what do you want to know?" Ron told him.

The next night they met in a Georgetown restaurant. Greg looked like he had aged another ten years. "You should have asked me to butt-fuck the Director. It'd probably be easier. You were right about Lawrence being involved in that mess at Squaw Valley. He was the agent in charge of the operation. But it wasn't his fault that Crane was mistakenly identified as the hitman. Lawrence was down in Sacramento when it happened. The big boys were really pissed off at him, not so much for the incident, but for letting the girl get away. Do you think the professor knows where she is?"

"I don't really know. Wouldn't Lawrence keep tabs on him?"

"He did just that for three years. For a while we kept him under such close surveillance that he couldn't crap without it being recorded, but I don't believe he knows anything."

"Does the Agency still watch him?"

"We do a routine check once in a while."

"You mean the girl's that important?"

"Yeah."

"Greg, could the CIA have ordered his..."

"You mean kill him? No. First of all, we don't go around shooting civilians. Anyway it makes no sense. He's still the best, and really the only, lead to the girl. We still keep hoping that maybe someday he'll take us to her. If Lawrence wanted to 'list' him now he'd only re-open the incident and believe me, that's the last thing he wants.

"What about hiring Vereste?"

"Negative. Ever since the Bay of Pigs we haven't talked to a mobster let alone hired one. It's probably what you said it appeared to be, and attempted gangland execution."

"Do you think I should give up and go home?"

"I do. Look Ron, we've been close for many years. I don't mind telling you that the kinds of questions I had to ask got me some dirty looks. But this shooting's just not the Company's scam. Personally Lawrence is too big for his britches. I don't like him, but he's clean where you're concerned."

The former LAPD officers parted and promised to keep in touch. Agent Albers went directly to his car and made a phone call.

"Did he buy it."

"Yessir," Albers reported. "At least for the time being.

He's a good cop though. If anything else happens he'll be on top of it."

"Keep an eye on him."

"Yessir."

Ron Mabra sank into the soft cushions of the Boeing 727. He watched the lights of the capital give way to the dark countryside as he headed home. Greg's story made sense and he knew he should let well enough be, but it was somehow all too convenient. How did Greg know he was in Washington and where to find him? He distinctly remembered Greg talking to the cashier and the man pointing, before his friend "accidentally" ran into him.

FOUR

Ian McGregor was an odd kind of recluse. The canny Scotsman had been the board chairman of a multinational company for many years. Then, one day in 1960, he surprisingly retired, moved from his Edinburgh flat to America and now spent the better part of his days fishing and sailing. Ian's face was weatherbeaten a deep brown from the sun. His eyes were wrapped in dark wrinkles, a striking contrast to his snow white hair and sparkling blue eyes. He was tall and slender with a wiry frame the envy of men much younger than his seventy-two years. As much at home on the water as on the land, he had at one time been the sole year-round resident of the lake and knew every cove, shelter, shoreline, and where the fish were always biting.

Andy and Ian became friends when the anthropologist moved to the country. As soon as he started dating Leslie, she became the third member of the trio and Ian easily accepted her as he would have his own daughter. They were sitting on Ian's deck, a redwood structure he had personally built. It sat on wooden pilings and extended ten feet over the lake itself.

"Eat up, lass," he told Leslie. "You're a bag of bones, ye need some meat on yer body." He was sharing a brunch of eggs, ham, and mushrooms with his young friends.

She hungrily obliged and dug into the enormous omlet. "Okay Ian, I can take a hint and anyway I couldn't refuse such a culinary masterpiece."

Andy was thinking. This is what we really needed, to get away from it all. He looked at the bright sun's reflections on the blue waters and eagerly anticipated exploring the north end of the lake.

Ian's boat sported a mainsail and a jib. When the March winds blew he would fly a spinnaker and his craft would literally fly across the water. Today the breeze was slight and the pace leisurely. While Leslie sunned by the bow, Ian made fast the rudder to the mainsail and tossed Andy a cold beer.

"Been awfully quiet lad. Want to talk 'bout what's on your mind?"

"Perhaps...later. Right now I just want to enjoy the life of a beachcomber. What made you trade the executive life for the waterfront?"

"Many things, but most of all the crazy pace. I was flyin' all over Europe and most of Asia too, always puttin' together deals, drinkin' and smokin', my life was like that movie, if it's Thursday, This Must Be Paris. When my wife died there was no reason for any of it. We never had the time to have children, so I buried Maureen, picked up my bags and left."

"Ever go back to Edinburgh?"

"Nooo, for the past five years I've not gotten further than Chicago and I don't mind tellin' ya, the trip was hardly worth the time."

"But doesn't it get lonely, Ian?"

"Aye, that it does, yet the solitude's comfortin'. I sit out on the deck drinkin' a brew and remember the old days. I'm at peace with the world and I cherish my memories. Seems most of the folks out there's a lot worse off, always fightin'n' hurtin' each other." He added with a twinkle "And I've got good friends too, yourself and Leslie. Twice a week I take supper with Clara Dinsmore, she's a mite spry for a widder-woman."

Andy envied this old-young man's adjustment to living, and wished he could be as philosophical.

They anchored off Partner's Cove, donned fins, facemasks and snorkels. Andy and Leslie spent a good hour exploring the blue-green expanse of the underwater world. Exhausted but feeling better than ever, they joined

230

Ian for another beer.

He pointed to an outcropping of rocks. "That's where it happened, you know. They said it was an accident but I seen the whole thing."

"What are you talking about" asked Leslie.

He settled back and re-lit his pipe. "T'was before either of you came here, back in '71. Caleb Franklin used to be President of your University. Every summer, he and his family would rent a cottage from ole Matt Dawson. Caleb was a big one for the fish, always wantin' to try out them new lures, used to make 'em himself, he said. Well, it was blowin' a bit and the surface was choppy. I was right about here when I seen him by the rocks. The water's pretty deep at that point and some of the really big fish stay back there. He was wearin his cap n' windbreaker and just sittin' when his boat started to rock. I mean really rock, back and forth, like it was caught in a see-saw."

"Could it have been the wind?"

"Nope. The wind was blowin', sure, but it'd never overturn the boat. Somethin' else was doin' it. Anyway he must 'ave panicked cause he stood up and all of a sudden went over the side, like he was pulled. I saw him struggle in the water and then it got real still. I come over fast as I could but he was floatin' face down. Then I saw it about twenty yards away. It was a black object, size of a man. He must have been wearin' a wet suit with all that underwater gear. I yelled to him, but I don't think he heard me. He just disappeared in the deep."

Andy was listening intently. "Did you call the police?"

"Not right away. I pulled Caleb aboard, but he was drowned. Called the coppers when I got back to the house. They came out 'bout an hour later and wanted to see where it happened but the wind was something fierce by then so we waited till the next day." His pipe had gone out, he strick a match and continued.

"The coppers were nice young men, two of 'em. They listened politely, but they never did anything about it. No one else seen the diver, and they didn't believe this old man's story. The papers called it an accidental drowning, but I know better."

"What would you call it?" inquired Andy.

"Murder, pure and simple. Just beyond the rocks there's an old road, you could drive right up to the lake and no one would ever know. I figure that's what the diver had done. Then he goes into the water real quiet like, swims to Caleb's boat and starts rockin' it. When Caleb stands up, he must've grabbed his foot and once he was in the water, he drowned him. After, he capsizes the boat to make it look like an accident."

"Have you told anyone else your story?"

"Started to tell his wife and kids but changed my mind. They had all the grief they could handle. Anyway, no one's likely to believe a daft old codger like me and I didn't want to waste my time. But my eyes are as good as ever and I know what I've seen."

The wind was really blowing now. Andy and Leslie put on sweaters as they shivered in the dampness of late afternoon, as Ian made for port.

"I know what you're thinking," Leslie said. "Franklin drowns in a mysterious boating accident and guess who becomes the new President. How convenient it all is."

Andy tried to imitate Ian. "You'd be damm sure of it lass, come the mornin' we're going down to the library. I've got more than a wee hankerin' to get at the back issues."

They both laughed, but underlying their merry mood was a darkening cloud of fear. It seemed certain that the people who had put Mansfield in the number one university position were also orchestrating his Senate campaign. If they killed to put him in power once, they would be likely to do it again to keep him there.

They returned home. Ever since the incident in Locust Valley, Leslie had moved in with Andy. There were two letters waiting for them.

"It's from my friend with the USIA in Taiwan. Here,

232

listen to this. 'The next time you ask me for a small favor I'm going to think twice about it. I checked out the address you gave me. It's a Korean restaurant. Nobody ever heard of a man named Sung. But when I got home that evening, two men from the Generalissimo's secret police were waiting for me. They wanted to know why I was asking for a Mr. Sung. First I told them it was none of their business but they were very persuasive, if you know what I mean. So I had to tell them about your inquiry. They wouldn't believe me till I showed them your letter. Seems they've been after your man for quite a while. When you find the time maybe you can tell me what this is all about. Don't write me at the Agency, use my home address.' "

"Looks like we struck a nerve, doesn't it?"

"I'd say so. You remember the conversation I overheard in the village. The prisoner they were talking about was also called Sung. I wonder if it could have been the same man. When Bruce gets back from Afghanistan, I'll have him look into it. And now, my lady of mystery, what's in your letter?"

"I called my ex-husband the other day, asked him to check out Congressman Duane Parsons but that's old hat now. Remember the Korean scandals, and Parsons disappearing in Argentina?"

"It's a bit strange," Andy remarked. "Parsons withdraws from the Senate race for no apparent reason making Mansfield the front runner. The people behind Mansfield must have gotten to Parsons earlier. Mansfield claimed he received an anonymous tip, but they must have supplied him with the evidence. Looks like they screwed Parsons twice. Did the Congressman serve in the Army?"

Leslie looked at the letter. It was typed by Dex's secretary. She noticed the wording; "Dear Dr. Pace", and "respectfully yours". She was surprised he bothered to initial it. "According to this, Parsons was a pilot during the war, he was a reservist called back to active duty. Hey, get this. In the second World War he also served in the Asian theater. His plane was downed and he spent over two weeks with the Chinese."

"When did he go into politics?"

"Right after Korea. He came home a war hero and upset the incumbent in a bid for the State Assembly. Four years later he ran unopposed for the House and he's been in Washington ever since."

Leslie continued reading. "This is interesting. When he was first elected he was against a strong military commitment to Korea, but about five years ago he switched sides and became a hawk. He's been to Korea four times since then, ostensibly to check on their military preparedness."

Andy was thinking. There's the connection, Korea. The three of us were there, but damned if I know what that means. His thoughts were interrupted by the ringing of the telephone. Leslie answered. "It's for you, Andy."

"Dr. Crane, this is President Mansfield. I've recently learned we have a lot in common. I think it's about time we got together. Could you come to my home tomorrow evening for dessert?"

"Can I bring a friend?"

"By all means, please do. We'll be expecting you and Dr. Pace then, about eight-ish."

FIVE

It was a balmy evening, hot and humid. The breeze that had been blowing had ceased causing Andy and Leslie some discomfort as they drove out to the President's home.

"You know we can't prove anything." Leslie was telling him. "Old Caleb Franklin's death was reported as an accidental drowning, and there's not even a hint that it could be anything else."

"You're right. The two officers who conducted the investigation are no longer with the Sheriff's department and even if we could locate them it probably wouldn't help."

"So we're right back where we started." Leslie sounded disappointed.

"Not quite. I have this strange feeling that the President doesn't even know about the 'so-called accident'. Perhaps we can enlighten him."

"Andy, I'm nervous, suppose it's a trap?"

"I don't think so. First of all we can't prove anything, or else we'd have gone to the authorities long before this. He knows that and his own home is hardly the place for...well, a double murder." Leslie shuddered.

"Besides," Andy continued, "from what we've learned Bliss is no killer."

"What about the Sergeant in Korea, he killed him, didn't he?"

"In the heat of battle, yes. Judging from what Fishbein told us, I'm not so sure I wouldn't have done the same thing myself."

"Andy!" she exclaimed, "you wouldn't. You couldn't

kill anyone?" Leslie wasn't so sure anymore; her voice faltered. "Could you?"

He remembered Su-lin and Squaw Valley. "No, I don't think so," he lied.

Fortunately she changed the subject. "I wonder what he's really like? I've never been invited to a President's house before."

"I think you'll find him quite a charming host. I just don't understand him. He's the last person you'd think would be involved in any of this. I want to know more about what kind of man he really is."

"That's why we're going tonight. Isn't it?"

Andy didn't respond to the question. He was puzzled. He knew a confrontation was inevitable but he didn't think it would come so soon. He wished he had been better prepared.

As a university President, Bliss was naturally expected to entertain in his own home. Recognizing this obligation, the Trustees helped subsidize his monthly payments, which on the Mansfield'd two-acre spread came to eight hundred and fifty dollars. Located in the semi-exclusive division of Monroe Terrace, the right to residence being a matter of money rather than creed or color, the house resembled an architect's version of "eclectic excellence."

Sloping beamed ceilings in almost every room gave the 3,500-square-foot structure a distinctively modern appearance, while two antique brick fireplaces dominated the oversized living room and complemented a collection of traditional furniture. A dining alcove enclosed on three sides by glass windows caught the last rays of the early evening and highlighted the stone-fenced flower garden and swimming area.

Mansfield's people had instructed him to meet with Professor Crane. Their purpose was two-fold; to find out how much he really knew and to make it clear to him that they were aware of his moves. It was a calculated risk but, they thought, a necessary one. Bliss readily agreed. It was time to know his adversary, to face the man who was attempting to ruin his life. Bliss, having initialed the call, and in his own home, would have the advantage.

The President greeted his visitors at the door. "Dr. Crane, Dr. Pace, please come in." He was dressed casually in an old workshirt and slacks and looked far less commanding than when he formally presided at univeristy functions.

"Please forgive my appearance, but I've been working in the garden. The evening is the best time to put in new plants." Leslie noticed the dirt under his fingernails. He introduced them to Alexa, an attractive woman with a remarkable figure and a generous smile. They exchanged greetings and went into the dining alcove. The table was set for six.

"If you don't mind, my son and daughter will be joining us. They're always too busy for dinner, but they wouldn't think of missing Alexa's dessert."

Leslie decided the children had excellent taste. The chocolate mousse was deliciously rich and the coffee even better. She kept wondering, how does she keep her figure with food like this. I'd be a blimp in two weeks. Bryan was eighteen, a husky good-looking boy like his father; Freshman at Williams, he was majoring in biology. Erin was a well-tanned, sixteen-year-old having trouble deciding whether to devote her life to "tennis" or "boys."

Were an outsider to watch the four adults and two teenagers, they could mistakenly conclude that they were old and dear friends. The conversation shifted from philosophy, to tennis, to anthropoogy, to politics, and back to philosophy. There was a healthy give and take of opinions, a surprisingly enjoyable arguing over principles and realities, a relaxed conversational atmosphere where, it seemed, sperficialities were quickly discarded.

When the youngsters left, Alexa adroitly suggested a tour of the house and gardens to Leslie. They left together chatting like old school chums.

Bliss poured brandy, and the men adjourned to his study. Andy was impressed. Bliss was knowledgable in many fields and an astute listener. A philosopher, Andy thought. He enjoys verbal dueling just for the challenge. They were alike in many ways. Both had played football in high school, came from a working-class background, struggled through graduate school and, he remembered, served during the Korean War. It's evident that he loves his wife and is very proud of his children too. He imagined they would be what his children could have looked like if Elaine had been able to sustain a pregnancy.

Mansfield was thinking along similar lines, under any other circumstances I'd like to have him as a friend. He appears to be casual but he's a more competent scholar with a wry almost sarcastic sense of humor and one hell of a tennis player. They made a smashing couple; him and Leslie. They reminded him of himself and Alexa when they were courting, no, not quite like Alexa, more like Jocelyn. Why did this man have to be his adversary?

The indirect lighting and soft leather of the study conveyed a false sense of security. It was perhaps an odd place for a battlefield, but appearances are often deceiving and the confrontation had started.

"I think we already know each other too well. Let's drop the formalities. I'd prefer to call you Andy."

"I'd be comfortable with that Bliss."

"You've been looking into my background. My mother told me about your visit; reporters...really! And Leslie spent a good deal of effort digging up my collegiate years." The memories still pained him. "Why?"

"You're an important man Bliss, possibly our next Senator. I've contracted with a magazine to do an in-depth portrait."

"What magazine may I ask?"

"Sorry, I'm not at liberty to say. While we're on the subject of your early days, when were you in Korea?"

"Fifty-one, fifty-two, three, same time you were there Andy, but then you already know that."

"Yes, but you were captured by the Chinese and didn't return for several months."

Bliss was cautious. "A Korean couple hid me in the mountains and then I fought with an ROK unit. I was debriefed by M.I. You were in intelligence yourself, weren't you?"

"I was a corporal stationed down near Taegu. Do you know the area?"

"Might have passed through once or twice."

"Were you ever in the village?"

"Village? Sorry can't say I have. Where are you getting you information from anyway?"

"I have some friends."

Bliss smiled. "Yes?"

"Do you have friends too?"

"Everyone has friends."

"Do your friends help you?"

"How?"

"Like tutoring you in Chinese or getting your book published."

"I don't know what you mean, my book was published by Alden."

"Then I suggest you see the social science editor and a reviewer named Nielsen. Didn't your friends tell you about that?"

Bliss was genuinely puzzled. He didn't know what Crane was talking about. He decided to remain silent, perhaps he would learn more that way. He refilled their glasses.

Andy was becoming braver, he pushed on. "And President Franklin's boating accident," he pronounced it like a question, "didn't they tell you about that either?"

"His boat capsized and he was drowned. Is there more to it?"

"Isn't there?"

Bliss was agitated. "If you've got something to say why don't you go ahead and say it?"

"Caleb Franklin was an experienced fisherman, and a strong swimmer. He was pulled from his boat. The boat 'capsized' only after he was already dead in the water."

"You say he was pulled from his boat? Who pulled him?"

"I was hoping you could tell me."

There was an uncomfortable silence as the two men studied each other. Bliss knew that Andy was baiting him but it didn't seem like he was lying about either the book or the drowning. This man knows a hell of a lot more than I do, he thought. He decided it was time for him to take the offensive.

"What did you hear in my office, Andy, when you 'accidentally' "—he pronounced it with an implied question—"overheard my conversation?"

Andy didn't hesitate. "Your Mandarin is excellent."

"Is that all?"

Andy wasn't about to admit knowing about the coded phrase. He changed the subject. "Where did you learn your Mandarin?"

"I learned it from a Chinese tutor in Chicago."

"I don't think so. You already spoke the language before you met Mr. Sung."

Bliss was shaking inside, but he maintained his composure.

"Did I, where do you think I learned it?"

Andy only appeared to be guessing. "In Korea...or China."

Bliss frowned. "Perhaps..."

The men were silent once again. Andy decided to take a chance.

"I think you're involved, somehow, either directly or indirectly, in the shooting incident. The bullet was meant for me, not Spaacklund. And my unexpected offer from Harvard, that was your doing too." He was not going to

240

tell the President about Leslie's experience.

Bliss replied. "That's nonsense. You really don't know anything about me."

Andy thought carefully about his next statement. "Why? Who's behind your campaign, who's been helping you ever since Korea?"

"Suppose I told you I don't know."

"Then I wouldn't believe you."

The president spoke softly now. "You're in a lot of trouble, Andy Crane, and because she's your girl friend so is Leslie. Why don't you forget it? Go to Hawaii. If you stop now I can promise there won't be any more 'accidents'."

"How did you know I was going to Hawaii?"

For the first time that evening Bliss relaxed. "Because Professor, I approved your grant." He returned to the question. "If you really think I'm involved in some kind of an insidious scheme why don't you go to the police?"

Andy remained silent.

"You don't have any proof, do you?"

Andy tried a bluff but he didn't sound very convincing. "Don't be too sure."

Bliss indicated that the match was over, it was at best a draw. Neither of them had won anything substantial. Bliss was however, extremely agitated. He wanted to believe that his people were not involved in the book or the boating accident but perhaps he was only fooling himself. Now for the first time since 1952 he had some serious questions to consider.

Andy, on the other hand, felt better. He didn't learn anything he hadn't already known or strongly suspected. He was sure he knew more about the book and the drowning than Bliss did. That gave him some satisfaction and maybe a slight advantage. Yet he had revealed what he had known. Perhaps it was too much. Bliss or his people might re-evaluate their strategy and decide that he was expendable after all. He desperately needed allies. He thought about Colonel Bruce Jones and Ed Fishbein, the Trenton attorney.

The intelligence officer was speaking to Major Dabney. "I still don't understand it, Chet. Why was I picked for this assignment?"

"Really, Bruce, you must be putting me on. Everytime we go out like this they always send a 'spook'."

Bruce was astounded. "You think I'm with the CIA?"

"You were added to the team at the last minute. Your orders came over from Langley, compliments of the Deputy Director. I naturally assumed you worked for the Agency."

"Jesus Christ, Chet, I'm Regular Army. I've never even set foot in Langley. What did they tell you about me?"

Major Dabney never had time to answer his question. The MATS flight carrying the team back from Afghanistan ran into unexpected engine trouble further complicated by extreme weather. The pilot sent out a distress signal seconds before the transport crashed in the higher elevations of the rugged, and usually inaccessible Hindu Kush mountains. The wreckage was never found and the Army assumed there was no survivors.

After receiving a phone call, Edward David Fishbein started packing his clothes. At eleven p.m. that Wednesday evening he moved from his furnished bachelor apartment. Christine Bates, his twenty-three year old girl friend didn't know he had planned to leave and sobbed hysterically for two nights. She thought she was pregnant and he had left no forwarding address.

SIX

Born in Chia Shang-wa, the fourth child and second daughter of a poor farmer, she was raised in the village of Heng-shen in Shensi Province, 2,500 feet above sea level on the eroded slopes of the plateau where the ground is not cultivated and where the hills are covered by scrubby brush.

When she was nine years old she was the first girl from her village to strike Lau Jang, the wealthy landlord, with a bamboo cane. The Communists had told her that he was responsible for the death of her baby brother.

She joined the youth brigade, outperforming most of the boys on her production team and proved an eager and diligent student at the new village school. In 1957, at the age of sixteen, being of proper peasant background and politically aware of her responsibility to her country, she entered the Chinese University. Selected by General Kao for special training, she spent four additional years studying English at the University of British Columbia in Vancouver, returning to China in '65 where she attended a select institute for promising party members.

In 1968, the delicate, dark-haired, intense young comrade changed her name to Su-lin and at the age of twenty-seven became the youngest member of the General's "committee".

On July 25, 1970, two months after her mother had been buried, Su-lin received permission to leave the country to visit her brother, a member of the trade delegation to an East African nation. Moments before she was to board her return flight to China she collapsed, suddenly stricken with "appendicitis", and was immediately rushed to a local hospital. Two hours later she had mysteriously vanished.

Leslie was upset. "Darn it! And I really wanted to go to Hawaii." She had just received a hysterical phone call from her mother. Mom was distraught and almost incoherent. "...Oh dear...he collapsed, yes, at the club. He was just playing golf at the club and then...What shall I do?...No, the doctor said he had a stroke...Oh yes, please hurry."

Leslie then called her sister. "Of course I'd come but Malcom's out of town on one of his business trips and the kids have the chicken pox. No dear, they're contagious." Being a dutiful and loving daughter, Leslie made plans to leave for New York immediately.

Andy was disappointed as well. He had looked forward to their vacation in the islands. They both needed the change and the rest. But, he understood. Orphaned in his twenties he, more than most, appreciated the importance of family. It was a time of crisis and Leslie was needed at home. He wouldn't have had it any other way.

His trip to Los Angeles was uneventful. "Can I be of service, sir?"

"Sure, another bourbon."

She smiled at him. "My my, but we do drink a bit, don't we?"

Andy told the flight attendant just what she could do with her broomstick. He was re-reading his presentation for the fourth time. Long suspecting that the assimilation of the Chinese minority into the American mainstream meant the annihilation of the Chinese as a viable cultural group, he challenged the theoretical basis of that assumption. It was a matter of perspective, he thought. Who really gains if the Chinese "melt" into the American dream, the Chinese or the rest of us? Perhaps nobody.

The flight to Oahu was better. He watched *All the*

Presiden'ts Men for the second time. The coverup reminded him of the Korean scandals, but unlike Watergate, which was strictly a domestic affair, Korea had international implications.

Exchanging business cards and chatting aimibly with his seat companion helped to pass the time. Mr. Hakato was saying, "this is my first visit to Pearl Harbor but not the first for my family. My father was a fighter pilot, he was there in 1942."

"How do you feel about your visit?"

"A little uneasy, thank you. I am going to your fiftieth state to help negotiate the purchase of another hotel for my Japanese company. Somehow it doesn't seem right."

Yes, Andy thought, it was ironic. Thirty-five years later the Japanese would buy what they did not win in a devastating war.

"Aloha, Andrew. What a pleasure to see you again, old friend." He shook hands with the program chairman, David Yee and accepted a traditional "lei greeting" from his pretty wife, Ai-li. They drove out towards the University of Hawaii's Manoa campus.

"Was your trip a pleasant one?"

"Perfect David, but I'm a little tired now, where am I staying?"

"We booked you into the Hale Aloha Dormitory where we are housing the conferees. Shall we meet for breakfast in the morning, say about seven?"

The view from the tenth floor was breathtaking. The university spread out beneath him appearing insignificant against the lush green vegetation of the surrounding mountains. Far to the right storm clouds had gathered, contrasting with the clear blue sky above. A rainbow was just beginning to appear and he wished Leslie was with him to share one of nature's most beautiful mysteries.

The Asian Studies On The Pacific Coast Conference

was held at the university's new campus center. Andy's session was particularly lively and informative.

The afternoon session was far less stimulating. Andy left early. He felt removed from it all. The concerns of academe were petty and shallow compared with the drama he was living. He felt like telling David, "excuse me, but I find it difficult to concentrate on Chinese-American identity because I am preoccupied with investigating how and why a university president, about to become a U.S. Senator, is working as an agent of a foreign power, probably the very Chinese we're talking about. He also knows that I suspect him and has attempted to have me killed, resorted to bribery, and terrorized my girl friend." He didn't dare.

His new and precarious life-style was also thrilling, the danger only making it more so. The hunt and the chase kept his adrenalin flowing. It was, he even admitted to himself, more exciting than doing fieldwork in the exotic Far East, his original reason for becoming an anthropologist. His thoughts drifted and he recalled his encounter with the CIA and tried to remember Su-lin.

The cold wind chilled his bones and his fingers almost froze through the thick gloves. It was late November and the snow had come early to the Lake Tahoe resorts. Goggles protected his eyes but minute icicles began to form beneath his nostrils. The wind whipped the falling snow around him and gave his blond hair a white frosting. In the valley far below, the Olympic Village and the new resort, resembled a Christmas card, advertising a winter vacation at a Swiss chalet.

The lifts had just opened and except for the Ski Patrol, he was the first paying customer to ride the chair up to "Kt-22". He raced down the hill, his "comps" flashing red and blue in the morning light. He tried to stay on the edges of his "205's" and use his poles to execute the difficult parallel turns.

He was free, he was alive. His muscles responded to his will as he blended with the trees and joined the arduous terrain. He was one with the earth and the sky, a part of God's universe. Pain became an abstraction. His mind refused to recognize the agony of his own grief, the sobbing of her parents, Elaine's body, stiff and cold in the open casket, and the emptiness of her final resting place in the crowded cemetery. He had shut out the reality of death and the false comfort of a life beyond. His world had been abruptly shattered and he ran to the mountains to escape and to be re-born. He skied until late in the afternoon when the lifts closed.

Bar No. 1 was a favorite watering hole for the Squaw Valley weekend ski crowd. Drinks were cheap, the music loud and the laughter and vivacity infectuous.

"Welcome back, Jean-Claude," the bartender teased Andy. "How's the snow?"

"Icy at the top and cold. How's the bar?" Andy had been a regular customer for almost every day during the past month. He drank and Billy poured, the chemistry of a profitable relationship.

"Remember the big blond from last night." He pointed to the stool she had occupied. "She told me she'd like to get it on with you. Interested?"

"No thanks, Billy, she looked like she wanted to eat me alive." The truth of the matter was that Andy was not yet ready for a sexual encounter with anyone, especially the "ski bunnies" whose body language often suggested quick and easy romance, or something like it. He had also tried alcohol to stimulate forgetting, but paid dearly the next morning. So he was content to sit at the bar and watch the perpetual apres-ski antics of the windburned, effervescent young people. He was grateful to the noisy mob for helping him not to remember. They acted like a sedative and prolonged the hours until he returned to a lonely room.

Friday night was a madhouse. The weekend skiers

were just getting started celebrating when he first noticed her. Petite, slim, almost to the point of being skinny, her long dark hair fell way past her shoulders. High cheekbones complemented her delicate features. She walked with the grace and assurance of an athlete, yet her eyes were sad. Her escort seemed out of place among the fun-lovers. He chainsmoked and nervously looked about the room as if he was expecting someone.

Andy had never seen a more alluring woman in all his life, and continued to stare at her. He knew it was rude but he couldn't help himself. Waiting until the man had left, he gathered up his drink making his way towards her table. He really didn't know what he was going to say when he noticed the jade watch on her wrist.

"Shemma shrhoula?"

She glanced at the Chinese timepiece and replied. "Cha budwo jyou dyan."

"Syesye."

"Bu sye."

And then she smiled, her pearl white teeth accenting a golden face. "Do your really speak Mandarin?"

"Some."

They exchanged a few phrases and she was pleased that his tones were good, that is, for a Caucasian. "What is your name?"

"I'm Andy Crane, what's yours?"

She hesitated. "You may call me Su-lin. Have you been to China, Andy?" She pronounced his name Ann-dee.

"To Taiwan and Hong Kong."

"What do you do?"

"I used to be a professor."

"Oh? And now?"

He looked down at the table. "I ski."

She accepted his answer. "Why did you speak to me?"

"Because you are very beautiful."

"No. I have been looking at all the American girls. They are much prettier."

What a strange girl, Andy thought. Their eyes met and told him that she was very lonely. Then she broke contact as if she were suddenly afraid. "If I am beautiful, why are you the first man who has spoken to me?"

"Your...," he searced for the right word, " 'friend', doesn't look like he appreciates competition."

"Yes, he would not. I am not so sure he is my friend either."

Andy couldn't figure out what that meant. Did he have a chance now? "Can you sit with me?" He leaned towards her.

Her face paled and she moved quickly away from him. "No!" Her eyes glanced nervously at the door. "Do you ski Siberia?" she asked.

"Yes."

"Tomorrow, when the lift's open. He will be there with me. Don't speak, just follow."

Stan Burris, the agent in charge of protecting Su-lin, which he interpreted as keeping everybody at arms length, saw her talking to the tanned blond skier. Oh well, he thought, she's not exactly a prisoner, but he was wary just the same. He had exaggerated his skiing abilities to obtain he assignment, and wasn't about to complicate his job. He was visibly relieved when Andy walked away.

The sun shone brightly on the fresh powder as the early morning buffs waited for the gondola. Andy searched the crowd and easily recognized Su-lin. She was wearing a blue down parka with red piping and yellow sportcaster pants which fit over her boots, indicative of the new styles. He was excited, and for the first time in long while a warm feeling spread over his body. Jesus, he thought, I'm going to have an erection.

If Su-lin recognized Andy she didn't show it and continued to talk to her friend who was having some trouble with his rented boots. Andy stayed two chairs behind them as they rode towards the summit. "Siberia" was less difficult than "KT-22", but was definitely not for beginners.

For a moment she poised at the top of the run, then she dug in her poles and was flying over the white mountain. Her companion tried to follow but he couldn't keep up with her. His skis went out from under him as he sprawled spread-eagled on the new snow. The safety strap must have broken because one of his ski's continued the descent alone.

Andy lunged forward and was soon skiing besides his mysterious friend. My God but she's good, he thought, as he struggled to keep up with her.

"Can we ski anothe run where he can't find us?"

"Sure, com'on."

They took the chair back up to the summit but traversed across the ridge to "Shirley Lake".

"Ann-dee, you are a very fine skier."

"No, not really, you're the expert. Did you ski in China?"

Su-lin was cautious. "How do you know I come from China?"

"I didn't, I took a guess. Perhaps it's your accent." He grinned and started to laugh.

She didn't think it was funny. "I went to school in Vancouver, that's where I learned to ski."

"What did you study?"

"English, of course." It was her turn to smile.

"Why are you afraid of your 'friend'?"

She looked over her shoulder, they were alone. "I'm not afraid of him. I just don't trust him, that's all. But he is going to help me."

"Help you with what?"

"You ask too many questions. Come on, I'll race you to the meadow."

She disappeared in a flurry of white powder as he followed. They didn't see the outcropping of rock ahead. Su-lin lost control and landed on her back beside him. They both lay in the snow oblivious to all around and were laughing hysterically. He ran his fingers through her hair and kissed her lightly on the lips. Slowly, almost reluctantly she started to respond. They were two lonely people who had found each other, and for a few brief moments were no longer afraid.

Later they lay on the bed and watched the snow continue to fall. Su-lin was both nervous but pleasantly excited as he played with the zipper on her pants. She had made love only once with the Canadian boy, but he was just as inexperienced and had hurt her. This handsome blond American on the other hand was strong yet gentle. She liked the way his fingers stroked her body.

"Are my breasts too small for you? I know the American girls are very large?"

"Your breasts are beautiful, small and delicate like the rest of your body." Rubbing his palms over them, her pink nipples stiffened.

"Would you like to kiss them?"

He answered by drawing them into his mouth. As her body became more sensitive he reached between her legs and she gasped with a hurried excitement. Her breathing was shallow.

"Ann-dee you are so big, don't hurt me."

She guided him to her opening and he carefully penetrated her lips. When he was seated inside her they began to move. Slowly at first and then faster. They could no longer control themselves and she shrieked as he came deep inside. The second time was better, more relaxed and with only a gentle urgency. Later they talked, or rather Andy did. She listened.

When Burris returned to the Lodge he found them in the restaurant drinking hot chocolate.

"Where the hell have you been, I've been searching all day?" He was very angry.

"She couldn't find you so I kept her company."

Burris recognized him as the skier from last night. And

251

when Su-lin spoke to him rapidly in Chinese, Burris didn't like it one bit. He was becoming increasingly suspicious, but said nothing. The CIA man left with her and they returned to their rooms.

Andy motioned to the waitress. "Make it a bourbon straight this time." He sat there and wondered what it was all about. It was obvious that Su-lin and this man were not lovers. They didn't even sound like friends. Why were they together? What was he going to help her with? Although he had told her almost everything about himself she had said relatively little, but it didn't really matter, all he knew was that he had to see her again.

Wu Ming-yin had been living in Hong Kong for the past three months. He was a muscular young man who trained daily in the martial arts. His English was good and he was an accomplished skier. He was also an intelligence officer in the Red Army.

Twice he walked past the building, and when he was sure no one was following, he left the streets of the Wanchai district and entered the hallway. General Kao, now dressed in a white shirt and dark blue business suit dismissed the prostitute and spoke to him.

"You are returning to America Comrade Wu. The girl has been located. She is being watched by her enemies at the ski resort in Squaw Valley. You will try to bring her back. If you cannot, you will eliminate her."

"Yes, Comrade General."

"We have prepared a kit for you." He removed a small plastic case from his jacket and opened it. "This is the needle. It is filled with a substance that kills instantly. Everyone will think she died of a heart attack. We prefer that you use it."

Wu nodded. The intelligence officer left for Tokyo and then boarded a Northwest Orient flight to San Francisco. His passport identified him as Mark Wu, a Hong Kong exporter.

The General did not tell him that Su-lin was a member of the "Committee" or that her disappearance was a matter even more important than the national security of the People's Republic. If Wu were apprehended, he thought, the American CIA would torture him and he thought it best if the man knew nothing.

Agent Burris had Andy checked out with his superiors in Langeley. They confirmed Andy's ID, but he was far from satisfied. It was obvious that he had spent the entire afternoon with the girl, and that she more than liked him. The fact that he apparently understood Chinese was more disturbing. Perhaps it was only a coincidence, but then again perhaps not. He had been warned about the possibility of an assassin and Crane thus far fit the bill. Stanley Burris had long ago learned to rely upon his instincts. They told him to watch out for the anthropologist.

Wu watched them for several days trying to follow their routines and understand their patterns. He remembered his last assignment. Get to know your victim, step inside her body and learn to think with her mind. He enjoyed the excitement of his trade. Removing an enemy of the people allowed him not to think of it as killing. I must get to the girl when she is alone he thought, yet the man watching her will be a problem. The best time is when they have finished skiing. She goes alone to her room to rest before dinner and always takes a shower.

He quietly but efficiently opened the lock. The shower was running and helped to mask the noise. Moving rapidly to the small bathroom, she wasn't even aware that he was there until he ripped the shower curtain away.

"Aieeii, what are you..."

He hit her expertly on the throat causing her to gag. Covering her mouth he spoke. "If you try to say anything I will strangle you. Now get out and put on your clothes."

Su-lin knew what this man was. She also knew he

253

would not hesitate to kill her, even if it meant forfeiting his own life. I must wait for an opportunity and meanwhile do as he says. She took note of the small needle taped to his palm, it was instant death. She dressed hurriedly, always watching him.

Burris barely heard the door open but he recognized the telltale click. He pressed against the wall and listened. The sounds of her dressing told him she was still alive. When the intruder tried to take her out of the room, he assumed that was his objective, he would make his move. He removed his shoes so as not to make any noise and waited patiently in the hallway just behind the door.

"We are going to walk out of the Lodge. You will put your arm around me and we will laugh and talk. The Americans do it all the time. They will think we are lovers."

No sooner had they opened the door when Burris swung his pistol butt at the Chinese agent's head. Wu released the girl and turned just in time to parry the blow with his forearm. Burris kicked him in the groin. The pain was unbearable. He screamed and lunged forward. The needle penetrated the operative's muscle. For an instant he was on fire. Then the poison spread and he felt no pain. His last thoughts were of his four-year-old daughter. She was crying because she had fallen from her red tricycle. He held her in his arms and made it all better.

Su-lin's screams had attracted attention. Doors opened in the hall as she ran for her life. She was breathing so hard she could hardly speak.

"Andy, Andy, please let me in," she cried as she banged on his door.

"Oh, please hold me." She clung to him and buried her head in his chest sobbing hysterically. "Stay with me. Promise. Please promise me you won't ever let me go."

Stanley Burris' death was attributed to a sudden heart attack. Only Special Agent in Charge Lawrence, and Su-lin knew better. Andy could sense she wasn't telling him the truth, but she seemed so helpless and when he tried to question her she would cry. Of course, Su-lin was far from helpless, but she was tired and frightened and tried not to think about the future. She knew there would be another attempt.

Lawrence was furious. His man had been wasted. The girl was still under surveillance but she never left the anthropologist's side. He also suspected that Andy was responsible for the agent's murder but he had to be sure. He dispatched another man to do just that.

It was a windswept and blustery day. Heavy snows fell and made skiing almost impossible. Andy and Su-lin sat and warmed themselves by the fire. She was leaning against his shoulder.

"Will you go back to the university Ann-dee?"

"I suppose so."

"You will be happy there. It is a good place for a loving and sensitive man." She kissed him.

"And what will you do?"

She was apparently in good spirits. "I don't know, I have a lot to think about. When I decide I will let you know, unless of course, you marry an American with enormous breasts."

"I wish for once you would be honest with me." But when she didn't respond he changed the subject.

"Come with me."

"Will you love me?" She was going to cry again.

"Always." It was too late, tears ran down her cheeks.

"Can I please have a handkerchief?"

Perhaps the gods were on their side or it just could have been an accident. Wu Ming-yin didn't see the car as he was walking back from the diner. He lay on the road thirty minutes before the ambulance could reach him because of the heavy snows. By the time he had fully recovered it was too late.

The next day, Andy and Su-lin's romance was also shattered. He had returned to his room earlier than usual. He wasn't feeling well and Su-lin wanted to continue skiing. It was the first time she had left his side since that frightful afternoon. Andy did not know it then but it would be the last time he would see her.

"What the hell are you doing in my room!" The man had just emptied the desk drawer and was starting on his suitcase. The agent, thinking that Andy might be Burris's killer, overreacted. He drew his revolver.

"Just stand where you are, freeze. Put your hands in back of your neck, if you move them I'll kill you."

Andy did as he was instructed. The man searched for a weapon, and when he was satisfied he commanded him.

"Lie down on the floor, spreadeagle." The man reached in his pocket and withdrew his wallet. When he was through, he threw it on the floor.

"Shit, not a fucking thing, I ought to kill you anyway you fucking son-of-a-bitch." He raised the gun, steadied it, pointing the weapon at Andy's head and seriously considered pulling the trigger when he heard a knock on the door. The man turned around and that was all the time Andy needed. He was on his knees and remembering his football drills hurled himself at the stranger sending both of them crashing to the floor.

"You fucking Commie," he yelled and went for Andy's eyes.

He wasn't sure just how it happened but Andy had the pistol in his hands. The gun exploded with a deafening roar and the man lay on the floor, the gaping hole in his chest was covered with blood that was slowly spreading, making a circular pattern on his sweater.

Andy screamed. "Get the police and a doctor, a man's been shot!"

At first the local authorities were suspicious, burglars at ski resorts are rarely armed. But the men from Virginia can be extremely persuasive, keeping Andy up for two nights and asking him, over and over again, about the dead man, Su-lin, and her chain-smoking companion. When they had no further questions they told him he was free to go.

Andy was worried. He knew he had accidentally shot and killed a CIA agent. The fact that it was self-defense gave him little comfort. But to charge him with the killing would mean that they were going to have to admit that their man was searching his room, and that would lead to more questions about Su-lin and her dead friend who was not really a friend. Somehow they were all related. But how? The CIA wouldn't tell him anything. Su-lin was the key. Who was she really and where had she gone.

The girl who knocked at the door, Andy was sure she had saved his life, had brought him a note from his Chinese friend. It was a brief three lines, hastily scribbled, almost as an afterthought, on a paper napkin. "It is because I love you that I must go. Do not try to find me. Su-lin." He tried anyway. She had taken a taxi to the airport and boarded a shuttle flight to San Francisco, but her trail ended there.

The next year Andy accepted a position at the university and the enchanting Su-lin, became just another bittersweet memory.

He heard his name being called. "Andy, where have you been. I've been looking for you everywhere?" exclaimed David. "We have an invitation for dinner at Spaulding House. Come on, we're already late."

SEVEN

His hair had been prematurely gray since his early twenties. Now at sixty-two, it blended nicely with the gaunt, almost emaciated frame of the towering green-eyed priest. Father Patrick Larkin sank to his knees as he bowed his head and prayed aloud to the Lord he had faithfully served for more than four decades.

President Chung Hee Park had declared him an "undesirable visitor, and had demanded his deportation. He was given one week to clean up his affairs. It was now three weeks later, and he still hadn't left.

Father Larkin had served mass that morning and was taking his ritual evening walk down by the river. Preoccupied with his thoughts he failed to notice the three young Koreans who followed him. Their knives were sharp and they did their work so well that he felt only the first thrust before he lost consciousness.

The brutal slaying of the American priest made the front-page headlines in half-a-dozen European capitals, and in every major American paper. His service to the Korean War orphans had been internationally recognized and praised for what it was, one man's prodigious if not fanatical efforts to bring love and living to the forgotten children of that war-torn East Asian penninsula.

The CIA Deputy Director was uncharacteristically nervous. "No sir, to the best of my knowledge the priest's murder has no connection to the congressional payoffs."

The man behind the desk in the Oval Office wasn't smiling. "What happened?"

"Well, Sir, we think two of the men who allegedly

stabbed Larkin were South Korean Rangers. We don't know who the third man was."

"You 'think', what does that mean?"

"We have no proof, at least not yet. Our informant is a highly-placed official, he's never been wrong before."

"Could Park have ordered Father Larkin's death?"

"It's very possible, sir. The priest's refusal to leave the country put him in on the spot. He's a politican. Saving face would be very important."

" 'You think', 'allegedly stabbed', 'it's possible', just what *do* you know?" The commander-in-chief made no effort to conceal his growing anger.

Lawrence started to sweat. "We're doing all we can, but Korea's a difficult place to pin down facts. It's a repressive society with secret police everywhere. The people are afraid to say anything. If you ask me sir, I'd like to get our men out and shut it down."

"And our military commitment?"

Lawrence knew he had overstepped his bounds and backed down. "That's not my province Sir."

The newspapers however were less cautious in their evaluation. The headlines screamed, S. KOREAN DICTATOR LINKED TO DEATH OF AMERICAN PRIEST, LARKIN MURDERED BY KOREANS FOR REFUSAL TO LEAVE COUNTRY, PRIEST KILLED WHILE U.S. MILITARY STANDS BY." And beneath the twelve point banners, articles and editorials reviewed and argued the American military presence in Korea.

Master/Sergeant Gerald Lacy, a twenty-five-year Marine Corps Veteran and winner of the Congressional Medal of Honor, refused to recognize his orders to Korea and announced his retirement.

Reverend Moon claimed his Unification Church's mansion in upstate New York had been firebombed. The State Police took their time with the investigation.

Theodore Kim, a Korean exchange student was beaten

in broad daylight as he crossed the USC campus on the way to his organic chemistry seminar.

In Des Moines, Iowa, vandals smashed the two rear windows of Mr. Lee's hardward store and wrote in block letters on the front of his door, "Koreans Go Home."

General Jason Carterett, chief of U.S. forces in Korea, fearful of reprisals, restricted all personnel under his command to military installations and declared Korean villages "off limits" to his troops.

The Pope made an unexpected appearance in St. Peter's Square and publicly condemned those responsible for Father Larkin's brutal slaying.

It was a hotly-debated diplomatic maneuver but finally Roland Stephenson, the United States Ambassador to South Korea was recalled to Washington.

Phase two had been a success. The long wait was almost over.

EIGHT

Midway between Ala Moana, the world's largest shopping center and Waikiki Beach, the Ilikai hotel-resort rises thirty stories to touch the white-tinted, blue skies of the Hawaiian Isles.

The conference was officially over. David, Andy and Ai-li celebrated with a gourmet feast at the "Top of the I". They were in exceptionally good spirits and had just finished a second bottle of Chateau Madeleine when the waiter approached Andy.

"The champagne is for you and your guests sir, compliments of Mr. Hakata." He started to pour the Cordon Rouge.

"Tell Mr. Hakata we graciously accept his gift and would be delighted to have him join us."

"Well, well Andrew, I didn't know you had such generous friends in Honolulu."

"Actually David, I don't. Mr. Hakata was my seat companion on the flight over. I'm just as surprised as you are."

"Shhh you two, the gentleman is coming over here."

"Dr. Crane, so nice of you to invite me. I abhor drinking alone."

Andy introduced him to his two friends and watched with interest as the Japanese businessman and the Chinese Director carefully executed almost imperceptible bows of their heads as they tried to establish their respective social positions.

The evening stretched past eleven. David and Iwao Hakata eagerly discussed Japanese investments abroad and Ai-li listened politely to Andy's amusing anecdotes of her husband's graduate days at Cornell. She was more interested however, in Leslie.

"Do you miss her very much Andrew?"

"Yes, she's a special person. I spoke to her earlier this evening. Her father's coming home from the hospital tomorrow."

"In a way I envy her; she's a professor too?"

"Yes, we both teach at the same university."

"Will you have children when you marry?" Ai-lin amazed herself. I must be changing, she thought. A year ago I never would have asked such a personal question.

"I don't think so. She's thrity-five and besides we haven't decided to get married."

Ai-li blushed.

Mr. Hakata was asking Andy. "Do you plan to stay long in Hawaii?"

"I don't know, perhaps a few more days."

"If you would do me another honor, please by my guest at the hotel."

"Is this one of your...I mean your company's acquisitions?"

Mr. Hakata merely smiled.

"How may I repay your kindness?"

"No, no. Consider it a gift, a gift from my father. I am interested in Chinese art and if you could find the time to accompany me, I understand your Chinese is excellent."

Andy extended his right hand. "Consider it done."

"Then the day after tomorrow, I will ring you at ten."

Andy smiled. Both men had been able to save face and repay their unstated obligations.

Waikiki Beach is a strip of sand that fronts the blue-green Pacific. The available space for each tourist has been estimated at two square feet per body by one of the more knowledgeable locals. Needless to say it is packed with visitors from almost every corner of the globe who seemingly ignore the increasing numbe of new hotels that obscure the view of Diamond Head, an extinct volcano that juts into the water.

Brown, muscular, Hawaiian "beach boys" offer outrigger canoe rides and rent folding chairs and tatami mats to sunworshippers. Hotel swimming pools abound for the more timid who fear the sand and the salt.

Andy enjoyed walking by the shore trying to picture the island before haoles came. The water stretched far beyond the endless horizon making the island itself appear insignificant. Billowing clouds started to gather in the distance and again emphasized the vast expanse of ocean. Around eleven he played one set of singles on the Ilikai's private courts, took lunch by the pool and let the sun and the sea caress his tired body. His reverie was occassionally and pleasantly disturbed by the bikini clad beauties who made the beach their second home. Almost asleep, he listened to the sounds of the surf breaking. Thoughts of Leslie gave rise to images of Su-lin as he closed his eyes.

When Iwao Hakata rang, Andy had just finished dressing. His blue and white flowered "Aloha shirt", worn outside white pants contrasted with a very dark tan. If it wasn't for his blond hair he could almost pass for a "Kamaaina', an oldtimer.

Mr. Hakata's interests gravitated to expensive Chinese silk screens. Andy's presence was hardly necessary; Hakata was a learned art connoisseur and the gallery staffs all spoke English. He suspected that he was invited so that he need not feel too guilty about his complimentary room. They lunched at a Chinatown restaurant where his language abilities were finally appreciated.

Mr. Hakata was strangely silent throughout the meal. He had been out to tour the U.S.S. Arizona Memorial in Honolulu Harbor. No doubt the visit included not too pleasant thoughts of a time long ago.

Trade winds were gently blowing as they left the

restaurant when Andy suddenly stopped. She was coming out of a shop across the street. Levis accentuated her still slim figure. Her hair was cut short and perhaps she looked a trifle older, but there was no mistaking the eyes. He was about to call out when he remembered the circumstances that prompted her to disappear. For a moment it seemed as if she recognized him. He hesitated just long enough for her to vanish into the crowd.

That afternoon Andy returned to Chinatown alone and went directly to the store she had left. It was a specialty shop and most likely had a regular clientele. He had rehearsed his lines carefully but now that the time had come, was afraid.

"Good afternoon, sir." The young Chinese girl gave him her full attention.

"Excuse me, but my girlfriend was in this morning and she must have picked up the wrong package. This isn't her's." He produced an item he had just purchased, hoping it was enough like the shop's merchandise.

"I'm awfully sorry, sir. One of our customers must have picked it up by mistake."

This was his chance. "I noticed a lady. She was wearing blue jeans and a halter top, slim with short black hair. She was carrying a similar bag."

The girl appeared puzzled. "I'm afraid I don't remember her." She thought about it. "Oh, you must mean Mrs. Chen."

It was now or never. "Perhaps you could call her, please."

The girl considered his suggestion. Andy watched and memorized the number she dialed.

"I'm sorry, there's no answer. Would you like to wait a while and we could try later, I'm off work at four." She was flirting with him but he declined the offer. "No thanks, I can stop by tomorrow." She escorted him to the door.

The phone rang three times before she answered. It had been more than six years, what could he say.

"Yes."

"Shemma shrhoula." Would she remember.

"I thought it was you, but I couldn't be sure. Don't say anything." She gave him an address in Makiki Heights. "In two hours."

At six-thirty he knocked on the door. It opened slightly and she released the chain. Removing his shoes, he stepped inside. She was wearing a rose-tinted mumu, a long Hawaiian robe which hid her figure. He just stood there and stared at her, she was the same Su-lin he had remembered. She looked up at him. There were tears in her eyes. Su-lin and Andy were suspended in time, each reliving their own private memories. It seemed like hours but it was only a moment before he spoke.

"*Mrs.* Chen?"

Her eyes sparkled. "Yes. My husband is away. Are you married too?"

"No. But I have a girlfriend, in New York."

The tension between them was gone. "Please sit down Andy. We must...how do you say it, catch up on old times."

They sipped a chilled white wine and tried to pretend they were only long lost friends having a private reunion.

"Why did you disappear?"

"I had to. I was afraid if I stayed you would become involved. It wouldn't have been right."

"It's been over six years, do we still have to talk in riddles?"

"I think it's best for both of us."

"*No.* Not for me. When I returned to my room a man was searching my luggage. He had a gun and I'm sure he blamed me for your friend's death, the man who had the 'heart attack'. He was going to even the score, when we struggled for his gun, it accidentally went off, but the CIA thought I deliberately killed him."

"Oh my God." She started to cry.

"Su-lin, Mrs. Chen, whoever you really are, I have a right to know what this is all about."

She stopped crying and dried her eyes. She was no longer a frightened woman. Her voice was calm and decisive. "All right Andy, perhaps I owe you an explanation. I was born and educated in the People's Republic of China. I believed in the new order and worked for my country for quite some time. Everything went wrong. We had only replaced one despot with another, but I stayed hoping things would get better. They didn't. When my mother died there was no longer a reason to remain. I received permission to visit my brother in an East African country. He helped me to defect and later I learned they had him killed. The CIA arranged my escape. They were going to give me a new identity. Squaw Valley was supposed to be safe."

"The man who chain-smoked, he was protecting you?"

"Yes."

"How did he really die?"

"The Chinese sent a man to take me back, but the agent surprised him and was killed."

Andy looked puzzled.

"He used an injection to make it appear like a heart attack. I knew he would try again. That's why I had to leave you."

"Where did you go?"

"To San Francisco, some people hid me and later I came to Hawaii."

"Su-lin, why would the CIA help you to escape? What were you doing in China?"

She became tense. "I'm sorry but I can't tell you that."

He knew she wouldn't say anymore, the subject was closed. He didn't really know why he said it but the words came out anyhow. "Chun swei dzu jyu ren."

She was pouring the wine when her glass hit the floor sending broken slivers everywhere. From the folds of her robe she removed a small revolver. Holding it in both hands she aimed at his chest. "What did you say?"

He didn't believe it, but he repeated the words. "Chun swei dzu jyu ren."

"Sit down," she commanded him. "Where did you hear those words?"

He told her, starting with the telephone conversation in Mansfield's office. She listened attentively, but didn't seem surprised.

"Did anyone follow you here?"

"No."

"Are you sure?"

"Ever since they shot at me, I've been careful."

"I hope so, for your sake and mine." She lowered the gun but her finger remained on the trigger.

"Listen to me, Andy Crane. Listen to me well and then forget everything I have said. When the Korean War started, the Chinese knew the North Koreans couldn't win, so they had to help them. You must remember what it was like then. Korea seemed to be dominated by foreign powers, especially the Americans. It was also a strategic peninsula, the gateway to Japan and to China. Of course this was all before Vietnam and Cambodia and that makes it perhaps even more important now.

"An influential man, a General Kao, foresaw the way the war would end but he was determined to win it. He envisioned a plan, a long range one. We were enjoying some success in our POW camps getting American prisoners to collaborate and convincing a few to become 'turncoats'."

"Yes, I know, you even sent some soldiers back as enemy agents."

Su-lin was impressed. She continued. "The General arranged for a special camp in the mountains. Its location was only known to a few officials. All told the camp held only six prisoners and never more than one at a time. They were all bright young men, potential leaders already disenchanted with American life. Somehow it was possible to convince them to act on behalf of the General and the PRC. We trained them as 'sleepers'. They returned to the United States and went undercover. They all worked hard to achieve responsible positions and we helped them to attain their goals. When the time came, they would receive instructions."

Andy was becoming nervous, although the evening was cool he started to sweat. He thought carefully before he asked the question.

"What time?"

"I don't know. The General had a schedule worked out but he wouldn't tell us. I think he was planning in terms of twenty or thirty years."

"But why so long?"

Su-lin smiled. "Andy, for the Chinese twenty years is not so long. We are extremely patient people."

"What happened to the six men?"

"One died." She saw the look on his face. "No, it was not planned, he died of cancer."

"And the other five?"

"Carrying out their instructions."

He was almost afraid to ask the next question. "Who are they?"

"Twelve people were originally assigned to the 'committee'. I was chosen in 1968. We were to coordinate and oversee the General's plans. Each person and a back-up were responsible for one man only. Except for our man we never knew their real names, only their codes."

"Chun swei dzu jyu ren?"

"Yes, your university President was my assignment."

"The other codes?"

"Apple-blossom, quiet turtle, beautiful flower and wise uncle. I don't know their identities but they are important people now. I think one of them works for the CIA. You see, the Agency was supposed to be protecting me, but when I was almost kidnapped at Squaw Valley I suspected they must have had an informer in their organization, possibly one of the five. I couldn't trust them any longer."

Andy was stunned. He had been focusing exclusively on Mansfield, not even beginning to imagine the scope of the conspiracy. If Su-lin was telling the truth, and he had no reason to doubt her, the President was merely one piece, a rook perhaps on a chessboard with an unbelievable game plan. Andy let the words sink in. They made sense. If he was allowed to continue to investigate Mansfield he might discover the link to the rest of them. They couldn't permit that.

"How do the men contact each other?"

"They don't. Except for the man in intelligence, the others are unaware that other agents even exist. They think they are acting alone."

"Do they understand what is expected of them?"

"Andy, I just don't know. Seven years ago Korea was still the ultimate objective, but things have changed since then. New leaders have taken over."

Andy thought for a moment. "I know Mansfield pretty well. I can even understand converting him back in '51. But more than two-and-a-half decades have passed. What if he or any of the others changed their minds?"

"We considered that possibility too. Remember, Mansfield killed his Sergeant. He also aided in the escape of a Chinese prisoner. Recall the conversation you overheard in the village. We have documented evidence and tape recordings as well. It would be easy to ruin their careers and if necessary...well, to have them killed."

She put the gun down. "Andy, sometimes I think you really don't understand your own people. Your President Mansfield has had more than his share of success and power all these years. Soon he's going to be a Senator. Do you think he's going to throw it all away? Let me tell you something about these men, they are very realistic and," she added "very dangerous."

"But you're asking them to betray their country?"

Su-lin just shrugged her shoulders. "That's no longer the question, they already have. Do you believe most Americans care what happens to Korea or the Koreans? Have you learned nothing from Vietnam? Will your Congress support a war to save a ruthless dictator like Park, a man who most likely ordered the death of an American priest?"

She's right, he thought. Most Americans couldn't care less. If I weren't so involved would I feel any differently? He returned to thinking about Mansfield.

"Mansfield has to have local contacts. How is that arranged?"

"There's a number he can call in Washington, a Barclay's Answering Service. Any messages are then relayed to the proper persons. There is also another number but it is only for the most dire emergencies."

"Suppose your people wanted to contact him?"

"Nothing unusual, special delivery, an innocent-sounding phone call. They'd use his code."

"You said one of the men is involved in U.S. intelligence work?"

"I think so. He apparently knows who the others are, but his identity is closely guarded. I once overheard the General talking about him. He's in a very sensitive position."

Andy knew he had to ask although he already suspected the answer. "Su-lin, will you help me?"

"I cannot. I tried that once and two people were killed because of it and they almost murdered you. I have a new life here, Andy. My husband knows nothing about my past." She looked tired. "I already betrayed my country once. What will you do?"

"I really don't have a choice, do I?" He thought of Leslie and of their future. "Su-lin, tell me everything you remember about the sleeping giant and the General."

They drank dark coffee and talked till three in the

The phone rang. "Yes." It was an anxious voice.
"We have found the girl."
"Excellent." He breathed a sigh of relief.
"Do we remove her...yes...and the American?"
"It must appear to be an accident."
"I understand."

NINE

Neither Andy nor Su-lin slept well. Their meeting had been unexpected and their conversation unsettling. They were acting in a drama in which they had started by playing bit parts, only to find that they had become the central characters. Having resolved nothing, they made plans to see each other again in the delightful sea cove at Koko Head Park.

Spreading a blanket on the white sand Andy scanned the horizon. "Which way is east?"

"Oh, Andy, those are mainland terms. In Hawaii we speak of 'Mauka', towards the mountains, and 'Makai', towards the sea."

The sun was bright and the sky, clear. They sat on the beach feeling the welcome warmth of a new day. The sinister conspiracy of last night not quite forgotten.

He changed the subject. "What would your husband say if he knew you were spending the day with a man who used to be your lover?"

She laughed. "I really don't know. Perhaps I'll ask him when he returns. And your girl friend?"

"I'm sure she would understand, and also be furious. Leslie's very possessive when it comes to those things."

"Before we start getting any ideas, why don't we cool off our rising passions." She was teasing him.

They ran hand-in-hand, into the beautiful waters of the bay.

"Su-lin, this is fantastic, there are fish all over the place."

They dove beneath the surface and tried to catch the multi-colored swimmers who easily eluded their grasp.

He had an idea.

"Do you scuba dive?"

"Why, yes."

"Can we rent equipment?"

"I know a dive shop."

Andy had not dived in over six years. The first sounds he heard were the incredible noises of his own breathing greatly amplified in the ocean depths. He tapped on his tank and listened to the resounding echoes. Schools of multi-colored swimmers passed him on the way to some unknown rendevous. He reached out to them and found that he could almost touch their slippery forms. Unlike snorkeling, a scuba diver has a good sense of distance.

Su-lin swam with the grace of a mermaid, moving in slow motion as she exploded the circular rock formations. She felt secure in touching the compact hardness of the rough coral.

They had been temporarily transplanted to another world, one of an eerie beauty that often defied description. They held hands and lay on the bottom, letting the tide rock them back and forth as they relaxed and chose to ignore the realities of the human domain.

Andy tapped her and pointed at a crevice in the formation. The creature was lying perfectly still, his thick five feet length mostly hidden, except for the head and the mouthful of razor sharp teeth. They moved away from the moray eel.

As they journeyed further out into the Pacific, they greeted a more varied assortment of neptune's creations, a school of small round fish with delicate butterfly wings, larger, beady-eyed, sharp-nosed predators, multi-banded angels, and there, beyond the coral, two ominous shadows. Andy tensed, sensing they were sharks, and the fears of a thousand ancestors made him involuntarily shudder. The dark shapes came closer and if it wasn't for his mouthpiece he would have sighed in relief. They were only divers.

He turned to tell Su-lin. She was choking, both hands were clutching her neck, the international signal that she wasn't getting any air. Dammit, why doesn't she do something? It seemed like an eternity before she reached back and then he saw the third diver. He had turned off her regulator valve and was holding her down. He swiftly moved towards her but the two divers were upon him cutting off his own air supply. He remembered instructions he had learned long ago. His right hand grasped the rubber handled knife. Jerking it out of the protective sheath he stabbed at the arm around his neck and watched the blood mix with the water. He was free for the moment but he wasn't getting any oxygen. He released the buckles and blowing bubbles to compensate for the lack of air started to rise rapidly. He wasn't fast enough. The second diver was holding onto his legs trying to drag him down. With a surprising burst of energy Andy lashed out causing him to lose his grip, then gasping for breath, he broke through to the surface.

It was too late to save Su-lin. He started to swim towards shore straining his every muscle and stretching his arms as far as they would go. He knew the divers would be following him.

He didn't remember how long he had been swimming. His body ached and he was at the point of hyperventilating. He started to say something but the words wouldn't come out. He was babbling incoherently when the life guards found him.

It was warm in the station but he wrapped the towel around his body. Soon there would be questions and he would patiently try to explain that he had viciously been attacked by three scuba divers. No, he didn't know why they would want to kill him or his companion. Yes, she was an old friend. They would take her body with them and the police would find nothing. He accepted a cup of black coffee and when the officer had left he started to cry.

The sun was at the midway mark and the trade winds gently moved the drawn curtains on his patio door. He remembered he had thrown up twice and his stomach still ached. He tried to light a cigarette but the taste of the pungent tobacco made him gag.

Who? Who knew his movements in Hawaii. He had been so careful but they had traced him to Su-lin. He didn't want to think about her. If...If only he hadn't noticed her on the street, if they hadn't gone diving, a thousand and one if's. He felt responsible for her death, and had like the fool he was, led them right to her. He wondered how Mr. Chen would react when he found out, but he didn't have the nerve to face him. Not now.

He knew that he would never be safe; not until Mansfield was exposed or destroyed. He thought about killing him yet it didn't make him feel any better. Bliss and four other men, sitting in important positions, in government, industry, journalism, the military? God only knows where. Five men who had sold their birthright years ago and who would dance to the music of their new masters. They would have the power and the authority to...to do what? Was Korea still the ultimate objective? How would they do it? He lay back on his pillow and fell into a deep, dreamless sleep.

When he finally woke, the sun was setting, an orange giant reflecting light as it seemed to plunge into the waters. In the lobby, sunburned guests were noisily celebrating their Hawaiian holiday. Their laughter hurt his ears.

Hakata, of course, how could I be so naive. It was amazingly transparent. He just happened to be his seat companion, and conveniently ran into him while dinning. And the trip to Chinatown...his suggestion.

"Excuse me," he said to the desk clerk. "Could you give me Mr. Hakata's room?"

He busied himself with the register. "Sir, we have no Mr. Hakata staying at the hotel."

"Tell me, do you know who owns this hotel?"

"Western International Sir, it's part of a world-wide chain. Say, you don't look so good, can I get you anything?"

"No thanks, I'll be checking out in the morning. May I have my bill?"

"Name?"

"Dr. Andrew Crane."

"Your bill's already paid."

"Who paid it?"

"Why you did sir, didn't you...?"

Isn't he a strange one, the clerk thought as he watched Andy walk towards the beach.

TEN

"Oh did I miss you!" She held him so tightly he could hardly breathe and smothered his body with passionate and demanding kisses as she pressed her soft body against his hardness.

"I don't ever want to leave you again." She stepped out of her pants and started to unbotton her shirt. They made love with an urgency born of desperation and longing. "More and more, I don't want to do anything but fuck all day."

Andy was strangely silent. He knew he was risking her life, but he couldn't tell her about Su-lin, not yet. He was still hurting inside. She sensed his mood and decided not to ask questions.

"How's your Dad?"

"He's going to be okay. The doctor's expect a full recovery, but it will take some time, and Mom's stopped all her social activities. I guess she realizes just how important he is to her. I think they'll make it."

At the club, Andy smashed the ball against the backboard for almost an hour. He was so tired but he wouldn't let up. Slowly he made his peace with his memories. His body succumbed to exhaustion and his mind began to accept the inevitable. That evening he told her everything and when he finished there were tears in her eyes.

"Oh, no, Andy, it must have been so horrible for you. What can you do now?"

"Not me Les...us. We're in this thing together. I'm tired of waiting for them to come after us, it's time we started calling the shots. We've got to stop Mansfield, and soon, before it's too late. I've got an idea but we need help. Tomorrow we're paying a call on Chief Mabra."

The chief sat back in his chair and adjusted his hearing to the hum of the air conditioner. He knew he should be grateful for the cool breeze but the noise was distracting. He lit up a cigar and patiently listened to his cautious yet compelling visitors. They were frightened, he could sense that, but their resolve was stronger than their fear. Jet-setters, that's what they reminded him of, the beautiful people who tanned in the sun and drank champagne while they hopped over continents to the next happening. No, that's just a surface impression. These people are very professional and very serious.

Their story would have sounded like a neurotic's hallucination if he hadn't known better. After his visit to New York and Washington he was ready to believe anything. True, the evidence was only circumstantial, but somehow the pieces fit together. He felt they weren't telling him everything but they had said enough. More important, he liked their determination and found himself eager to help them. He hadn't been so excited since his rookie days on the force.

"If what you're telling me is true, Andy, Leslie." They had insisted on first names. "We've got to find at least one corroborator. Think back now, is there anyone who can verify even part of your cut-and-paste version?"

Leslie was trying to remember. What was his name, the lawyer, the bachelor who had seen him shoot the Sergeant?

But it was Andy who spoke first. "Edward Fishbein served with Mansfield in Korea. He witnessed not only the shooting but he can also testify that Bliss was captured and brought to a P.O.W. Camp."

"Where is he now?"

Leslie answered. "We don't know. One night he packed up all his things and took off. No forwarding address."

Mabra thought for a moment. "Okay, if he's still

practicing law we can find him. Lawyers have to register with the State Bar Association and if the state is non-reciprocating, pass an exam."

"And if he's not." Andy and Leslie exchanged glances. They were thinking the same thing. If Fishbein was permanently missing, if he was already dead...then what?

"Just give me the details and let me work on it. I've spent a good deal of my time trying to track down missing persons. I can use some of my contacts."

"Let's assume we find him, then what?" inquired Leslie. "Force him to testify, where? We're not a court, we don't have any legal authority."

Neither Andy nor Ron knew what to say. Leslie got up and walked across the room. She put her hand on her forehead and her eyes flashed. "That's it. Look, Bliss is an agent of a foreign power. His usefulness to them depends upon keeping his identity and his past a secret. If we confront him publicly, we could raise questions. Sure, he'll answer some of them and try to call our bluff. But he won't be able to do that. If we can publicize our suppositions, someone else is bound to become curious. In any case it will all come out in the open."

Ron vetoed the idea. "Negative. First of all you need a platform to give your 'speech' and you don't have one. Even if you did, both of you would come out looking like kooks. Our President is a hero. No one would take you seriously."

"Well, it sounded like a good idea." Leslie was depressed.

"Ron, you presumed that I was the sniper's intended victim and that the CIA was behind it because of the incident with Su-lin at Squaw Valley. You said you had a friend with the CIA. Could he help us?"

Ron lowered his eyes and frowned. "I thought about that too, but my 'friend' was a little too convenient, like your Mr. Hakata. I don't think we can trust him."

Andy and Leslie looked at each other. Su-lin had said

that someone high up in the intelligence service was involved. Was Ron's life also in danger?

"Wait a minute, Ron, you say we need a witness, but maybe not. It's only Bliss who has to be convinced. His people haven't been completely honest with him. They didn't tell him about the book or the former President's drowning. Chances are they didn't tell him about Fishbein either. So if we can't produce the lawyer, maybe we can manufacture one. Leslie, remember, you took pictures and we have a tape recording of his voice. I'll bet Bliss won't be able to tell the difference. The important thing is that he thinks Fishbein is legitimate."

Ron interrupted. "You know what you're thinking of doing is against the law."

Andy grinned. "So...arrest me."

The three conspirators agreed that the Chief would attempt to located the bonafide lawyer while Andy and Leslie would work on a replacement. The key to the operation however, was the opportunity to publicly confront Mansfield. TV cameras and news media were essential. They would wait for just the right moment.

While Andy was in Hawaii, Bliss was busy campaigning. By exposing the congressional scandals he had become a national figure. The death of the American priest only added to his prophecies.

Two days ago his token opposition had dropped out of the race and Bliss would be unopposed. Yet for all his success, the President was not entirely satisfied. He had been hesitant to ask about the "book" and the "drowning", they were events, he decided, that he really didn't want to know about. When he finally found the courage, they told him it was nonsense and to forget about it. But they did not deny Crane's accusations and that's what bothered him. It was a situation he didn't like.

What went wrong, he kept asking himself. Back during the Korean War everything seemed so simple and in the ater years he had been so busy enjoying his success he had had little time to think about it. Yes, I am an ambitious man. I love the power, and as a Senator I'll be able to make policy. But I am not my own master. Funny, I never believed it but I haven't been for a long time, it's just that I'm now realizing it.

For a fleeting moment he thought about revealing everything, but the thought passed quickly. He would be ruined. No Washington, no presidency, and he would have to face military charges. He imagined himself in a stockade wearing a blue denim shirt with a white "P" emblazoned on the back. He pictured a firing squad...ready...aim...It was just like that play, he had made a deal and now the devil had come to collect.

"Alexa, do you really want to go to Washington?"

She smiled at him. "Of course dear, why...are you getting nervous."

"I guess so I've looked forward to this day for a long time, and now that it's suddenly about to happen I'm not so sure."

"Not sure of what, darling?"

But he was already thinking about the home they would buy and the swearing-in ceremony, his office in the Capital.

"Nothing Alexa, nothing at all."

Mr. Chao was back in the rugged mountains of his native land. He was truly a citizen of the world and probably the most traveled man in the country. At home in the luxurious capitals of the old and new nations, his soul remained in the small village where untold generations of his ancestors had lived and died. Before the change he would have been a farmer like his father before him. It would have been a good life.

He was speaking to his nephew, his brother's youngest son and a member of the select "committee".

"What news do you bring from Peiping?"

"There are quiet rumblings, comrade."

Chao wished he would call him "Uncle" but settled for the term that promised equality. He was after all a child of the revolution. "And the opposition...?" He knew his plans did not enjoy everyone's support.

"They hold their tongues. Many do not wish to risk a confrontation. After Nixon's visit they had hoped to follow another path."

The old man thought back to the former U.S. President. But presidents come and go and policy always changes. Now that the Americans had been defeated in Southeast Asia they would not want to risk another debacle and certainly not over that madman Park. There would be one final incident and then...

He noticed his nephew pacing nervously. He wants to say something, but he is unsure of himself. He recalled the time he had wanted to discuss certain matters with his father. He too had been hesitant. Perhaps some things will never change.

"Speak up, something's on your mind."

The younger man averted his eyes. "I think we should terminate the 'sleeping giant'. He will only cause more trouble. The anthropologist is a clever man. He is not so frightened that he will not act again. We should have finished him in Hawaii, but those goons we hired only make things more difficult now."

"You make it seem worse than it really is. The girl has been silenced. Without her he has no proof and can do nothing. No, the 'sleeping giant' will soon be an American Senator. His work has only begun."

"I don't trust him."

"It does not matter, he will do as he is told. You have arranged for the nuclear accident, yes?"

"Yes."

"Good, when the Americans realize they can no longer trust the Koreans, it will all be over."

"And the American anthropologist?"

"Soon, but not yet. We will continue to watch him as before."

"He must know the others."

"Nephew, does he know their names? Does he know who they are? Or what they are doing? Who can he turn to? If he goes to the police they will not believe him. And if he tells the CIA then he really is a fool."

The younger man knew better than to argue with the old fox. Perhaps he was right after all.

ELEVEN

The debate was actually Mitchell's idea though Bliss believed he thought of it first.

"You know you don't really have to do it."

"Ah, but I want to. It's too good an opportunity to pass up."

Mitchell cautioned him. "Let's not be so hasty. As it stands now you're an odds-on favorite to win. What you'll be doing is giving your opponent an unexpected chance for some TV coverage, and he needs it. He'll jump at the offer."

Bliss sipped twelve-year-old Scotch and watched the sun set beyond the hills. "Mitchell, my friend, I see it differently. My opponent, the honorable James Parrott is a very unimposing challenger. Seeing us side by side should convince the voters that he's no competition at all."

If Bliss was overly confident, he had good reasons, having just received a packet from his friends, documents which detailed South Korea's military strength and emphasized the ROK Army's ability to defend her borders in the event of an enemy attack. The information would surely make him appear more knowledgeable than he really was. He wondered if the President of the United States had access to the same data. He doubted it.

"Okay, but it will take a while to set it up. We want coverage on both the state and national levels and a large audience. Perhaps we could use the Union Hall where you first exposed the Congressional payoffs?"

"No. I've got a much better idea, the university theater. It's my home ground and Parrott will be even more nervous than he usually is facing a partisan audience."

Mitchell thought about his suggestion. Superb. He had been concerned about Bliss' participation in national politics. After all the man had never held an elective post before. But this candidate was now a fighter, a persuasive speaker whose oratory demanded respect. After he finished his first term he would be fifty-seven, young enough if he aspired to higher office.

"Fine, I'll make the arrangement. When can you be ready?"

"Give me about two weeks and let's get all the publicity we can. This will be our last big show before the election."

"Andy wake up! Look at the paper." Andy didn't hear her, he was asleep on the couch dreaming about Bliss addressing Congress. But all the Senators were small Asian ·men with straight black hair and Bliss was speaking in Mandarin.

"Andy, listen to me." He was dead to the world. Leslie smiled and thought to herself, how happy I am since this mysterious man came into my life. Would it be quite the same if things were different and we were just two people living an ordinary life. What will it be like when all this is over? She shook him.

"Huh?"

"Here, sleeping beauty, read this."

He did. They looked at each other.

"We'll never have a better opportunity."

"I'm not so sure, lover. Remember, this is a debate and the audience really doesn't get a chance to participate. Ron also telephoned while you were sleeping. He's had absolutely no luck locating the lawyer. Apparently Fishbein's dropped clear out of sight."

Andy realized just how tenuous their position was. No lawyer meant no witness, and while his idea about an impersonator seemed brilliant at the time, the more he thought about it, the less pausible it became. The debate on the other hand was a perfect platform, but only if you were a debater. That's it! He had an idea but first he had to find out more about Assemblyman James Parrott.

285

James Thadeus Parrott appeared to be the most unassuming and umpretentious elected official in the lower house of the State Assembly.

"Well, I would have preferred a more forceful man, but Parrott will just have to do. He's honest and from what I can gather, clean. Apparently a bit of a Mr. Milquetoast in public, but it's just possible he'll listen."

"Listen to what?" Leslie and Ron were almost afraid to ask.

"To us, to our story. We can supply him with the right questions and if he'll use them effectively, it's good-bye Senator Mansfield."

"And what in God's name makes you think he'll listen, or for that matter even see us?"

Andy smiled. "Not us, Leslie, you. I've been doing my homework on the good Assemblyman. He's quite a 'gallant', almost a little old fashioned. He'd never turn down a chance to meet a beautiful woman."

"Oh really, Andy. How can you be so sure?"

"Because you have an appointment with the gentleman in two days, at his home, and his wife is away visiting her sister."

Leslie was bewildered and a bit angry, but she agreed to go. It seemed like the only hope.

James T. Parrott sat at his desk pretending to read the Finance Committee's report but all the while nervously glancing at his watch. He had just shaved and was wearing his best leisure suit. His hair was scrupulously combed in the three-way mirror to hide his noticeable bald spot. He had also liberally doused himself with cologne.

Maybe it's a mistake, he thought. I should call and cancel the appointment. His underarms continued to sweat and he continuously ran his tongue over his thick lips. He thought of the Playgirl centerfold and that ludicrous picture of Burt Reynolds. He practised flexing his muscles and holding his breath so that his paunch hid beneath the jacket. Maybe I should change, perhaps a sweater.

But it was too late. He heard the car pull off the gravel path and turn into the driveway.

Leslie was also noticeably apprehensive. She abhorred the tasteless charade that degraded both the men and women who played games, preferring a straight forward approach to both sex and politics. Her disguise as a Playgirl reporter was clearly Andy's idea but it had suggestively worked to gain a private audience with the President's opponent. It was now up to her to enlist the Assemblyman's aid without offending his masculine sensitivities.

Ron had been more than just concerned about the meeting. "Leslie, I'm worried. Bliss' people have been watching you as well as Andy since the attempted assassination."

"What makes you so sure?"

"First, because it makes sense. If they know what you're doing they can plan accordingly. You really don't think the lawyer vanished all by himself. Secondly, they followed you to the club the day you were almost ran down. If I were in their position, I wouldn't let you out of my sight, at least not until the election is over."

Leslie thought he was being a bit melodramatic but then she remembered the two men in the car and agreed.

Andy and Leslie drove downtown to Martindale's Department Store. It was the last day of the half-price clearance sale and the store was jammed with bargain hunters. She left Andy looking at the microwave ovens and excused herself. In the woman's rest room she exchanged her tan overcoat and wide-brimmed hat with the campus policewoman.

Wearing a wig and dressed in Leslie's attire, Detective Alice Carlsen easily might pass as her look-alike. Waiting

287

five minutes after the policewoman had left her she hurriedly exited out a back door and into the unmarked car Ron had left at the curb. The keys were in the ignition and seconds later she was on her way to Hidden Valley. It took the man following the detective fifteen minutes to realize she was not the same woman, but by that time it was already too late.

"Ms. Pace." He opened the door greeting her with a slightly exaggerated bow. "So good of you to be my guest." God, but she is striking, he thought. The way her hair frames, yet almost hides, her face. The white pants hugging her body, the fit of the black sweater suggestively outlining her femininity. She smelled like fresh roses, reminding him of the models who appeared carefree and sensuous on the cover of fashion magazines.

"It's my pleasure, sir, I'm privileged to be here." Her smile was warm and generous although she was momentarily overwhelmed by the aroma of his cologne and aware of his eyes busily removing her clothing. She felt better when she noticed he was still wearing his gold wedding band.

"May I offer you a drink?"

"Please do."

"Your pleasure?"

"Scotch."

He poured her a double and sat behind his desk. He was sweating profusely but once seated in his familiar chair felt his confidence return. "Well, where shall we start?"

Leslie had been dreading this moment. She had rehearsed her lines but found herself unable to begin. It seemed like an eternity before she finally spoke.

"Sir, I'm not with Playgirl."

"What do you mean?" He was obviously confused.

"I pretended to be a reporter in order to see you. You're the one man who can help us."

He was becoming angry. "If you're not a reporter then who are you, Miss?"

She hadn't planned on crying, it was such a shallow ruse, a disgustingly sexist ploy. But the tears came, streaking her make-up as they ran down her cheeks.

His anger vanished and turned to concern. His voice was gentle. "Tell me about it."

Leslie began her story. At first he seemed merely curious, surprised of course but refusing to consider seriously her incredible tale. Yet soon his bewilderment became interest and he was no longer amused.

"Excuse me for interrupting Dr. Pace, but would you mind starting at the beginning. I want to record this conversation." He turned on the tape deck.

When she had finished he poured them both another drink.

She's very convincing. Either she's a consummate actress and a rather good one or what she's told me is the truth. He realized the unstated inplications and what they could mean in terms of his own career. He would have to be careful.

"Dr. Pace, can you prove any of this?"

She lowered her eyes. "Some, we made a recording of our conversation with the lawyer. Do you want me to play it?"

"Please do."

He listened intently. "Excuse me a moment." Unlocking a desk drawer he withdrew a folder prepared by his campaign staff. Her story seemed to chronologically correspond with the brief his people had hastily compiled on Mansfield. Why was it so hard to believe an American university chief, a senatorial candidate, as an employee of...of who really knows?

Of one thing he was certain. This was no practical joke. The young lady seated before him was hardly a clown, she was a very frightened woman.

"How come you haven't gone to the authorities before

now?"

"We didn't have evidence. They would have laughed at us."

No. She wasn't telling him everything. It's obvious she doesn't trust the authorities either.

"What do you want me to do about this alledged conspiracy?"

"Mr. Parrott, next week you are going to debate the President. We want you to use the information. Once the issue is out in the open he'll no longer be a threat to anyone."

"Really, if I confront Mansfield as you have suggested and can't back up my claims, remember, I don't have proof, he's certain to sue me for libel. I can't see how that will help anyone."

Leslie was ready to give up. It had been foolish of them to think that she could convince him. "You're our last hope, sir. After the election it will be too late. I know you think I'm a bit mad, but if I'm not then this country is going to be in a pretty sorry state."

Parrott thought about that. She's right, of course, I can't sit here and pretend I never heard about it. He also realized the consequences in terms of his political ambitions. Sex and power. It's strange, I started the afternoon fantasizing about sex and end it by dreaming about a U.S. Senate seat. "May I see you to the door?"

Leslie knew she had failed. They had missed their only chance. She meekly followed him and was about to get into her car.

"Just a moment, Doctor. Would you mind leaving me a number where you can be reached?

Ladies, man or not, James Parrott was a skilled politician who had represented his district for over twelve years. During that time he had done a goodly amount of compromising and had accumulated more than his fair share of owed favors. That afternoon and evening he called them in.

Forty-eight hours later he had gathered enough additional data on Bliss Mansfield to seriously consider the attractive professor's story. But why hadn't anyone questioned Bliss before? True, the proof was only circumstantial, but when you added up each coincidence there really did seem to be a pattern. Of course you first had to know where to look.

It had also occured to the cautious Assemblyman that the people behind Mansfield's candidacy were ruthless, quite capable of even murder. He involuntarily shuddered. His life could be in danger and those of his family as well. It was a frightening thought and he managed to dismiss it.

The debate was a chance for a political upset, a miracle, the only hope for victory. The promise of power was greater than all his fears. It was also the first time he realized the extent of his ambitions.

Leslie Pace was about to devour an unbelievably large piece of chocolate cake topped by a rich, creamy, frosting when the phone rang.

"Yes."

"Dr. Pace?"

"Speaking."

"I've decided to explore the possibilities we discussed last Thursday."

TWELVE

The university theater was not the most attractive building on the campus nor was it the newest. It had been originally designed ten years ago when student riots were common but the funds for its construction had been appropriated late in 1973 Thus its exterior resembled more a stone and glass fortress rather than an enticing monument to art and beauty.

The senatorial debate was scheduled to begin promptly at seven. It was free for all univeristy employees and students while the general public was charged an admission of one dollar. A full house was expected.

Although scheduled for the evening, preparations for the debate started in the early hours of the morning.

"Christ, what the hell are we doing here at this ungodly hour?" Officer Rizzo usually took the evening shift.

"Damned it I know," answered his companion. "The Chief said to guard these doors starting at six-thirty. Anyone who doesn't have proper ID just doesn't get in and we're supposed to check everyone."

Acting President Hadley had received a bomb threat the night before and was taking no chances, nor were the City Police.

Commissioner Blake personally addressed the four man bomb squad. "I want you to take the building apart and I don't care how long it takes. Anyone who's mad enough to tell us there's a bomb hidden inside is crazy enough to put one there. And after you're through don't go home. I want the building checked out again in the afternoon."

By two the green-garbed janitorial staff was busy

sweeping between the isles and setting up the stage. TV technicians and cameramen were beginning to arrange their equipment and the lighting crews were similarly occupied.

Chief Mabra briefed his staff as well as the city and State authorities who would supplement his campus force that evening. Outside of Leslie and Andy, only Ron knew of the Assemblymna's plans, and he was understandably nervous.

"Anyone who even acts suspicious, and only God knows what that means, will be detained. I want the plain-clothesmen and the detectives to mix with the crowd and stand in line like everyone else. Uniformed patrolmen can check thier assignments on the board."

Lieutenant Mackay sat in his State Police car by the west gate and remarked to his driver. "With all the fucking cops here, you'd swear the President of the United States himself was the speaker.

Bliss spent the afternoon swimming in his pool and pruning the rose bushes. He was relaxed and confident. Mitchell Potter, his political mentor, had spent the lunch hour with him going over last minute details.

"When this is over you will be the most celebrated politician across the country."

"Fine, but will I win the election?" Bliss was, of course, joking.

"Are you kidding, I predict a victory with no less than seventy percent."

"You two are sure optimistic," Alexa beamed. "I'm going to the beauticians and after that to the caterers. Then out to the airport to pick Bryan up." Alexa was planning a post-debate party. Her son was expected and he had surprised her by insisting upon spending his own money for the flight. She was very proud of both her men.

After a leisurely shower, Bliss sat alone in his study and dreamed of Washington. "Senator Mansfield," the name had about it a ring of sincerity and authority. A cloud started to block out the sun and cast its shadow over the terrace. The only disturbing note to an otherwise perfect afternoon was Mitchell's lack of curiosity about where he had obtained the information on Korea's military preparedness. It was almost as if he knew.

James Parrott also sat alone, in his hotel suite. He had agonizingly rehearsed his opening statement. It would be a rather innocuous speech except for the closing sentence "...there is more to this university president that meets the eye, more than he wants us to know."

That should at the very least spark the audience's curiousity and more important, unnerve the President. He knew that this debate was the single most significant event in his career as a public official. It was also a risk, a gamble, but he had to take it. Please, dear God, he thought. Let Dr. Pace know what she is talking about.

Then, like Mansfield, he too turned to fantasizing about his life in Washington.

Andy and Leslie sat on the deck of their lakefront home.

"I have before me a bottle of a very rare Chateau Lafitte. I have decanted it and let it settle. I would like to propose a toast to this evening and to the fascinating and lovely lady who made it all possible."

They were really celebrating not so much the forthcoming debate, but something infinitely more precious. They brought their glasses together in a silent salute to the hopes they shared, two ordinary people whose uniqueness lay in their commitment to each other, to a bond forged out of trust and tenderness.

By five-thirty the line stretched around the theatre, across the paved road and back to the co-ed dormitory parking lot. Acting against the Chief's advice, "President" Hadley was persuaded to allow standees, an action for which he was later severely chastized by the Trustees.

Despite the warm day, the evening was cooler than expected and the crowd shivered in the chill of the Autumn air. They were noisy and boisterous and had come to the debate with an excitement usually reserved for a homecoming weekend. They greeted each other with hugs and kisses and handshakes. They exchanged gossip and discussed concerns of a common interest, while they excitedly proclaimed their partiality for the university president. Though the lines were long, the crowd was orderly and the police who watched them carefully were relieved.

The candidates arrived ten minutes apart and parked in the Administration lot. They were then escorted across the campus and quietly entered by side entrances. Both men reluctantly submitted to the make-up crew who prepared them for the live camera.

While Bliss joked with the security people. Parrott tried to disguise a growing case of nerves by visiting the men's room—twice. Finally the waiting was over.

The lights at first hurt his eyes and he squinted trying to shut out the glare. Parrott was impressed with the size of the crowd but they clearly indicated that Mansfield was their favorite. He placed his briefcase by the side of the table and removed his papers. The lights were too hot. He took off his glasses and wiped his brow with a paisley handkerchief. His throat was dry and he tried to resist the temptation to loosen his tie. Dammit, there should have been a water pitcher already on the table.

Bliss looked past the spotlights and studied the audience. He was thrilled with the standing ovation he had just received, and continued to smile. Look at the red light on the console, the TV man had told him, you have a much larger audience at home. But he focused instead on a single individual, a blond co-ed with large white teeth, remembering his mentor's advice pick out one person in

295

the crowd, forget about the others. Make her face your only focus, talk to her alone.

"Ladies and gentlemen, the university is proud to sponsor the senatorial debate between Dr. Bliss Mansfield and Assemblyman James Parrott. It gives me great pleasure to introduce first, the president of the University and a candidate for United State Senator...Bliss Mansfield."

The President rose and walked to the center of the stage. He was standing perhaps six feet from the front row orchestra seats.

The slender young man wearing a cheap and slightly stained sportsjacket with an open collar white shirt joined the cheering crowd in giving the speaker a rousing ovation. Long black hair fell across his face and for a moment obscured his vision. His horn-rimmed glasses made his eyes appear too large for his face but he didn't mind. He had worn then since childhood and was practically blind without them.

Surprisingly no one noticed his right hand move towards his waist and before he could be stopped he quickly withdrew the small handgun he had illegally purchased for two hundred dollars only two days ago. He gripped his right forearm with his left to steady his aim. He remembered to breathe out and hold his breath while squeezing the trigger.

The sounds of the shots echoed throughout the theater as he emptied all six bullets into the president.

He was still screaming incoherently when he was apprehended by a city detective and a campus peace officer.

THIRTEEN

President Bliss Mansfield died thirty seconds later.

It was an appropriate day for a funeral, an overcast sky shut out the sun and distant thunder gave notice that a storm was brewing. The air was humid and occasional showers marked the solemnity of the event. Alexa would have preferred a small family gathering, but her late husband belonged in part to the public, which turned the grisly affair into a state occasion.

Andy and Leslie had foregone the crowded memorial church service but huddled together as the casket was lowered into the red earth. His death was so shocking and unexpected, even his enemies were moved. It was as if they too had been cheated out of a more meaningful finality.

Tears rang down her cheeks. "Oh Andy, somehow it doesn't seem fair."

"I know. But perhaps sooner or later it was bound to happen." He reached for her hand and pressed it against his own.

"The Korean student, what will happen to him?"

"I guess he'll have to stand trial for murder, although I hear there's talk about returning him to his government."

"He'll be better off here."

The drizzle had turned to rain. Andy opened his umbrella and drew Leslie closer. "It's an ironic twist of fate, Bliss is killed by the boy whose life he once saved."

"And for all the wrong reasons," she added.

He was born in a small Korean village in an area that

was later known as the "Iron Triangle". His father had been a poor farmer but somehow there was always enough food to eat. When he was two, the senior Mr. Kim was forced to serve in the Army and he didn't see him very much after that.

His days were spent playing with his little sister and enjoying the warmth of his mother's smile. He tried desperately to become the man of the house after his father was killed. He was four.

When the American soldiers came, most of the residents had left the village. His mother was also planning to leave but took sick the day of the shelling. He remembered hearing the loud bursts of the cannons and watching the mud huts crumble in the aftermath. A man was screaming in a language he couldn't understand. The family went outside to see what the shouting was all about. He was terrified, the soldier raised the rifle and was aiming at his mother, but he couldn't move.

Kenneth Kim had been only six-years-old when Sergeant Killebrew brutally executed his mother and his sister. He didn't remember that it was the Lieutenant who had saved his life by shooting the soldier-killer. But he had seen the officer and he would never forget his face. All those years he had held him responsible for denying Kenneth a normal family life.

"He couldn't have been in the country more than a month when he saw Mansfield's picture."

Andy nodded. "A lifetime of resentment, all the hostility and anguish he must have felt. It was too much to handle all at once."

He studied harder than the rest of the students at the University of Seoul, and when he completed his mandatory military service, applied for graduate study abroad. His friends gave him a party the night before he left.

Naturally shy and introverted he found his first week at the university a frightful experience. American students were so carefree that they even laughed at their assignments. He would never understand them. The foreign student advisor didn't help either. He was too busy to realize how lonely Kenneth was. His roomate was worse, a Japanese, much younger than Kim, and a bigot who regarded all Koreans as "yellow monkeys."

The first day of instruction he had so much trouble understanding the professor that he left the large lecture hall twenty minutes before the end of the class and wandered aimlessly about the campus.

"Did you speak with Parrott?"

"Well I tried to, but he had convinced himself that all's well that ends well. He reminded me that after all we had no proof, and now that Mansfield was dead, what would we gain by exposing him. He also told me that he was very impressed with you and even hinted that once he was in Congress, he might find room for a position on his staff."

"I spoke to Ron the other day. He thinks we ought to let the whole thing rest. He's even given up trying to find the lawyer."

"It figures. Alice, Bliss was a dangerous agent, but now he's dead he's a national hero again."

"What are we going to do now?" The rain was falling harder and the sounds of thunder almost obscured the Minister's words.

"Ashes to ashes, and dust to dust..."

"Get married, run away, apply for a Sabbatical, Jesus, Leslie I just don't know. Su-lin was positive there were five agents altogether, Bliss was only one. His people will assume that I know about the others."

"But you don't know who they are."

"I haven't the foggiest notion, but they don't know that."

Lightning flashed and illuminated the fresh grave. The dark heavens sent down torrents as if to formally recognize the passing of another life.

Across the seas, Mr. Chao was watching the water flood the rice paddies below the hill where his dear friend and comrade, General Kao had been laid to rest. Although the party had denounced the practice as superstitious and decandent, the gravesite had been carefully determined by an old geomancer, who had made sure that man and heaven would maintain their proper relationship for all eternity. He took one last look and went into the cottage.

"Comrades, the work of the 'committee' is almost completed. The killing of our man an unfortunate accident but it serves our purposes well. The Americans will suspect the student of being a South Korean agent acting under orders from his government. The university president was an outspoken proponent of withdrawing American troops. His death will no doubt be linked to his political stand. There are already plans to bring the U.S. soldiers home. Yes?" He nodded to the gentleman smoking his pipe.

The chairman's emissary rose to speak. "Comrade Chao, what will happen to the nuclear accident?"

"It is no longer necessary."

"And the anthropologist, Crane?"

"For the time being, nothing. It would be foolish to eliminate him now, it could only raise embarrassing questions."

When the meeting was over his nephew came over to him and put his arms around his shoulders. "I am proud of you, Uncle. We are all proud of you today."

The old man thanked him graciously and returned once more to look at the burial ground atop the hill.

Once again CIA Deputy Director Lawrence was seated

before the President.

"Lawrence, what have your people found out about the Korean student?"

The Deputy was finding it difficult to swallow. He had grown to intensely dislike these sessions now that the Director was in the hospital. "He completed his undergraduate work in Seoul, served with the ROK Army as an infantryman and was accepted as a graduate student by the university. There's not much else in his folder sir."

The President continued to stare at him.

"I know what you're thinking, Mr. President. Yes, it's possible that he was instructed by the Koreans to assassinate Dr. Mansfield. The story about Mansfield shooting his mother and sister when he was a boy seems a bit farfetched. Mansfield's military records certainly don't confirm it."

"Ridiculous," The man in the oval office was tired, exhausted and resigned to the inevitable. It was almost as if he didn't really care anymore. "Do you believe him?"

"Frankly sir, no. The Korean was apparently a trained marksman. Even if there is some truth to what he says, he's still a perfect candidate for the mission."

"I'm inclined to agree with you." He stood up. "You'll have to excuse me, the White House has been receiving calls about this for the past seventy-two hours. If the military recommend it, I think our days in Korea are over. Goodnight."

"Goodnight, Sir."

Jason Carterett was summoned to Washington and met with the Joint Chiefs of Staff. Admiral McDaniels began.

"General, you know everyone here."

Jason nodded.

"I'll come right to the point. Can the South Koreans withstand and defeat a North Korean attack if we withdraw our troops?"

Jason thought for a moment. "Yes, they can. That is if North Korea wages a traditional war and if our estimate of their military preparedness is correct. The South Korean armed forces are stronger than they've ever been. Their equipment is superb." Everybody laughed—"their" equipment was of course "ours."

"...and as far as I'm concerned they can stand on their own two feet. General Lancaster?"

The World War II Air Force ace was also silent. "Jason, how would you assess the morale of Park's armies?"

"Excellent. Despite what we may think about Park, he enjoys the support of his officers. The ROK soldier is as dedicated and as skilled a fighting man as I've ever known."

"What about discipline?" The question came from the Marine Corp's Ian Michaels.

"I wouldn't worry about that, General. You know as well as I do what happens to anyone who refuses to follow orders. It's the same as it was back in '51. They shoot 'em."

"Can you document troop strength and readiness?"

"Yessir." He passed out a thick folder to each man. "It took us four months to prepare this, it's accurate and current."

It was the Admiral again. "Jason, we've known each other for quite some time. I've always respected your opinion. Are you telling us we can get out?"

"I sure am, and as goddamm soon as possible."

The military leaders were satisfied. Their staffs would examine the report and if they concurred, then the Joint Chiefs would present their recommendations to the President. As they were about to adjourn, General Deighton asked a final question.

"What if the Chinese were to join the attack?"

Jason tensed. "I'm afraid that's another ball game sir."

The rain was coming down so hard that the windshield wipers were practically useless. Leslie was curled up next to him looking like a little girl who had just lost her favorite doll and was afraid to ask for another. Andy kept his eyes on the road but his thoughts were elsewhere.

"Things can't ever be the same Les, at least not for us. Oh, they'll wait a while, at least until the public forgets Mansfield, but they'll come again."

"Andy, I was just thinking, why don't we go someplace just the two of us, maybe to Colorado. It's only another month till winter recess and you can teach me how to ski."

"Sure, we can go to Aspen or would you rather go to Vail instead?"

"I don't care, either one. I'm so tired." She closed her eyes and a moment later was fast asleep.

Yes, Andy thought. They would go away together. They would keep looking over their shoulders and suspiciously watching the cars behing them. They were in no immediate danger now, but one day, after they had been lulled into a false sense of security...

EPILOGUE

General Sung slowly sipped the hot tea. His hands were shaking and he didn't know if it was the cold or because he was excited. He lit a cigarette and watched the smoke rise in the early morning darkness. He had said goodbye to his wife and the experience had been unsettling; this time he did not promise he would return. Last night he gathered his men together and they talked about old times and of the days to come. He smiled as he thought of his son, a young lieutenant who had yet to experience combat, and like the boys of his generation had never known the humiliation of defeat. He checked his watch and it was time. He gave the command.

At four on a gray winter morning the snow began to fall and surround the mountains with a lacy curtain of white mist. The air was chilled so, that their breathing would have given away their positions if anyone had been watching. It was a slow and steady march, but the men and machines with the red star made good time on the recently-improved roads. Their lines seemed to stretch endlessly over the horizon. Assuming their current rate of travel, they would soon see the river and not very long after, cross the thirty-eighth parallel.